# Buried Tales of Pinebox, Texas

# PINEBOX, TEXAS

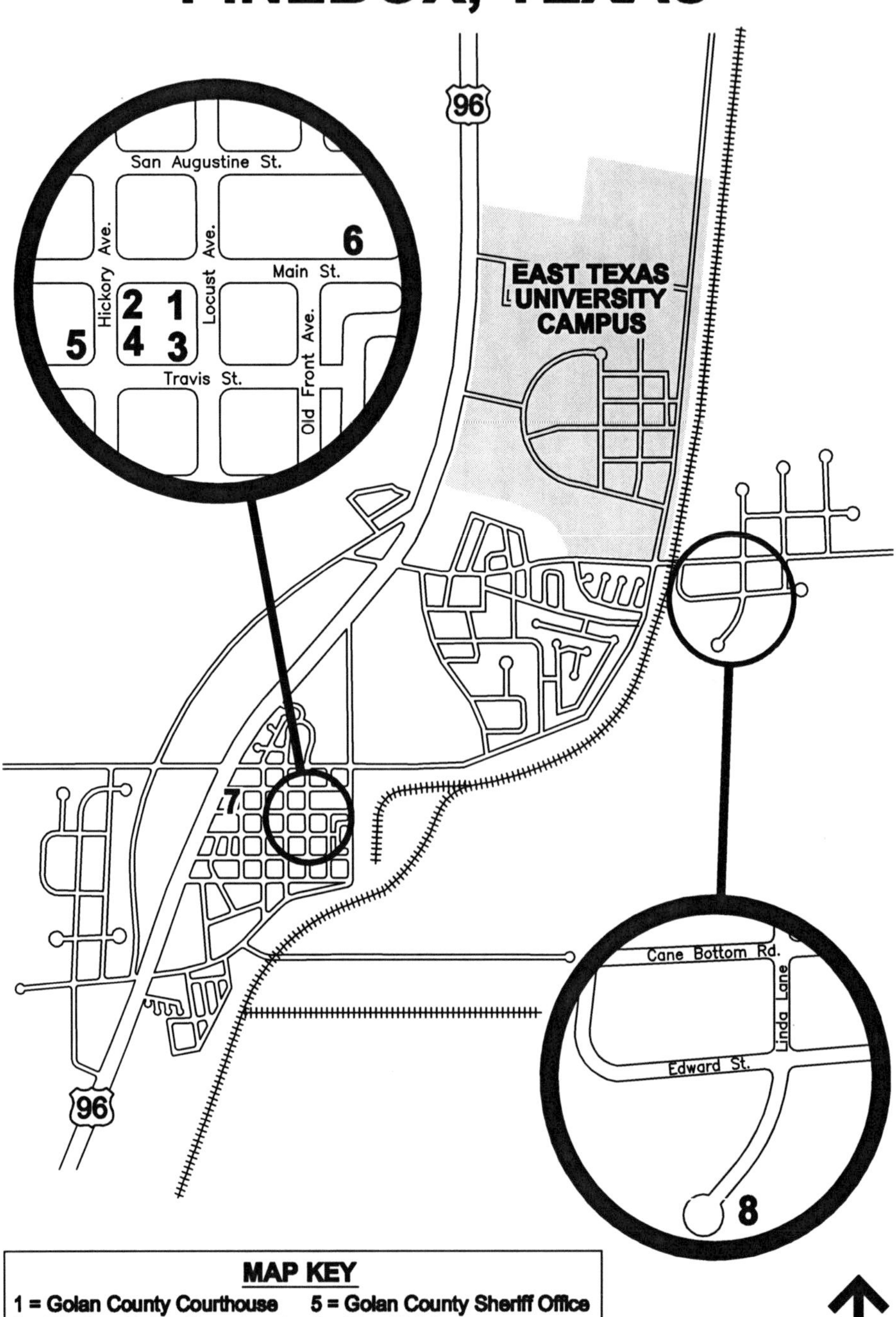


**MAP KEY**

1 = Golan County Courthouse
2 = Pinebox Police Department
3 = Post Office
4 = Pinebox City Hall
5 = Golan County Sheriff Office
6 = Pine Hotel
7 = Mom's Diner
8 = Witch's House

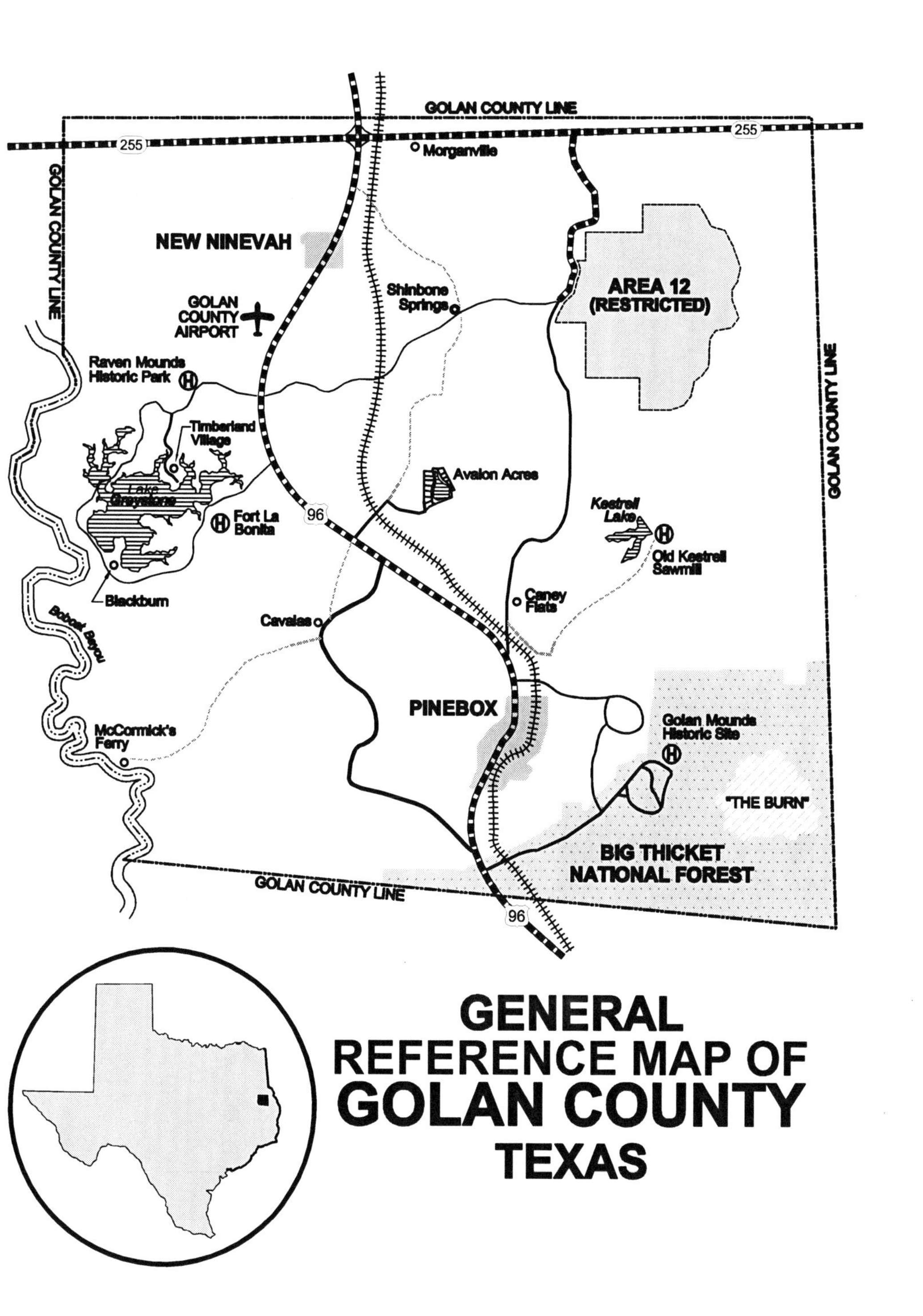


# GENERAL REFERENCE MAP OF GOLAN COUNTY TEXAS

## ~Other Pinebox, Texas books~

*The Beast Within*
*Last Rites of the Black Guard*
*Brainwashed*
*Chickens in the Mist*
*Skinwalker*
*Bloodlines*
*The Prodigal (Fall 2009)*

# Buried Tales
## of Pinebox, Texas

**Edited by Matt M. McElroy**

Cover by Jeff Varnes
Maps by T.C. Largent
Copyediting by Ed Wetterman

This product is purely a work of fiction. Any similarity to actual people, organizations, places, or events is purely coincidental.

Buried Tales of Pinebox, Texas



A Pinebox Book
Published by 12 to Midnight
2522 Bridge Hampton Way
Sugar Land, TX 77479

**12tomidnight.com**

**12 to Midnight** and the 12 to Midnight logo are trademarks of 12 to Midnight.

ISBN-10: 0-9819637-2-2
ISBN-13: 978-0-9819637-2-3



First Edition: June 2009

# Contents

# ~Take a Tour of Pinebox~

I first encountered Pinebox, Texas way back when Preston DuBose asked me to review the Bloodlines adventure for my Flames Rising website. I thought the idea of creating a series of modern horror adventures was pretty cool so I dove in and started reading the adventures 12 to Midnight had to offer.

Pinebox is an interesting little town. It has all the usual little shops, restaurants strip malls and even a state college. What you don't see, not at first, are the creepy things hiding in the shadows. There are legends overheard at the pub and stories told by the campfire by those in the know. Thing is, many of these tales are true, a warning to those that will listen. Monsters in Pinebox are real and they are not going away anytime soon. Pinebox does have a few heroes, brave souls who hunt monsters and protect the innocent. Most of them don't quite make it to old age, either driven away from the town or worse. For a while though, they manage to make a difference, driving the monsters back into the shadows.

I had been following the development of the Pinebox setting over the years and using a few of the adventures in my own modern horror games. *Buried Tales of Pinebox* came about after some conversations with Preston about the future of the setting. The collection of adventures had offered up plenty of mysterious monsters and twisted antagonists, yet there were plenty of shadows yet to explore.

I wanted to see what would happen if a dozen authors had the chance to visit Pinebox, each one exposing just a little more of the setting. Some were already familiar with the folks who live there, having worked on the adventures. Others were visiting for the first time and adding a new tale to the town's collective lore.

*Buried Tales* offers new horror fiction from 12 dark souls who have walked the streets of Pinebox, Texas. Each of them is offering a peek into the shadows, meet the monsters, and listen to the whispers of the dead. It is almost midnight and the bus is filling up fast, so take your seats. The ride is about to begin…

Matt M. McElroy
*Editor*

****

*Matt M. McElroy is the Editor-in-Chief of the Flames Rising webzine, an online resource for fans of Horror and Dark Fantasy entertainment. Matt also works as the Marketing manager for DrivethruHorror.com. His writing includes a story in the Tales of the Seven Dogs Society collection from Abstract Nova and an upcoming vampire novel.*

# ~The Jennifer Ridge Transcripts~

Pinebox gossips were set abuzz with excitement when reporter Jennifer Ridge checked into the Pine Hotel and conducted a series of interviews for a tourism feature. The article is unpublished, but transcripts of those interviews offer rare insight into the character of the sleepy, rural town named Pinebox, Texas.

## Interview 1: Chamber of Commerce

**Jennifer Ridge:** This is Jennifer Ridge at the Pinebox Chamber of Commerce. Would you please state your name?

**Dorothy Green:** My name is Dorothy Green.

**JR:** And do you I have your permission to record you?

**DG:** Sure!

**JR:** Thank you, Dorothy. As I explained off tape, I'm working on an article for Texas Travel Destinations. Would you mind telling me a little bit about Pinebox?

**DG:** I'd be glad to. Well, Pinebox is located in the heart of East Texas off Route 96, and we've got a population of roughly 18,000 full time residents. I say full time because I'm sure you know we also have East Texas University here and they add an extra 12,000 students.

**JR:** You know, from what little I've seen this doesn't strike me as a college town.

**DG:** No, we keep a tight reign on trouble. I think we have something like 22 police officers and eight police cars now. And that's just the Pinebox Police Department. That doesn't include the county Sheriff's Department. Pinebox isn't a very wild place and the kids learn pretty quick that there's not much trouble to be found in town. Most of them stay near campus where there's more to do.

**JR:** Huh. What about crime around campus? Do they have a problem with robbery or assult around there? Or maybe people disappearing?

**DG:** Not particularly. You're not really going to write about petty crime in your tourist article, are you?

**JR:** Nah. I was just curious. Speaking of being curious, I've just got to ask. Where does the name Pinebox come from?

**DG:** Well, for almost four decades we were the biggest lumber supplier in all of East Texas. At height of operations, there were 23 lumber mills in the area. Today we only have one and that is Whitmore Timber. They are the county's second biggest employer behind ETU. Anyhow, with lumber being so important to the early settlers I guess Pinebox seemed like a good name.

**JR:** That makes sense, I guess. So what should I make a point of seeing while I'm here in town?

**DG:** Let's see... you should definitely visit the Cecil Greystone Memorial Library. We have an excellent archive with lots of old pictures, and usually someone from the Pinebox Historical Society volunteers there during the week.

**JR:** Okay, I'll be sure to check that out.

**DG:** Of course you'll want to visit the university. I'm told ETU is known all over the world for their history and folk culture departments. It would sure be nice if their football team did better though. Not many folks bother to visit Pinebox for ETU football games. I hear places like College Station get 50,000 visitors for their games. Can you imagine 50,000 people here in little old Pinebox? That would be a nice boost for local businesses.

**JR:** Maybe this article will help some too.

**DG:** Oh of course you're right. I'm sorry. Sometimes I just go off on a tangent. I love working for the Chamber of Commerce, so sometimes I get a little carried away.

**JR:** That's okay. Why don't you just tell me about some of the businesses here?

**DG:** Well I've already told you about Whitmore Timber and ETU. We're also fortunate to have some branches of big industrial businesses such as Borden Chemicals and The Golden Mark Corporation. Then there's Garland Industries, which works one of the most productive tin mines in Texas. The southeast station of the Texas Forestry Service is in our county. Oh, and the headquarters to the world famous Lewis Catfish King restaurant chain is right here in Pinebox.

**JR:** Really? I've eaten there before.

**DG:** Well sure. It's one of the fastest growing restaurant chains in Texas. Just last night Don Lewis—he's the owner—presented the Wolfhunters Club with a check for five thousand dollars.

**JR:** The wolf cub?

**DG:** Ha-ha, no. That's CLUB, not CUB. The Wolfhunters Club is one of our local community organizations. It started out as a hunting club back in the forties and fifties, but as the members got older and wolves got scarce it turned into a social club. They are Pinebox's biggest fundraising group. They give money for local activities like the high school, humane society, and the Pinebox Hospice.

**JR:** Pinebox has its own hospice?

**DG:** Oh, yes. ... But are you sure you want this for your travel story?

**JR:** Don't worry. I'm just looking for background information so I get a good feel for your beautiful community.

**DG:** Okaaaaay. Well, the Pinebox Hospice Society runs a home on the edge of the lake. It's a very beautiful place, and believe it or not it's getting a reputation as a lovely place to pass away. You know–surrounded by nature and all that. Still, that's got to be one hard job. They have a dedicated staff. I know I couldn't do it. Raising money is one thing, but staring death in the face every day is something else.

**JR:** No kidding. Well, thanks for your time. I think I'll take your suggestion and visit the library.

**DG:** Great! Let me give you one of our maps. (paper rustles). Okay, we're here. And let's see... here's the library. So when you pull out of the parking lot you're going to want to turn right. Then at the light you're going to want to take another right, then you'll go three blocks. It's a white building across the street from the grocery store. You can't miss it.

**JR:** Thank you very much.

[interview ends]

## Interview 2: Pinebox Library

**Jennifer Ridge:** Okay NOW it's on. See? The little green light is on.

**Norma Wallis:** Oh yes, I see that now.

**JR:** So now that I am recording, would you mind giving me your name and stating whether or not I have permission to record this conversation?

**NW:** My name is Norma Wallis. I am a librarian for the Pinebox Library. I work here part time in the archives. I am also Treasurer for the Pinebox Historical Society.

**JR:** Thank you Ms. Wallis. And you don't mind my recording this?

**NW:** I suppose not.

**JR:** Thank you. So, can you tell me a bit about how Pinebox got started?

**NW:** Well, Empresario Greystone settled this area in 1826—

**JR:** I'm sorry. Who? Did you say Emperor Greystone?

**NW:** No no no. EM-PRES-ARE-EE-OH. Didn't you ever take Texas History in school?

**JR:** Actually, I just recently moved to Texas.

**NW:** And you're writing for a Texas travel magazine?

**JR:** Think of it this way: I can write about Pinebox from a fresh perspective.

**NW:** I suppose... Well, back in 1822 or so, Mexico passed a colonization law. Under the law, contractors were issued large tracts of land to colonize. Empresarios were like recruiters, land developers, and governors all in one.

**JR:** So Pinebox was colonized by one of these Empresarios.

**NW:** Right. Carter Greystone. Before getting an Empresario contract he was a fairly successful farmer and businessman in Virginia. But after his wife and son died of pneumonia in 1823 he decided to leave his old memories behind and start fresh out on the frontier. Of course, after he settled down out here he changed his mind and had their bodies brought to Texas to be buried near his new home.

**JR:** Wow, really? Back in the early 1800s that must have been a messy job.

**NW:** He was a rich man by the standards of the day. After getting his Empresario contract from the Mexican government in 1825, Carter didn't waste any time. He recruited 400 families. Think about that. Four hundred FAMILIES all willing to pick up and move out into the wilderness for the promise of cheap land they'd never even seen. No roads. No towns. No civilization except what you make.

**JR:** Cheap land? I can see how that would be a draw.

**NW:** Well, there is that. Each family got something like 100 acres of land. Anyway, by the end of 1826 the first families had arrived and settled around the lake. By 1828 over 600 families had been lured here with the promise of fertile land. Things were getting a bit crowded, so Greystone applied to the Mexican government for more land.

**JR:** ...

**NW:** Well, he applied but he never got a response. Finally in September of 1829 he took matters into his own hands. He took a dozen families into the Big Thicket with the intention of building another settlement upriver from Lake Greystone. He left his younger brother William in charge of the settlement. William had come to Texas in 1827 with his wife and daughters.

Weeks went by, then months with no word from the new settlement. William got worried that his brother had been attacked by local Indians and sent a request to Mexico for troops to protect the settlers and to locate Carter's lost colony. Needless to say, his request went unanswered too.

**JR:** This is really interesting. Someone could make a movie based on this.

**NW:** You haven't even heard the ending yet. The next spring, William formed a militia to search for his brother's outpost. They traveled upriver into the Big Thicket, where they found scraps of clothing and some busted trunks. No other evidence was ever found of Carter or the families who traveled with him.

**JR:** Wow! So do you think they were attacked by Indians or what?

**NW:** I guess it depends on who you talk to. Most historians assume the Carter party was attacked by the Indians. But there's also another explanation. All the local school kids can tell you about the creature in the woods. It's like a local Bigfoot. Maybe Carter disturbed something in those woods. Something that fought back.

**JR:** You're kidding me, right?

**NW:** Well, it makes a fun story, doesn't it? Anyway, when Texas won its independence from Mexico in 1836, all those old Empresario contracts became void. William continued to run the settlement until it officially became the town of Pinebox in 1855. Even after that he was Mayor until he died in 1875. As a matter of fact, there are still descendants of the Greystone family in the area.

**JR:** So why is the town called Pinebox and not Greystone?

**NW:** Well, the first colonists came here for farming, but pretty soon it was clear that this was timber land. By the time the city was chartered, timber was the major economic force. There was already a town named "Pine", so Greystone named us Pinebox. Maybe it was a kind of nod toward his brother's death, or maybe not. Nobody really knows for sure and we probably never will.

**JR:** Well Ms. Wallis, thank you so much for your time. It has been fascinating hearing you talk about the history here.

**NW:** Well I hope some of this makes it into your story. My name is spelled N – O – R – M – A – W – A – L – L – I – S.

[interview ends]

## Interview 3: Parks & Recreation

**Jennifer Ridge:** Would you mind starting over now that I'm recording?

**Jonathan Connelly:** Sure thing.

**JR:** First of all, please give me your name and tell me I have permission to record you.

**JC:** MY NAME IS JON CONNELLY AND I WORK FOR PINEBOX PARKS AND REC.

**JR:** ...

**JC:** OH YEAH. YOU CAN RECORD ME TOO. ANYHOW, PINEBOX HAS SEVERAL ATTRA—

**JR:** Jon-

**JC:** ATTRACTIONS. WE HAVE THE GOLF COUR—

**JR:** JON!

**JC:** YEAH?

**JR:** You don't have to shout into the recorder. It has a sensitive microphone. Just talk normally.

**JC:** Oh. Sorry.

**JR:** That's okay. Now what were you saying about the microphone? I mean, about the golf course?

**JC:** Heh. We have a very nice 18 hole golf course that is owned by the city. I think the real name is the Dan Travis Golf Course. It's one of the nicest in East Texas. The school holds a big tournament here every year.

**JR:** The school? East Texas University?

**JC:** Yeah, ETU. Anyhow, next to the golf course is the Golan Fairgrounds. We have all sorts of events out there. There's the annual rodeo, the chili cookoff, the 4-H show and auction, uh... and other stuff.

**JR:** Someone was telling me there's a—

**JC:** OH, and the Swap Meet! It's the East Texas Swap Meet and Festival. It's a big deal around here. We hold it every Halloween weekend. The swap meet is like a big flea market out at the fairgrounds. But there's also a parade through town on Saturday morning, and a carnival, and a beer garden, and a costume contest. And a bunch of other stuff. Then Saturday night they have the Moon Dance. They fence off one of the streets downtown, set up a stage at one end, and charge $20 a head to hear crappy country and rock music. But if you're single, it's the place to be. There, or the beer garden.

**JR:** Sounds... fun.

**JC:** Yeah, you should come back and see it. Or, hey! That would be a good thing to write for your magazine. Folks from all over East Texas come to the Swap Meet!

**JR:** I'll be sure to write about it.

**JC:** ... Uh, what else should I talk about?

**JR:** How about you tell me some of the things to do outdoors, Jon? I hear there's a lake, and the woods...

**JC:** Duh! Yeah! Pinebox is a National Tree City. I'm not really sure what that means. But it's on all our brochures. We've got all sorts of walking trails crisscrossing Pinebox and the university. Some of them go right into the Big Thicket past some historic old homesteads and gardens. If you really want a hike, there's the old El Camino Real. That's Spanish for King's Highway. You can hike it all the way to the Louisiana border. It's got all sorts of scenic views, campsites, animals, and plants.

**JR:** Jon, that reminds me. I keep hearing people talk about the Big Thicket. Just where is it?

**JC:** (snort) Jen, you're *in* the Big Thicket right now! It's all around us. All these national forests and stuff in this part of the country—they're all just pieces of one big forest we call the Big Thicket. It's hundreds of miles big.

**JR:** Oh. I feel dumb.

**JC:** You're not from around here, are you?

**JR:** Nope. I came here just for this article.

**JC:** So where are y—

**JR:** Hey Jon, how about you tell me about some of the other things to see around here? Tell me about the local lakes and parks.

**JC:** Okay. Let's see. Uh. Most folks think the Caddo Indian Mounds Park make for the best camping. There's lot's of trails to hike on, if you're into that kind of thing. Then some folks ride their horses in the Burn. That's a piece of forest east of here that burned up in a forest fire in the 50s or something. Nobody knows what started it, but it's about 25 square mile where stuff still won't grow to this day. I'm not really all that into camping though, unless it's for hunting. Now fishing is a different story. I'm saving up for a killer fishing boat. It's gonna have–

**JR:** That's great, Jon. Why don't you tell me about the lakes around here.

**JC:** Oh man, Pinebox has got some of the best swimming, fishing and boating in Texas. We're just 10 minutes from Lake Greystone, about 20 minutes from Sam Rayburn and forty minutes from Toledo Bend. Uh, let's see. Lake Greystone started out as a natural lake, but during the depression the CCC came through and built a dam and made the lake bigger. Up until the 70's Pinebox got some of its power from a turbine out there, but the equipment was really old and there was some sort of accident.

**JR:** Really? What kind?

**JC:** You know, I don't really know. Folks don't talk about it much.

**JR:** Oh well.

**JC:** Do you know why it's called Lake Greystone? See, back when Texas was still part of Mexico there was this governor named Carl Greystone and he–

**JR:** Actually Jon, someone at the library told me about him.

**JC:** Really? I'll bet they didn't tell you how he disappeared. See–

**JR:** Actually—

**JC:** there had been attacks on some of the settlers. Some people were killed and some just disappeared. Carl Greystone took a bunch of folks upriver into the Big Thicket to track down whatever was responsible. Only, he never came back. Finally his brother took some trackers into the woods after them, but all they could find was some bloody rags and strange prints in the ground. They say the hunting dogs were so scared they ran off the opposite direction and showed up in Pinebox half a day before the people. Bet they didn't tell you THAT at the library!

**JR:** You're right, Jon. They sure didn't tell me that. So who killed all those people?

**JC:** ...

**JR:** What?

**JC:** You'd just laugh.

**JR:** No! Tell me.

**JC:** Promise you won't laugh.

**JR:** I promise.

**JC:** (indistinct)

**JR:** What?

**JC:** Piney Devil! I said it was the Piney Devil!

**JR:** The... Piney Devil? I haven't heard of that. What is it?

**JC:** Well, it's just what we call it. Imagine Bigfoot, but sixteen feet tall and with horns. That's the Piney Devil. The Indians all knew about it and they knew better then to go trespassing. Greystone pissed it off somehow and they all got spanked for it.

**JR:** That's really…interesting, Jon. But tell me, how do you think his brother got all the way in the woods to find the rags if the Piney Devil was after him?

**JC:** I knew you'd laugh! Look, there could be all kinds of reasons. Maybe it was just Carl that pissed it off. Maybe the Piney Devil was in a different part of the forest when his brother came through. Maybe the Devil was busy baking Indian pot pie. I don't know! But don't tell me it's not real. I've seen it myself!

**JR:** You've… seen the Piney Devil?

**JC:** Yeah, I seen it. Me and my brother were out hunting one night and uh…I'm not saying anything more. I'm done here. This don't have nothing to do with a tourist story for a magazine. You're just laughing at me.

**JR:** Jon, I'm not laughing at you. I just…

**JC:** Maybe not laughing, but you're thinking I'm just a dumb hick. I can tell. Well I'm not. And I'm taking away my permission to record me!

[chair scuffling]

**JR:** … huh…

[interview ends.]

## Interview 4: East Texas University

**Jennifer Ridge:** This is Jennifer Ridge at the office of University Public Relations. Would you please give me your name and if I have your permission to record you?

**Terry Easton:** My name is Terry Easton and you have my permission.

**JR:** Thank you, Terry. Would you mind doing me a favor and start by telling me a little bit about ETU's history?

**TE:** Not at all. East Texas University was first founded in 1888 as East Texas Women's College. For whatever reason, the college wasn't very successful. By 1905, enrollment had dropped from a peak of 18 students to only five. Fortunately for us, just down the road at Beaumont, a little oil well by the name of Spindletop turned out to be the biggest oil discovery of its time. One of the early wildcatters who got rich off the discovery was Howard O'Brien, whose wife just so happened to be an ETW alumnus. After the O'Briens went from rags to riches almost overnight, Mrs. O'Brien convinced her husband to donate a million dollars to her alma matter.

**JR:** No kidding!?

**TE:** Yeah. Think about it. For most people today a million dollars is a lot of money. Back then, it was *really* a lot of money. Of course, nobody gives away that kind of money without some strings attached. Mr. O'Brien insisted that enrollment be opened to men as well as women. Of course that meant they couldn't keep calling it a women's college, so they eventually settled on the name South East Texas Institute.

**JR:** But... aren't we closer to the northern part of the state than the southern?

**TE:** Hmph. I guess it's just one of those regional peculiarities. Everyone refers to this part of the state as southeast.

**JR:** Oh. I'm sorry to interrupt.

**TE:** Not at all. You just stop me if you have any other questions. Anyway, South East Texas Institute served this part of the state for several decades. In those days, the students came from mostly rural families and studied forestry or geology. Aside from oil, there used to be silver in this neck of the woods and there's still an operating tin mine.

**JR:** So when did the name change to East Texas University?

**TE:** Actually, not that long ago. It was in 1987. In 1985 a news magazine listed the top ten party schools in the country, and we were on it. President Patterson was hired to clean house. He fired faculty who turned a blind eye to cheating, he helped the city clamp down on underage drinking, and he raised the minimum qualifications for admission. He also lobbied the state legislature to change our name to distance ourselves from the old reputation. We'd grown quite a lot from the days of being a forestry and geology institute, and he felt like our name should reflect our greater scope.

**JR:** I'll bet the students weren't too happy about all that.

**TE:** Heh, yes, he was a pretty unpopular person around here at the time. But he had his supporters and he did what needed to be done. Today East Texas University serves more than 12,000 undergraduate and graduate students in almost sixty fields of study. Our anthropology and folklore departments are ranked in the top ten in the country and ETU is rated in the top 20 best education values for a public university. You'll see a statue and two buildings named for the O'Briens, but ETU owes what it is today to former president Patterson.

**JR:** Neat!

**TE:** Let's see… what else would you like to know? We have students from more than twenty countries. We also have a nationally ranked ROTC program and we were just recently awarded a grant to become a Homeland Defense Training School. We also have a very active Journalism department. We have a student operated cable television station, radio station, and newspaper. The newspaper is also online at theravensreport.com, so our alumni can stay connected with campus happenings no matter where they are in the world.

**JR:** Let me ask you something. ETU may not be a party school anymore, but surely the students must have some way of blowing off steam? I've spent the day in town, and it doesn't really look like a college town. In fact, it doesn't seem very… hospitable to students.

**TE:** That's because we try to give the students what they need right here on campus. We have five rec sports facilities and an indoor Olympic-sized pool. We have our own movie theater and bowling ally. We have two new dorms that are less than five years old. By comparison there's not much in Pinebox to interest students, and that is at least partly by design. They don't want much to do with us, and we don't need much from them.

**JR:** Well, you say "us" and "them", but you must live here too?

**TE:** ... I don't want to read this in your travel article, okay? This is off the record. Got it?

**JR:** Got it.

**TE:** Most ETU faculty and upper-level staff live in Timberland Village. It's a planned community about a quarter of the way around the lake. We have our own grocery store, post office, gas station, and so on.

**JR:** Wow! Really? It sounds like there's not much love lost between Pinebox residents and ETU.

**TE:** I don't think I want to comment on that. Let's just say Timberland Village is just a nice place to live. It's a private, gated community, and crime is almost unheard of.

**JR:** Speaking of crime, is it much of a problem with your students? I mean, I'm sure there's the usual amount of petty theft, but anything more serious?

**TE:** What does this have to do with a tourism article?

**JR:** Not a thing. That's just my own curiosity speaking. This seems like a such a nice, quiet place to live and go to school.

**TE:** Oh, it is. Sure there's the usual rowdiness every once in a while, but overall these are pretty good kids.

**JR:** So nothing too serious? No bodies found in the roommate's dorm fridge or anything?

**TE:** Haha, no nothing like that. Every semester we have a few students who just disappear, but most of them turn up either back home or hung over in a Mexican jail. I'm sure it's the same at every University.

**JR:** ...You're probably right. Well Terry, thank you for your time. Do you mind if I take one of these brochures?

**TE:** Please do. And let me give you an ETU t-shirt as a souvenir.

**JR:** Thank you!

## Interview 5: Henry Urbina

**Henry Urbina:** –sorry about that. I wanted to strangle Dwayne when he told me that he let Jon Connelly talk to you.

**Jennifer Ridge:** Oh, that's okay. He was an interesting character.

**HU:** Well that's a polite way of putting it. I'm glad you gave me a chance to meet with you and set things straight.

**JR:** Yeah, I was surprised when the hotel told me I had a message. I'll be honest. On the phone I almost turned you down, but when you said you'd show me what Pinebox was really like, I–.

**HU:** Heh. Yeah. No one can resist the mighty lure of—THE PIZZA BARN!

**JR:** Haha. And here I thought you were going to let me in on some deep, dark community secret.

**HU:** Oh, I am. The Pizza Barn is Pinebox's best kept secret. Did you notice the stage over there? They have live music and dancing a couple nights a week. This is THE place to be on a Saturday night.

**JR:** Hahahaha. I hope you're joking.

**HU:** Heh. I wish I was. So tell me what local sights you've–

**JR:** Oh great.

**HU:** What?

**JR:** Jon Connelly just came in. Crap! He just saw me. He still looks pissed.

**HU:** Part of me wishes he'd come over here and give me a reason to fire him, but I wouldn't want you in the middle. Do you want me to tell him to leave?

**JR:** No, I don't want to cause trouble. Why don't we just cut this short? Maybe I can meet you tomorrow.

**HU:** No way! I'm not going to let that little weasel spoil your visit to Pinebox. I'll tell you what. I'll go get them to make our order to go. You just head outside and get in my pickup. I'll take you on a driving tour of Pinebox and we can eat pizza as we go.

**JR:** Oh, I don't—

**HU:** Come on! We've already ordered the food. And you can't ask for better research for your article. What kind of reporter would pass up this kind of opportunity?

**JR:** ...Okay. Which one is your truck?

**HU:** It's white and has the Pinebox Parks and Rec logo on the door. It's not locked.

**JR:** Got it. ... [long stretch with no distinguishable speech]

**HU:** Hi. Ready for a wild ride?

**JR:** Sure, why not? If I end up dead in a ditch at least I told the hotel clerk who I was meeting, so you'd better take care of me. ...

**JR:** Sorry. That was supposed to come out funny.

**HU:** ... That's okay. You're in Pinebox. You *should* be cautious.

**JR:** Okay, you're not making me feel safer.

**HU:** Sorry. ...

**JR:** So what's on the itinerary for this evening?

**HU:** Well, we're going to make a left right here at Hamburger City, aaaaaand then we're going to make a quick right. Now just a couple blocks down this street is Crenshaw's Woods. This is a good example of how Pinebox has incorporated native flora into the city landscape. Jon probably didn't tell you, but we're a National Tree City.

**JR:** What does that mean?

**HU:** It's a program run by the national Arbor Day foundation. Basically to be a tree city you have to have a forestry board, you've got to adopt a tree care ordinance, you have to maintain a forestry program with an annual budget of at least two dollars per capita, and you have to host an Arbor Day observance.

**JR:** Hmmm.

**HU:** Okay, so maybe that doesn't sound very exciting. But it was a big deal to us at the time. Anyway, we're heading to Crenshaw's Woods, which is one of the nicest natural areas here in town. It's got several hiking trails, and in the middle is the Lost Pond.

**JR:** ...Okay, I'll bite. What's lost about it?

**HU:** Haha! Well, since you asked... Back in about 1852 there was an awful drought in these parts. The lake levels got so low that the water was unfit for drinking. Eli Crenshaw was an early settler here in Pinebox and he was desperate to find water for his cattle and family. And here on your right is Crenshaw's Woods. If you don't mind, I'm just going to drive real slow and make the block. I just thought of somewhere else really cool to take you, but we've got to get there before the sun goes down.

**JR:** You're the tour guide. So what happened with the drought?

**HU:** Well, according to the legend, Eli made a pact with the Devil and the next day he found a pool of clear, cool, spring water in his woods. The whole community celebrated Eli's discovery, but Eli himself was found dead exactly a year later. He was found floating in the Lost Pond.

**JR:** What a story! But I don't see the pond.

**HU:** It's in the middle of the woods. You can't see it from the street, but if you come back tomorrow you can find a hiking trail that leads to it. Of course, the woods used to be a lot bigger in those days so it's a little more understandable why the pond would be hard to find. Now I'm just going to head back the way we came and get on Highway 96.

**JR:** So what's next?

**HU:** Oh, I'll let this one be a surprise. I hope you don't mind, but I'm gonna have to step on it. It's getting pretty close to sunset.

**JR:** Oh, you should see me drive.

**HU:** I'll bet! Anyway, I can tell you about some other places of interest on the way. There's Lake Greystone, of course. It began as a natural lake, but back during the depression the CCC came in and built a permanent dam. A lot of native and settler historical sites ended up under water, but the Texas Historical Society has sectioned off a few areas around the lake. You've got Fort Greystone and the Ravens Mound, to name a couple.

**JR:** What are those?

**HU:** Well, Fort Greystone really isn't anything other than a long mound of dirt. See, back when Pinebox was first settled, some people went missing and the mayor was convinced that Pinebox was on the verge of being wiped out. So he convinced some folks to put together an earth and timber fort as a last defense. But as far as anyone knows it was never used in a battle. These days it's just a pile of dirt. I know I work for Parks and Rec and all, but even I think it's pretty boring.

**JR:** So what about the Raven Hills?

**HU:** The Ravens Mound? That is a burial mound of Cherokee Indians. This story's a bit more interesting. Back after the Texas Revolution but before we joined the US, a war band of Cherokees set up camp a few miles from Pinebox. The Cherokee had driven off the last of the Karankawas from the area by that point, and these natives weren't as friendly to the new Texans.

**JR:** Can you really blame them? We were taking their land!

**HU:** I don't think I'll touch that one. Anyway, they didn't attack right away so the mayor sent out messengers to see what they wanted. Unfortunately, the only ones brave enough were a few of the rougher lumberjacks, and they didn't speak a word of Cherokee. They go out and meet with the chief, and through sign language the lumberjacks figure out that they're talking to a war band there to pick a fight with someone named "Golan". Sound familiar?

**JR:** The name of the county!

**HU:** Right. Well, the lumberjacks try to tell them that there isn't anyone in Pinebox named Golan, but the Cherokees are determined. So the lumberjacks go back to town and report to the mayor, and everyone spends the night waiting for the attack to come.

**JR:** Okay, where are you taking me? I didn't say anything when we got off the highway, but a gravel road?

**HU:** Heh, don't worry. It's just another mile or so.

**JR:** Okay, so the Cherokees attacked Pinebox?

**HU:** Actually, they didn't. The morning dawned with no attack. Then the cavalry arrived—literally. At the first sight of trouble the mayor had sent a runner to the nearest Texas Ranger outpost, and a whole troop rode into town that morning. A couple of them spoke Cherokee, so they went down to the encampment to try to sort things out. As they got closer, it looked like the whole Indian encampment was covered in some sort of black blanket. When they got closer still, they realized they were looking at a whole flock of ravens. The entire campsite was covered in them, and every Indian in the war party was dead.

**JR:** What? Who killed them?

**HU:** Nobody knows. But the funny thing is that the Rangers explained that the word for raven in Cherokee is golanv. The lumberjacks couldn't pronounce the last vowel, so it came out Golan. If they were there to fight the ravens, it looked like the ravens won. The Pinebox folks dug a shallow mass grave and piled it with lots of dirt like some Indian burial mounds they'd seen. And that's how the Raven Mound got its name AND how the county got ours.

**JR:** Amazing!

**HU:** In the 50s, the historical society put up a monument shaped like a raven out there. It had one word inscribed on it. Can you guess what it says?

**JR:** Golan?

**HU:** Nevermore.

**JR:** Oh...you jerk! I can't believe I fell for that. Was any of that story true?

**HU:** Every word, up to the part about the monument. And here we are.

**JR:** Is this another joke? Wilson Quarry?

**HU:** Just a sec. [sound of vehicle door opening and closing, then opening and closing again a minute later]. Don't let the looks of the place fool you.

**JR:** Oh, I'm fooled alright. I'm not sure what worries me more—all the no trespassing signs on the gate, or the way you slipped the chain off the post without unlocking the padlock.

**HU:** Well, technically we shouldn't be here. But people come out here all the time. The quarry has been closed for decades and the owners live in Houston so they don't really care as long as nobody hurts themselves and sues.

**JR:** Henry, you're not making me feel very comfortable here. What are we doing alone at an abandoned rock quarry? This is something straight out of a movie. The kind where the girl is never seen again.

**HU:** Oh please. This is a local landmark. Half the people I graduated from high school with lost their virginity out here. We're just going to pull up here, and… I'll tell you what. Let me turn around and back up instead. Then we can sit on the tailgate and I'll tell you all about Wilson's Quarry as we watch the sun set.

**JR:** Watch the…? Look, Henry, I'm sure you're a nice guy, but I just met you. I don't know if I gave you the wrong impression, but—

**HU:** No, no. It's not like that. I promise. Wilson Quarry really is a local landmark. You've got to see it to believe it. I swear, just come watch the sun set and as soon as it's done I'll take you back if that's what you want. Come on. The pizza's getting cold.

**JR:** …I must be crazy.

**HU:** Good. You hold the pizza, and I'll let down the tailgate. Oh, and there's an ice-chest in the back. You want coke or beer?

**JR:** Coke definitely.

**HU:** Suit yourself. Have a seat here and I'll grab the drinks.

**JR:** Alright. I'm here miles from civilization sitting on your tailgate eating cold pizza. Are you going to tell me why it was so important to watch the sun set? And if we're supposed to be watching the sun set, why are we facing a sheer rock wall? If you tell me this is where you lost your virginity, I am SO out of here.

**HU:** Hahaha. No. That would be Crenshaw's Woods.

**JR:** Too much information.

**HU:** Sorry. Anyway, look at the quarry wall right in front of us. Do you notice anything...odd? Here's your Coke. Sure I can't offer you a beer? Mmmmm. Beer yummy.

**JR:** No thanks. The Coke is fine. What am I supposed to be looking for?

**HU:** Keep watching. The sun isn't quite low enough. So let me give you a bit of history. This used to be a sandstone quarry started by a guy named Henry Wilson in 1921. I think he was a descendant of one of the original settlers–John Henry Wilson. Anyway, the operation only lasted until 1929 when part of the excavation collapsed and crushed him. It was that part over there, back behind us.

**JR:** Somehow, I'm not surprised. Why does it seem like Pinebox isn't such a safe place to live?

**HU:** Because it isn't. Even before Wilson died, eight other workers died in on the job accidents. After Wilson died, his widow moved back with her family in California. She tried to sell the quarry, but the depression was coming on and nobody would touch it. So it—

**JR:** Mmf! I see it! Holy sh–.

**HU:** Cool, huh?

**JR:** It's a huge face! It's like looking at a movie screen.

**HU:** Yeah.

**JR:** How is it doing that? It's a perfect silhouette. I see the eyes, the nose, the mouth, the ears.

**HU:** Yeah. We're lucky the weather cooperated. It's a good, strong sunset. Keep watching. It's not done yet.

**JR:** How can the sun be doing this? I mean, it's too perfect!

**HU:** Take another look over your shoulder at the rock formation where Wilson was killed. When the sun dips down that notch in the rock and shines on what was left standing after the accident, it projects this face on the wall.

**JR:** Ooooh, that's kind of freaky. The way the shadows are growing makes it looks like his face is changing.

**HU:** Just wait.

[a few minutes pass]

**JR:** Uh, Henry? I think I'll take that beer after all.

[Silence, followed by sound of can opening.]

**JR:** That absolutely can't be natural. I mean, the teeth. The eyes.

**HU:** ... You know, I haven't been out here in years. I thought it would be something funny to show a reporter, you know? Seeing it again, it doesn't seem so funny.

[several minutes pass]

**JR:** You're awfully quiet.

**HU:** Oh, sorry. I was thinking about alligators.

**JR:** Alligators?

**HU:** Golan county has one of the highest rates of alligator attacks in the country. Higher than most parts of Florida or Louisiana. But you know what? I've lived here all my life and I don't think I've seen an alligator more than ten times.

**JR:** ...What are you saying, Henry?

**HU:** You were right, what you said earlier. Pinebox is a dangerous place. About ten years ago, the mayor was found dead in his office. At least, they found the top half of him. The bottom half was just gone. Do you know what the police ruled it? Alligator attack. In his office.

**JR:** You're kidding me.

**HU:** Do you know why we're called Pinebox?

**JR:** Something to do with the timber industry, right?

**JR:** Oh please! Is that what they told you? Back in the 1860s, one third of the town died in one night. Some people woke up, and some just didn't. At least one from every household. It was like a plague or something, but there'd been no sign of illness before or after. Even the town's first mayor, William Greystone, was one of the taken. The saw mills had to build nothing but coffins for three whole days. After the funeral, the new mayor called a town hall meeting and the whole town voted to rename the town Pinebox from Greystone.

**JR:** So why give me the runaround?

**HU:** It's hard to explain. Most folks just don't like talking about the things that go on around here. It's almost…embarrassing. We don't even like thinking about it.

**JR:** But you are.

**HU:** Yeah, it's funny. I guess it's Wilson's Folly up there that got me talking. Or maybe it's the beer. Anyway, any time someone dies and there's parts missing or the body's tore up, they write it up as alligator or a bear. See, it keeps the official murder rate low. Either that, or they declare it a missing persons case.

**JR:** Missing persons? Look Henry, do you remember a couple of years ago hearing about— what was that?

**HU:** I don't know. It sounded like someone yelling. Oh hell, it's probably someone down at the pit.

**JR:** Is that good or bad?

**HU:** It depends. We'd better go check it out though. We'll have to walk. Come on. The pit is a small spring-fed pond down at the other end of the quarry. Kids sometimes go skinny-dipping there, but it really isn't very safe. Once you get in it's not easy to climb out, and the water is ice cold. Kids have cramped up and drowned because they couldn't get out.

**JR:** How deep is it?

**HU:** Good question. Really deep. They say that back in the 70s a high-school girl murdered her boyfriend and drove his car into the Pit. A few days later she broke down and confessed and the police called in a scuba team to recover the car. The divers said they went straight down something like sixty feet without finding the bottom. They had to give up because the water was too cold on account of being spring fed.

**JR:** What is it about this place? Why does every story involve a gruesome death?

**HU:** I don't know. I guess growing up here it didn't seem that strange. You just get used to it after a while.

**JR:** There it is again!

**HU:** I can't tell if that's laughter or crying, can you?

**JR:** No.

**HU:** Let's pick up the pace. Someone could be hurt or in trouble. It's around that outcropping there. It's getting dark quick, isn't it? I should've grabbed the flashlight out of the glovebox.

**JR:** I'm not getting any cell phone signal.

**HU:** Yeah, forget it. Coverage sucks on a good day, but the walls are too high to get anything from down here. Okay, it's just around here. ... WHAT THE—

[recording ends]

## Postscript

Jennifer Ridge's rental car was discovered abandoned the following morning roughly a mile from the Golan County line. All her belongings, including the tapes from this transcript, were found in the car. According to the hotel clerk, Ms. Ridge returned to the hotel alone late that night and checked out early. That is the last time anyone admits to having seen Ms. Ridge, dead or alive, in the two years since her disappearance. With no physical evidence of foul play, the authorities still refuse to classify the case as anything other than a missing persons incident. Henry Urbina is also listed as a missing person and is wanted for questioning in conjunction with Ms. Ridge's disappearance.

*Texas Travel Destinations* magazine denies assigning Ms. Ridge an article on Pinebox, or even of knowing her.

Two years before her disappearance, an ETU freshman by the name of Michael Ridge disappeared mid-way through the fall semester.

These transcripts were acquired the through the Freedom of Information Act. The Golan County Sheriff's Department still refuses direct access to the original tapes.

# The Hanging Tree

*by Filamena Young*

Louis Rainer, attorney, started his new career in the little Texas town of Pinebox by running late. Despite the courthouse's location, so-called Main Street proved more difficult to follow thanks to a convoluted one-way road his directions didn't mention, and the fact that Pinebox was a much larger quaint 'little' town than he was expecting.

It was 9:20 a.m. when he made his way into the courthouse, and despite his rush, the clerk sitting in the front room gave him a slow, easy smile. "You must be Mr. Rainer. Mr. Perkins said you'd be here, but we weren't sure when. He's in court now, handling some little thing. You wanna go ahead in there and have a seat?"

Louis Rainer was young, smart, handsome, and eager. He wanted all of those traits–except the last–to speak for themselves when he walked into that courtroom. So, he nodded to the clerk, straightened his tie, checked his hair, and pressed into the courtroom quietly.

Any hopes for a controlled first impression vanished as the door to the courtroom squeaked with unimaginable volume and all talking within went silent. All eyes, maybe ten pairs, were on Rainer when he slid sheepishly into the room. He raised a hand and said a light apology, closing the door quietly behind him. It did not squeak again, and all eyes shifted from Rainer to the judge as if the interruption had been all but forgotten immediately.

Judge Howard Lindsey sat at an oak bench with marble inlay, a touch too decorative to suit the country feel of the rest of the cedar wood courtroom. He wasn't an old man, not as old as would be expected with his years on the bench, but he was an intense figure. Rainer thought that he looked like a hanging-judge, despite the fact that there hadn't been a hanging in Pinebox in a hundred years. His face was drawn and serious, and despite the glasses that Lindsey wore, Rainer could see one of his eyes was milky white with a cataract. That milky eye fixed on the man in the defendant's chair as the judge began to speak. A giant painting of an archangel, flaming sword pointed at the ground, hovered behind the judge. The angel's luminous wings sometimes formed a halo around the judge when he stood. Rainer suspected that was no accident.

"You've been in front of this court five times, twice in the last year, Mr. Conroy. You've gone and put that poor woman of yours in the hospital. They don't know if she'll ever recover. I sit here and listen to you snivel on about how it isn't your fault? How many times has the Pinebox Police Department helped you dry up?"

Rainer passed through the aisle to a bench behind the defense table. He identified Perkins by his positioning next to the defendant, but did not interrupt. The defendant, Mr. Conroy, looked abjectly terrified. He'd been sobbing, and snot still stuck to his upper lip where he hadn't wiped it all away yet. His swarthy complexion was white and sickly around the edges, more like tallow then flesh, and his hands clenched and unclenched themselves with a desperate rhythm.

Rainer had seen some big cases out of law school in Austin. He had never seen a defendant that terrified.

Perkins, a small man in an ill-fitting suit, seemed not to notice it. Across the courtroom, the Prosecutor leaned back in his chair, hands clasped under his round belly, with even less regard.

When the Judge gave Conroy the chance to speak, the defendant blubbered incoherently for a while, a panicked tongue tripping over his words. He never claimed innocence. With Lindsey's bad eye barring down on him, the man confessed completely but said that this time he'd "get better".

"Better at covering up your crime, maybe." Lindsey waved his hand dismissively, ordered Conroy to his feet, and announced his verdict. In exchange for allocution, the county jail would hold him until he could be transferred up to state prison for fifty years on a multiple offender statue in the county. Conroy started to sob hysterically when Sheriff's Deputies cuffed him and walked him out of the room. Lindsey nodded to Rainer once, and then dismissed court.

It was then that small-framed Franklin Perkins turned to Rainer and smiled wanly. "Sorry about all that mess. Wouldn't have pegged Conroy as a crier. The Judge doesn't have much patience for criers who beat their wives."

Rainer cleared his throat. "I can't imagine who does." Beside them, the prosecutor laughed, nodded, and kept walking without giving any time for an introduction.

"That's Dennis Holloway. He's sort of a good ol' boy. He'll warm up to you if you give him time. Anyway, why don't you walk with me and we can talk a bit about what you're getting yourself into here?"

****

Franklin Perkins was retiring, among other concerns, because his heart was in bad shape. He'd had a recent scare, and started looking for a replacement.

"Things have gone downhill a bit since then, you see. Doctor says I should be all right if I just walk away from all this nonsense right now. I hate to hand it over to you so abruptly, but the ol' ticker demands I do. You understand?"

The walk along Main Street was quiet, the mid-day heat discouraging much activity. It was still–oppressively so–and but for the two lawyers walking to lunch the street would have been as dead as midnight.

"I do." Trying to make points was reflexive with the young lawyer. "My wife Carmella, she's got these breathing issues. That was one of the primary deciders on taking this job. We had to get her out of that big city air."

"You could make a lot more in private practice."

"Maybe, but Carmella's health comes first."

"And yours too, I hope." Perkins wiped his forehead with a handkerchief and clapped Rainer on the shoulder. "Damnation if it isn't hot. You just take it easy and remember at the end of the day this is still a small town with small town issues, you'll live a long full life serving the public good. You got some petty crime here and there, violence when people drink too. We have a justice who handles the family court cases, but you might be asked to represent one party or the other since we aren't chalk full of fancy divorce attorneys. Still, compared to Austin, I imagine all of this will be a little like sleepwalking."

"That's fine with me, Mr. Perkins. Like I told you over the phone, I didn't get into law because I enjoyed big fancy cases and lots of money, I got into it because the process interests me and I would have made a lousy doctor."

Perkins raised a brow at that. "Squeamish, Mr. Rainer?"

"I've been known to get a little pale around blood, I guess." Wind whipped through a young tree nearby, sending a shower of leaves and hot air across their path.

Perkins laughed. "Well, not a lot of blood spills out on this courthouse floor, I assure you." He coughed after he spoke, like a strangled chuckle. "Look, I'll give you one more piece of advice before we move on to the happier side of the job, okay? You won't see a lot of legitimate felonies out this way. When you do, you do what you have to do. If you think they're guilty, and you'll know, just tell them to plead. It'll save everyone a lot of time and grief. No one expects you to save the world here. The best you can do for some of these people is explain the situation; explain to them how much easier life will be if they just allocute."

****

It was Monday before Perkins had finally packed up the office and turned everything over to Rainer. By three, he was elbow deep in those files, familiarizing himself with Perkins' recent cases and how Lindsey's verdicts trended.

He came across Conroy's paperwork; the man's curious hysterics in court were enough to coax Rainer to take a second look at the file. Something caught his eye.

Court records had Conroy listed with two different places of birth. A tiny hiccup, but enough that Rainer thought he'd take a walk down to the hall next to the courthouse and double check with Conroy.

The public defender's office was on Hickory, a block or two from Main, so it was a short walk to the jail and courthouse. The air was warm and thick with humidity, but cooling as midday turned to evening.

When Rainer pushed on the door to the Sheriff's office, he found himself wiping at his face the way the locals did. No one sat in the room immediately inside the door, though a card celebrating the 'World's Greatest Secretary' suggested it might normally be a woman named Gwen.

Leaving the empty room, Rainer went through a door that opened into the rest of the building. To the left were a set of doors, offices and workrooms where the deputies worked, and to the right another hallway. He turned into this, seeing first an intake desk with a computer, both of which were unmanned. Behind the desk were lockers for storing prisoners' belongings. Behind that was one big holding cell that could hold maybe thirty men at a time. To the left of that, a row of individual cells for people staying a bit longer. Three or four deputies stood outside of one of these individual cells, peering in. One of the men had his hat off, stuck to his chest.

Rainer scowled for a moment and cleared his throat. "Excuse me, gentleman. I was hoping maybe I could finish up some paperwork with Mr. Conroy before he's handed off to the state?"

"I'm afraid that's not going to be possible. Mr. Rainer, was it?" One of the senior Deputies, a Captain by the gold bar on his sleeve, shook his head before looking to the young attorney.

"Why not? Something's happened?"

"See for yourself." The Captain stepped back and motioned for Rainer to come have a closer look at the cell.

Against his better judgment, Rainer stepped forward, peeking before looking into the cell. Just as he was doing so, an older woman in a jumpsuit with a stethoscope around her neck held up a white sheet. Under it, Rainer could see Conroy lying on the floor. His head was twisted to the side, eyes wide and dull. The rest of his expression was pure suffering; in fact, his finger had dug into the ground enough to snap off at the nail. His mouth was a pit of satiny drying red-brown blood. It'd been a pool, now drying.

Rainer turned away as quickly as he could and made it back to the desk with the computer before retching. A few of the deputies started to snicker before their Captain hushed them. It wasn't uncommon for Rainer to skip lunch while he was working. For once the lawyer was glad of it, since he didn't have anything in his stomach to lose.

Rainer heard boots next to him and felt a strong hand pat his shoulder once in masculine sympathy. "Sorry, there, I figured you were a criminal defense attorney in Austin and you must-a seen this sort of thing all the time."

Rainer stood, wiping his mouth with a handkerchief and shook his head. He swallowed. "No, not really. I pushed a lot of paper work, and you can skip looking at crime scene pictures when you're at the bottom of the totem pole."

"Well, I reckon you're at the top of it now. I'm Captain Martinez. I'm sort of default in charge when the Sheriff's out on business."

Rainer nodded, offering a hand. "Louis Rainer, but you all seem to know everything about me already. So, what happened to Conroy? This isn't common, is it?"

"Common? Oh no." The Captain put a hand on Rainer's shoulder again. "Takes a lot of dedication to go out the way he did. Not an easy suicide, that's for sure."

"Suicide?" Rainer blinked. "That didn't look like a hanging by shoelace or anything."

Martinez shook his head. "No, nothing like that. With the way he flipped out in court, we were watching him for that sort of thing. We took anything out of the cell he could possibly hurt himself on."

"So then how..." Rainer tried not to fill in the gaps, when a helpful young Deputy with a medical waste bag chimed in, holding the baggy up so the lawyer had no choice but to look at the meaty chunk of red flesh inside.

"Bit his own tongue out. Never seen a damn thing like it! He'd gotten some Tylenol at the courthouse, said he had a headache from crying. Doc says it thinned the blood, then when he did the deed he ran around the cell to get his heart going. Dedication, that's for sure," the Deputy said helpfully. Rainer turned to retch again.

****

Captain Martinez saw Rainer out of the cellblock and down to one of the interview rooms. Martinez came into the room, armed with a folder. "I'm glad you came in. All ugly stuff aside, turns you you've got your first real case to deal with, Mr. Defender. And this one is just plain ripe."

Happy for the distraction, Rainer smiled and took the file, finally in control of his equilibrium. "Felony murder. This is a state case?"

The Captain nodded. "Assuming he doesn't plead out."

"Which you assume he will?"

The other man shrugged noncommittal and leaned against the door jam casually. "They usually do. Three of my deputies came on him beating the victim with a tire iron; eight or nine blows post mortem. He's about as guilty as they come."

Rainer sighed, rubbed his nose with a thumb. "Yeah, give me a few minutes to read over this, and if it's alright, I'd like to talk to him to get this all wrapped up."

Martinez waved a hand. "Not a problem. We'll have him in here in ten. Take your time, and watch out. There are crime scene pictures."

Rainer thought he saw Martinez smirk, but only barely, as the Captain stepped out of the room.

****

At 9 a.m. sharp, Rainer sat next to Dennis Holloway and across the desk from Lindsey. Outside of the courtroom, without his robe on, much of the Judge's righteous aura faded, leaving just a normal older man with a milky eye in a cramped law office with more pictures of grandkids than evidence of a bloody history of Draconian rule. Unsettling, maybe, but not upsetting the longer Rainer talked to him.

"Change of venue? No, of course not." He laughed, and it was genuine. "I can't try him, anyway. He pleads not guilty and he takes his chances with the state judges."

"I understand that, sir, I really do. I think the request is strange to say the least, but he seemed legitimately afraid of you. I don't know why, but he seemed to think if he sees you in court that you'll be able to talk him into asking for the firing squad or something."

Lindsey and Holloway exchanged a look. Dennis Holloway was a touch of a cliché, and Rainer felt guilty for considering him so, but there it was. He stood tall, maybe six foot tall, with a barrel chest that had long ago settled into quite the fantastic beer gut with age and southern cooking. He spoke slow, deliberating on each word, and had the general air of smug condensation about him, even if he didn't mean to.

"Well, now, son," Holloway said, folding his hands behind his neck. Hands like ham hocks. "You have to understand, Judge Lindsey comes from a long line of gentleman judges. They've been cultivating something ya'll city folk might call infamy in the criminal sector. Of course the bad guys are afraid of him. The guilty are always afraid of judgment."

****

At a little after 9 p.m., a rumpled and over-tired Rainer left his office to walk home.

Only he wasn't alone.

A block from the office in the still, humid air he was growing accustomed to, every small noise echoed like thunder to ears normally deafened by big city white noise.

A dog howled in the distance and Rainer imagined a hoard of slobbering wolves running to dine on his flesh. He was letting his imagination get away with him, maybe, but that didn't explain away the footsteps.

Rainer was sure he heard multiple sets of footsteps somewhere in the gloom behind him. If he walked a little faster, they followed suit a half second later, and if he slowed, they did likewise. The pause between tempo changes was enough to convince Rainer he was being followed.

As he processed this, his heart began to pound and he had to wonder what really damaged to Perkins' heart. The job, the food, or the place? And of course, as his heart beat faster, he walked faster, one quickening pace feeding the other until he was in a light jog and his followers weren't far behind. He spared a glance behind him in a darkened storefront window, and thought he saw the glint of a badge. If this were a hazing, the Sheriff would hear from him in the morning. If it wasn't, well, likely no one would hear from him in the morning.

"Rainer, sir, get down!" someone shouted. When Rainer looked back, he saw two things. Something tall and black was streaking towards him, and just past the streaking figure a Pinebox police officer was lifting a shotgun. On either count, he hit the ground.

The sound of the shotgun firing shattered the night. Whatever was running at Rainer staggered but kept running. A few young uniformed patrolmen followed in hot pursuit. One of them shouted, "Direct damn shot. I can't believe he's still running."

Rainer's stomach churned at the thought, but he got up anyway. His budding curiosity turned him, dragging him in the direction the officers had run.

A half a block down, past the bus depot, Rainer slipped and nearly lost his footing. Looking down, he noticed his shoes smudged with something dark and shiny. Blood, only too viscous and darkly colored in the bus depot's 24-hour flood lights to be any kind of blood he'd ever seen. Puddles of it led in the direction the cops had gone. Despite his stomach lurching again, he followed the puddles.

In the middle of the intersection of San Augustine and Hickory, Rainer caught up with them. A crowd of four young men huddled around a figure all in black whom they were trying to subdue. As he stepped out onto the sidewalk in full view, one of the men fired suspiciously 'wild,' taking out the nearby streetlamp, plunging the section of the street into darkness. Whatever they were struggling with seemed to redouble its strength and let out a howl that sounded like a dozen screaming men. Sparks and light filled the huddle for a moment, tell-tail signs of a taser being fired. The figure howled again, this time with more pain, and stopped struggling. In its twitching and flailing Rainer thought he saw a limb, bare, not in black clothes after all, but with strangely blackened skin like it was burned all over. Or born from ashes.

After it stopped squirming, one of the young men broke away from the others, shotgun over his shoulder, and jogged to where Rainer stood against a red brick building, catching his breath.

"You okay?" the officer, who couldn't have been more than 20, asked with all the poise and confidence of a trained killer.

"Yeah, what the hell was that?"

The man looked over his shoulder as the rest of the cops started escorting the prisoner back down Hickory. "Transient. We had reports of some tramp hanging around the bus depot at night, that he'd attacked a woman. A couple of guys headed out to patrol for him when we saw you were being followed. Kinda wanted to catch him in the act, you know? I figured, officer of the court, you wouldn't mind so long as you didn't get hurt."

Rainer shook his head. "Yeah, sure, glad to help." He watched the man explain it with the practiced ease of a natural liar, or worse yet, someone telling the truth. "I'm just going to head home then. Don't worry about me."

The officer looked over his shoulder at the moving men and looked back to Rainer with a nod. "Yeah, we'll book him for questioning. Hell, you might be seeing him tomorrow morning."

Somehow, Rainer doubted it. More so, when as he waited, he saw that the crowd wasn't headed for the jail, but next door to the courthouse. Whatever was going on in this little town, the cops were in as deep as the sheriff's department.

****

Ten minutes later, once more against his reason, Rainer crept up on the basement of the courthouse. The officers had dragged his would-be attacker to a storm door that led underground, and then dragged him in. Next to the storm door, Rainer spotted a little window, next to which he crouched.

Unfortunately, it wasn't a full view of the room, which seemed remarkably big, and much of the window was covered with paper on the inside. What he could see was a concrete floor with something sticking up out of the middle of it, and a dozen feet standing around the edges of the room.

Rainer nearly jumped out of his skin when he heard Judge Lindsey speaking. "...Which is why we won't tolerate your kind of evil, not in this town. We had a deal, and you've broken it. That makes you forfeit to our kind of justice. Bleed, and feed the tree."

The captive screamed again, more so as men grunted, apparently forcing it in some direction. The scream reached a peak, running Rainer's blood cold, followed by a grinding sound, like wood in a wood chipper without the engine noise. A gush of the blackened blood sprayed up against the window Rainer peered through. He sat back gasping, and then fled.

****

Two days later, Rainer sat beside a convicted felon being arraigned for capitol murder, who sat with his face in his hands weeping. He'd come in to court, the docket had been announced, Judge Lindsey took one look at the man, and he'd spontaneously admitted to everything. He'd beaten a rival dealer, a 16-year-old boy, to death with a tire iron because the boy was selling pot to some friends. Rainer couldn't stomach the terrible crime scene photos. His client went on to admit that he had been trying to set up a meth lab to service East Texas University.

"I sent you away for ten years the last time you darkened my courtroom. Someone upstate let you off for 'good behavior,' but it won't happen again. In fact, I mean to make sure of it."

The slow, perpetual smile on Holloway's face fell away. He nodded, some of the other court officers nodded, and Rainer felt sick all over.

****

Hours later, Rainer approached the courthouse from the back, armed with an old .22 pistol and a digital camera. He nearly choked when he saw Holloway's giant frame leaning on the wall by the storm door. "We were just starting to worry you weren't going to make it." He tossed a cigarette away and crushed it under foot. "If you need a cigarette later, just remember, city ordinance prohibits smoking in a public building."

"I don't smoke."

"You might start. Anyway, come on. We figured we couldn't keep this secret from you forever. Didn't figure you'd be on to it so fast, though." It almost sounded like a compliment, but not one Rainer was sure he wanted.

When they reached the bottom of the steps, Rainer had to force himself to look up from the concrete floor he'd already seen. Sure enough, much of what he expected was there. A pair of muscular off-duty officers from the Pinebox Police Department held his bound and gagged client up by the scuff. The judge, out of his robe, calmly cleaned his glasses.

What he didn't expect was a good look at the thing in the center of the room.

A tree stump, maybe six feet in diameter, with tangled, mean roots wrapped up in the poured flooring as if the stump had pushed its way up through the floor and then rooted back through it. Much of the bark was dark and wet, as if recently stained with dark red blood.

"When my great-great-grandfather was a boy, this spot was a gallows, you see. This was a hanging tree way back when, back before the Civil." Lindsey explained. He finished the polish on his glasses and placed them back on his nose. "A lot of justice was dealt out on this spot long before the courthouse was built. A lot of injustice too. The year my family cut it down, you see, the Klan was brand new and angry because the war was over. They hung 16 young black boys from this tree for no crime greater then being black in intolerant times. Things were different then, true, but crime was crime, and my great-great-grandfather's father was a Judge. He ordered the tree chopped down to prevent it from ever being abused like that again. Last people to hang on it were the Klansmen they caught. Maybe a generation later, a new courthouse was built on this spot, so the tree stump was dug up and the courthouse built.

"Only, the tree didn't take kindly to being uprooted. My grand-dad said years later that it regrew itself, pushed itself back up in the center of this here basement. Took over until it was about the size it was when first chopped down—and it wanted balance."

Rainer started to open his mouth to protest, the story was as far-fetched as he'd ever heard.

"I know, I know. If I hadn't grown up here, seeing the things I'd seen, I'd have thought this was crazy too. But I come from a long line of Judges in this town, and if there's one thing we understand, it's justice. See, this tree was so put off by what was done on it, it sort of opened a kind of sink hole to Hell in the root system there." Lindsey pointed causally to a pit barely visible under some roots at the stump's base. It looked vaguely oral.

"Near as we can figure," said Holloway, finally speaking up. "The only way to keep that hole from spilling something out—like it did the night you got caught up in that little downtown dustup—is to occasionally deposit some of our 'trash' down inside." He patted Rainer's client's shoulder and grinned. "A little blood of truly guilty men, and the tree's appeased. Not a bad deal really, considering what a mess the criminal system is in this state."

"You mean to tell me you're killing people down here?"

"Guilty people." Lindsey corrected. "Guilty people who've confessed in open court. Bad men who're on their way to Hell anyway. Just think of this as a quicker trip that's less of a burden on tax payers." He nodded to the officers. "Fellas, if you would?"

The men nodded, and grimly forced their victim forward, though he dragged his feet like a toddler. It didn't take much effort—he was facing Hell and hadn't much fight left in him. Close to the stump, roots lifted and reached out, taking the man's legs and coiling up around his body until they had a firm hold. Then, root by root, they passed him down into the pit at the base of the stump. As soon as his feet disappeared from view, a grinding noise started. The man screamed in too much terror to feel the pain. By the time he was thigh deep, he'd passed out. When his head vanished beneath the roots, there was a sick popping sound and a belch of blood splashed up from the hole, spraying half of the room.

Rainer promptly passed out.

****

When he came awake a few hours later, he was stretched out on the floor of the Judge's office with a towel on his face. "I called your wife. Told her you met up with us to discuss some questions you had with my methods. We had some drinks, and you're just cooling off so you don't walk home a real mess. She sounded relieved."

"You aren't going to kill me?"

The Judge looked genuinely confused. "And have to find a new Public Defender and go through all this again? Can you imagine the paperwork?"

He shook his head, and Lindsey handed him a glass of bourbon on ice. "So what am I supposed to do now?"

"Well, it looks like you have a few choices, some good, some bad, but at the end of the day you're the one who has to live with yourself. You're the one who has to take care of your family and look at yourself in the mirror in the morning before work."

It didn't sound like a threat, not to him or Carmella. Like this guy was such a true believer in his 'way of doing things' that he saw no way anyone could see the truth and not accept it.

"So what are you going to do?"

"I don't know yet. I have to think about it."

Lindsey nodded. "That's about what Perkins said too. So I'll see you in court on Thursday?"

Rainer nodded weakly. "Yeah, I guess you will."

****

*Filamena Young writes fiction and freelances as a game writer. Her fiction has made rounds in a number of 'zines and twitter fiction publications, and her freelance work appears in a number of books from White Wolf Publishing. She's a mother, a wife, and a geek living just outside Philadelphia. Find out more and read her blog and book reviews at filamena.com.*

# ~The One That Got Away~

*by Preston P. DuBose*

It was plain as daylight that something was eating at Clay. Most days, he would have cussed up a storm after hooking two turtles inside an hour. Instead, he just reeled in the second little thief close to the edge of the boat and cut the line. There were times when we'd had almost unnatural good luck fishing at the Lake Greystone dam, but on that hot, smothering, August afternoon the only things biting were the mosquitoes and the turtles.

"Pete, there's something I been meaning to talk to you about," Clay said while starting on a new lure for his line.

Best friend or not, I swear he was trying to get me to strangle him. I already had a pretty good idea what he was going to say, and I didn't particularly want to hear about it. I was out there for one thing, and it wasn't sharing feelings.

"How about first you reach around behind you and grab me another Hussy?" I asked as I picked up the old, solid wood paddle.

Clay gave up threading the line through the lure and swiveled his chair to face the foam cooler in the front of the boat. The ice water sloshed loudly as he groped for a bottle. Six empties already rolled around the bottom of my near-antique aluminum bass boat. You could tell which ones were Clay's because he liked to peel off the labels, but my two with the big breasted Brazen Hussy girl were still intact.

I was thinking about her inviting smile and eyes full of promise when Clay jumped up and sent the boat wildly rocking. "Hey, what's that?" he used my beer bottle to point out to our left, "Is that a body in the water?"

Off balance and tipping dangerously in my seat, I clumsily whacked him in the butt with the oar. Just my luck, I didn't quite manage to pitch the sunofabitch face first into the water.

"Sit down you pecker-head, or we'll be in the water too!" I said.

Even after we got the boat back under control, Clay was still focused on what he thought he'd spotted. At first I couldn't see what he was talking about, but Clay just wouldn't let it drop. He kept right on pointing until I saw it too. It was just a speck way out in the water and at first I thought it was an ice chest. I was just about to say so when the ice chest weakly waved at us.

At that point, I did some more cussin'. I could see that my plans for the rest of the evening were shot.

The engine caught on the fourth try and grumbled to life. When I was sure she wasn't going to die, I gave her a little throttle and the boat bumped over the water toward the floater. Once under power, we reached the guy in only a minute.

"You okay? What happened?" Clay shouted as I cut the engine and drifted up near the guy.

He didn't look so good. He didn't have a life jacket or even a seat cushion, just a green and white floating tackle box. He was damn lucky me and Clay found him.

"Thank God you found me. I hit something big," he said. "It ripped up a hole in the bottom and sank."

The man grabbed the side of our boat with one hand, making it dip toward the water. I threw myself on the opposite side and hung a leg over into the water to keep the idiot from capsizing us, too. I wondered if I could talk him into hanging onto a rope while I towed him to shore. It was going to be a royal pain in the ass getting him into the boat. He looked to be in his early 50s and not exactly in shape.

I lost rock-paper-scissors, which meant I got to hang half my body over one side of the boat while Clay tried to haul up the swimmer on the other. It took every bit of five minutes of pulling and cussing before Clay eventually got him on board. Once inside, he lay on the bottom with his arms still locked around his plastic tackle box and gasping like a fish out of water. I rolled back into the boat a little more gracefully.

"Looks like I landed a big one," Clay joked.

"Might be over the weight limit," I said. "Sure you don't want to throw him back? Cleaning him's gonna be a bitch."

"Don't mind Pete. He's been sore ever since his wife left him. You all right? Want some water or something?" Clay asked.

The man looked up at us from the bottom of the boat and clumsily propped himself up against the side. "I've had my fill of water for the last few hours, thank you. Got any beer?"

****

It turned out that Bob was a Yankee from Pennsylvania or Connecticut or somewhere like that. He was some kind of professor visiting East Texas University who figured to get in some fishing at Lake Greystone. Some of his university friends had promised to take him out on the lake, but they'd left him high and dry at the last minute. Bob was due back up North to Boston or Chicago or wherever, so he'd just rented a boat and went out on his own.

Of course, Bob didn't know about all the underwater stumps left from trees swallowed up by the lake when the dam was put in. One had peeled open the bottom of his boat like a tin can and he'd had just enough time to grab the first thing that floated before it was all gone. He said that he'd started paddling for shore, but he had lost his glasses and couldn't see more than 20 feet in any direction. He must have been following the shoreline the whole time.

Even though he was a Yankee and an egghead type, he seemed like an okay guy.

"I appreciate you guys giving me some time to recover before I have to go back and tell that rental place I sank their boat," Bob said. He sat sprawled in the bottom of the boat between me and Clay, resting his cramped legs.

"No problem, Bob. Josh Lang still owes me for some engine work I did for him five years ago. I hope he's not insured," Clay said.

"You know the worst part? Not only do I have to explain how I sank a boat, but I've got to go home empty-handed. I didn't even get a chance to catch a fish," Bob said.

Clay and I both nodded solemnly. That sucked.

"You know…you may think I've got sunstroke, but I swear once or twice I felt something big brush up against me," Bob said, tipping back the last of his beer.

"You'da known if it was an alligator. You'd be missing body parts," I said. "It was probably a gar. They get pretty big. You want another beer?"

"Maybe it was Bessie," Clay grinned.

"Sure, Pete. What's Bessie?"

"Aww, Clay's just having fun with you," I said. "Bessie is Pinebox's Lock Ness monster."

Bob didn't laugh. "No kidding? Have you seen it?"

"Sure have! Man, were we ever plastered. That was the same day Pete talked me into trying to water-ski behind this clunker. I still got the scar." Clay grinned. "Hey, you know Bob, it sucks that you got to go back empty handed. Maybe me and Pete could help you get that big catch. I mean, we're already out here on the water."

"Not to fart in your 'fridge Clay, but his rod's at the bottom of the lake," I said.

"Then let's take him to Flathead Bayou."

"Are you kidding? That's our secret spot!" I said. "Anyhow, Bob's a Yankee and a professor to boot. He don't want to go there."

"Aww, come on! Are you telling me you're gonna deny Bob's God-given right to go fishing? Even if he could find it again on his own, he'd keep it a secret. You want to catch some big fish, right Bob? I mean, like a 75 pound catfish?"

Bob's eyes bugged out and he spewed a little bit of his Hussy down his damp shirt. "That sounds pretty good to me. But Pete's right. I lost my reel. Unless you're going to loan me one of yours," he said, gesturing toward my rod.

"Bob, you're an okay guy, but ain't nobody touches Trish but me," I said, giving Clay a hard look.

"You...uh, you named your rod?"

"Yeah, after his ex-wife," Clay said. "Pete here is an honest-to-God professional fisherman. He won second place in the state River & Lake regional tryouts. That there rod and reel is worth more than this whole damn boat. Course, while he was winning it Trish was busy changing the locks."

As Clay talked, I felt my face get warmer and warmer. It was all I could do to keep from giving my friend a taste of what Bob had just gone through. Instead I turned away and checked to see how much fuel we had left.

"Oh, I'm sorry Pete. That stinks," Bob said.

I cleared my throat and shook my head. "It ain't no thang. I'm better off with the fish."

"You're righter than you know, my friend," Bob said.

After that, nobody spoke for a couple minutes. We just sat in the boat, wrapped up in our own thoughts and the soft numbness of a cold Hussy. Finally, after I finished mine, I cranked up the engine and shouted to Bob.

"Clay's right. We can't send you back up North empty handed. We're gonna give you the fishin' story of your life!"

****

Half an hour later, we'd left the boat pushed up on a bare shore and the three of us stood barefoot and waist deep in a lonely bayou. The sun had just dipped below the tree line, casting long, cool shadows across the water. With the snarl of the Big Thicket fencing us in, the only reminder of civilization was the occasional white noise hiss of a car going down FM1224 a couple miles in the distance.

Even though it was a far cry from how I'd expected to spend my evening, I couldn't help but grin as Bob's expression changed from disbelief to downright shock when Clay described what we were about to do.

"Okay, this here is what you call Noodling," Clay explained. "I've also heard some folks call it catfisting. See, here at Lake Greystone the catfish hide from alligators by digging holes in the mud. Holes like the ones here around where we're standing."

Bob's face turned two or three shades paler and near broke his neck looking around. "What a second. Did you say alligator?"

"Aw, don't worry. For some reason the 'gaters don't like it around here. Me and Pete been here a dozen times and ain't never seen a single one," Clay said. "So anyhow, here's what we're gonna do. Two of us are gonna be spotters. That means we help find a hole and stand by while the noodler dives down and sticks his arm in it. The catfish tries to get out of his hole and latches onto your fist by instinct. Even when you get him out of his hole, he'll still hold on to your arm. Then you just yank him up. Once you break the surface, the spotters will help you wrestle your fish to the shore. Carrying a flopping 75 pound catfish through the mud and water ain't as easy as it sounds."

Bob looked at Clay like he had grown an extra head. "Look Clay, I know Southerners like to have fun with us Northerners, but I've heard of a Snipe hunt before."

Clay grinned that shit-eating, lady-killing grin of his and shook his head. "Oh you of little faith! Watch and learn!"

With that, he took a deep breath and sunk under water to the hole he'd already found. The water rippled out from the spot where Clay had plunged. Bob tried to catch sight of him, but it was like staring into a cup of coffee. Just as Bob looked up at me with a question in his eyes, Clay stood up with a whoop. He levered his arm to the surface to show off a 40 pound catfish that had locked its mouth around his fist and halfway up his forearm. I couldn't get a grip on the mud-cat's slick, grey skin, until I managed to hook my fingers through its gills and take it in a headlock. Between the two of us, we crab-walked through the mud to the beached boat and lifted his catch inside. After prying its mouth off my best friend, I looked over to see what Bob thought. He was still standing exactly where we left him, his mouth hanging open like he'd just seen the Virgin Mary playing strip poker.

Clay caught sight of Bob and laughed. We waded back over and Clay slapped him on the back. "Whad'ja think of that? Bet you ain't never done nothing like that in Lake Michigan!"

Bob closed his mouth and shook his head. "No, you got that right. I've never seen anything like it. Doesn't it hurt? Let me see your hand."

Clay held up his arm, which was red and scratched in places as if he'd been picking dewberries. "It stings a bit, but it ain't that bad. No pain, no gain, right? You ready for a try?"

"Um... how about we let Pete go next so I can watch one more time. In fact, I've got a camera in that tackle box of mine. Let me get it so I can take a picture," he said.

"Alright, I'll take a shot." I said. "But we're not leaving here 'till you've caught yourself a trophy to show off to those dickless ETU eggheads of yours."

We spent a few more minutes wading up and down the bank trying to find another catfish hole. We had to wade out deeper into the bayou to find a likely spot. The water was chest-deep here, but from what I could feel with my toes the hole felt pretty big. By then Bob was back with his tackle box, so I took a deep breath, screwed my eyes shut, and sank under the water.

Lake Greystone is one of Texas' few natural lakes. Back during the Depression, engineers from the college in Pinebox built a hydro-electric dam that grew the existing lake by hundreds of acres. I know old folks who will tell you about losing their family land and homes to the lake. It ate up acres of Pine, Oak, and Cyprus, but brought electricity to our part of the boondocks. The Big Thicket left its mark, though. In still, quiet bayous like ours, all those pine needles claimed by the lake stained the water like dark tea.

Even if Flathead Bayou's water hadn't been dark as night, all the mud and silt we'd been kicking up by wading up and down the bank would have made opening my eyes or using a facemask useless. Totally blind and mostly deaf, I felt around the muddy bottom until I found the hole.

With no time to waste, I shoved my arm up the hole, felt around for the tale-tell slick, rubbery skin of a catfish, and braced for a sudden sharp pain on my fist that would mean I'd scored a fish. After a few seconds with no hit, I pulled myself deeper underwater and shoved my arm further into the hole, wiggling it from side to side. Still nothing. Finally, just as the air burned the insides of my lungs and I couldn't stand it anymore, my fingers grazed against the soft flesh of my future catch.

I yanked my arm out and shoved against the mud with my feet as hard as I could, rocketing up out of the water and gasping for air.

Water and mud streamed from my hair and into my face. "Sonofabitch! That's one sneaky catfish. I felt him, but he wouldn't..."

It was just about then that I wiped the water from my face.

Dark crimson blood ran down Clay's face from a gash on his head, and I realized he was weaving a string of curses long enough to stretch across the bayou. Bob was backing away behind him, trying to cover us both with a .45 I hadn't seen before. His open tackle box floated lazily beside him.

"Sorry I gotta do this, fellas," Bob said, licking his lips. "Just hold still, Pete, and don't try anything funny like Clay here."

Clay started up a new, stronger string of curses and turned back toward Bob. His profanity was cut off by a sharp pop from Bob's gun, and I watched as Clay's face went about three shades lighter in time with the spurt of blood from his shoulder.

"Damn it Clay, look at what you made me do!" Spittle flew from Bob's mouth and he jabbed the air with his gun for emphasis. "YOU'RE MAKING ME SCARE THE FISH!"

The abrupt, heavy silence pressed down on us like a wet burlap sack. Even the cicadas paused their droning call for a heartbeat. Bob didn't look like such a soft, harmless egghead any more. He had a slightly wild look in his eyes; the kind where you saw way too much of the whites. I'd seen that look in cornered animals that were one sudden move away from snapping.

Clay tried to choke back a low moan. My heart hammered an ache into my chest and my brain spun drunkenly over words I could use to talk my way out. That was always Clay's thing. He was the sweet talkin' lady's man and I was the strong, quite type. We were the dynamic duo. Only, Clay wasn't in shape to do much talking and I could never reach Bob before getting shot.

I tried using the same quiet, level tone I used when working cattle. Somehow, I couldn't keep all the nerves out of my voice as I asked, "What is it you want, Bob? You know me and Clay ain't got no money. And just so you know, I'll die before I let you go Deliverance on me. Though maybe Clay here..."

"What do I want? What do I want? ...I want the granddaddy of all granddaddy fish. I want Ur-sumthinoranother. Now shut the hell up and stand next to Clay before I make you cut out your own intestines for bait."

I shut the hell up and stood in the dark, bloody water next to Clay.

While Bob pulled odds and ends from his tackle box, my best friend kept getting more and more pale. His hand was clamped against his shoulder and snot ran down his face as he struggled to keep his sobs from drawing Bob's wrath again.

Luckily for Clay, Bob had other things on his mind. Clay flinched as Bob suddenly called out something in a foreign language I ain't never heard before. More words tumbled one after another, in a sing-song chant like a nonsense nursery rhyme. With a free hand he dumped a plastic baggie of grey ash into the water, not once stumbling over the gibberish he chanted. The words twisted in my ears and left a taste like mud in my mouth.

I realized that the cicadas had stopped droning again, for good. We couldn't have been more alone on the moon. Bob's chanting drilled into my brain, but watching him pull things from his tackle box was even worse. Some of them, like the tail from a cat, I recognized. Others, like the green and black bullfrog with six legs, I'm still trying to forget. Some went in the water, some (like the cat's tail) he burned, and one thing he ate in three long, crunchy, juicy bites.

Even while doing his mumbo-jumbo, Bob made a point of showing us that his pistol was always close at hand. If we'd been standing on dry land I might have risked rushing him, but there was no way I'd get to him wading through 10 yards of chest-deep water. The rhythm of Bob's crazy chanting wound down, and I dumbly realized that my time was almost up. All I could think to do was dive under and swim like crazy to the other side of the bayou while Bob shot at me. I looked over at Clay. The bleeding on his head was just a scalp wound from where Bob had conked him with the pistol butt, but the shoulder wound was still oozing blood between his fingers and into the water. He was definitely fading. If he didn't get help soon, he'd be gone.

I took a deep breath, but it was too late.

Two long, thick snakes slithered up through the murk on the other side of Clay and the water violently pushed and pulled at my legs. I dug my toes into the mud and managed to stay upright, but Clay nearly pulled me under again when he reached out with a bloody hand and steadied himself on me. The water swirled and eddied all around, and even Bob seemed caught off guard. Just like he'd done when Clay was noodling, Bob tried to stare through the murk into the depths below. A gray triangle mast sliced the surface nearby. Maybe the chanting muddied up my brain, but as it kept rising out of the water I pictured the upside down hull and keel of a fishing rig. That's when the top of its head broke the surface and I found myself looking into a deep, black eye the size of a softball.

I was being sized up by a catfish as big as a killer whale.

The edges of my vision twisted, and I felt myself falling forward. It was the helplessness of a nightmare and the tunnel vision of being really wasted all rolled into one. The ball of black ink grew bigger and deeper, reeling me down into its depths until nothing else existed. I was inside the eye, and the eye was looking inside me. I was floating in outer space, and stars winked in the darkness around me. For just a second, I thought I understood what infinity meant.

And then it was over. I wasn't in space, I was thrashing under the dark surface of the bayou. My feet found the muddy bottom and I pushed up into the air, sputtering out the taste of mud and lake water. Clay and Bob still stood hypnotized nearby. If they'd noticed my blacking out, they didn't give any sign.

The monster still floated in the water nearby. Its skin was the color of mottled ash and was crisscrossed and pockmarked with dozens of scars. At least three hooks and fishing lines hung trailing from its skin like Christmas lights dangling from a tree. What I had mistaken for snakes were its long, black, whiskers, and they restlessly probed the water around us.

I don't know where he found the nerve, but Bob slowly waded forward to the monster's head, chanting in a low, even tone like I had tried using with him. About the time he came even with me and Clay, damn if he didn't bow to the thing. And damn if I didn't catch myself doing the same thing.

As far as I could tell, the fish didn't respond, but I guess that was good enough for Bob since he reached out and gently touched it. I shuddered at the thought of feeling that skin, which would be soft and rubbery, slick and slimy. He stroked its head slowly and steadily, right between the eyes.

"Wise Ur-somethinoranother, Spirit of the Deep, Guardian of Secrets, Key to the Fifth Gate, in accordance with the ancient pact between spirits of the air and spirits of the deep, this day I have sacrificed a child pure, a man in his prime, and an elderly man in his dotage. Their bodies feed your children at the bottom of your domain, sent in the boat from which they sought to reap your kin."

Bob kept up the steady stroking, and cocked his head to the side like he was listening to something. It seemed like if I concentrated hard enough, maybe I could almost hear it too. Only, I didn't want to.

"Ancient Ur-somethinoranother, your domain holds many secrets, but one belongs in the world of Man. It is small, round, and blue like a jewel. In the name of the pact, release this item from your care."

Bob kept right on stroking and listened to something only he could hear. I wanted to turn away. I wanted to turn and swim as fast as I could...but I just couldn't bring myself to do it. Bob nodded, then jerked his head toward me and Clay.

"Yes. In exchange for the lens, I have brought a gift to fill your belly."

A gift of...and that's when things clicked into place. I felt another little moment of vertigo and the universe threatened to swallow me whole again, but I forced it down. I'd be damned if I was going to go down like that. Since sticking my arm down that catfish hole, I'd gone from fear to disbelief to terror to something else entirely, all in the time it takes to play a game of dominos. Now I was just pissed, and I didn't care what I said. Even the truth.

I cleared my throat and forced a lighthearted tone that I didn't feel. "Well Bob, it seems to me you got more bait than you need. Just dangle Clay there on the end of your line or however this works. Heck, if you need help getting' him on the hook I'll even stick around and help."

Bob turned to face me, never stopping the steady stroking between the mudcat's eyes. I hoped he wasn't looking at me the way you look in a box of worms trying to figure out which one to pick. My "best friend" shook his head, likely thinking he was hallucinating. "Whaaaaaat?" he slurred.

"Just be sure not to hook him through any place vital," I said. "That way they stay alive and wiggle longer."

"Don't give me trouble, Pete." Bob said to me. "We both know you'd turn on me the first chance you got. Just keep quiet and I'll do what I can to make it quick."

"Hear me out, Bob. Now, you only need one of us for whiskers here. The way I see it, you'd be doing me a favor. If you hadn't shown up when you did, I was gonna have a little sacrifice of my own. See, I was just about to clobber Clay with a paddle, hamstring him, and dump him in the middle of the lake."

Clay shook his head again, but something in my tone broke past the fog and his eyes locked with mine. In that instant I felt the smoldering satisfaction of watching him realize that I knew everything. It felt almost as good as I'd fantasized. I wouldn't have thought he could get much more pale, but somehow he did.

"No no no no no," Clay whined. "Don't listen to him. Shoot him! Shoot HIM. I can help you get away. You can have his truck, his boat, whatever you want."

"Why'd you do it, Clay?" I said. "Why Trish? We might have patched things up, but you had to go tomcatting around. Did you strike out with the coeds at the Pizza Barn one Thursday night and so you said 'Hey, I think I'll sleep with my best friend's WIFE!'"

"It wasn't like that. She came to me--"

The creature twitched in agitation, sending a small wave rippling out in all directions. Bob renewed his calming strokes on the fish's head, but he growled at me and Clay.

"Enough redneck tabloid news already! I don't give a damn who did what. You're both staying right there."

That's when Clay panicked. Bob had set down the gun inside the tackle box, then let it float out of reach with the catfish's wave. Clay made a weak, floundering dive for the prize. Bob jerked toward the box, then back to the fish as it twitched in irritation again, then finally back toward the gun again. Me? I started truckin' it for shore.

Bob gave it a good try, but the fight against chest-high water must have been like running in a nightmare. That's what it felt like to me, anyhow. Clay reached the box and scrambled for the gun. Bob shouted out something. I don't remember what. But that big fish he'd turned his back on must have had enough. It happened so quick, it was barely a blur. It lunged forward, opened its mouth, and Bob was gone. Just like that.

Clay didn't go down so easy. He managed to point the pistol in the thing's general direction and get off a single shot, but I don't know if he hit it or not. It sure didn't slow the thing down none. It flounced forward again, but it took two gulps to get Clay down its gullet. Probably on account of Bob already being down there. I'll never forget his legs kicking at the water for that brief, endless moment before he disappeared forever.

All the careful plans I'd made for getting away with killing my best friend were for nothing. In the end, the sunofabitch was eaten by a big fish.

And that, Judge Lindsey, is what really happened to Clay. So help me God.

****

*Preston grew up in Pinebox, Texas...or at least someplace similar. He is a co-creator of the Pinebox setting, and his writing credits include Brainwashed and Bloodlines. He is a Christian, a Freemason, a husband, and a father. His blog can be found at flametoad.com.*

# ~Pie~

*by Monica Valentinelli*

Wrapping her coat around her dying, borrowed skin, "Gloria" stood in a streetlamp's electric glow just outside of Mom's Diner, waiting for her FBI contact. She wasn't sure if the agent she called was going to show; already she had counted three police cars speeding past her down Main Street.

It'd be great if she could suck the memories right out of her victims' brains, but a Skinwalker's powers didn't work that way. Still, she wondered if the police were speeding toward yet another poorly-skinned body or if they were finally going to do their job. Too bad she didn't know how to work the police scanner. If she did, she'd have a clear idea of what was going on.

Irony forced her to smirk. The Skinwalker's life was a hard one, because she never just found a skin to wear -- she was temporarily stepping into a life, too. Usually she took her sweet time about it, but over the past few months she took on more lives than usual. Why? Because a murderer in Pinebox—a *rookie*—kept pointing fingers in her direction just to save his own ass. *"Well,"* she thought gleefully. *"At least he's too stupid to know I'm after him."*

"Gloria" was grateful that the evening air in Pinebox was crisp and clean. When the wind picked up, she could usually smell the blood on it. The Skinwalker always imagined that the wind moving through the trees was alive and it could speak to her, revealing her enemies or her future victims. Maybe some day she'd learn that particular trick, but for now she had to settle with the ones she had.

She wasn't quite used to the body she was wearing yet. One way or the other, she would find the monster responsible for forcing her to go on the run. When she did? There were ways to prolong a skinning to keep the body alive for weeks, maybe even months.

"A bit unusual for Pinebox, don't you think?" a wiry man asked as he walked up to meet her, flashing a badge.

The Skinwalker tried to size up the federal agent, but there wasn't much to him. Thin and practically swimming in his clothes, she thought he was just a touch too young to be working in law enforcement. She read him quickly, and saw that his aura was wreathed in the colors of love and innocence: vibrant pinks and shimmering silver. Yeah, he was young, a lot younger than she was.

"Isn't that why you're here, Agent..."

"Buchanan."

*Buchanan.* If that Irish name had popped up on the cell phone she was carrying, she probably wouldn't have bothered calling the FBI. 'Course, with her skin peeling off the way it was, she didn't have much time to begin with, so anything she could do to point them in the direction of the real murderer would end her need to run like a frightened animal. If they pushed her, she'd start killing their pets.

"You like pie, Agent?" She tried to shoot the kid an innocent smile, but it was tough. She was nowhere near the thirty-some odd years old the real Deputy Gloria Waddell was. 'Course, he didn't need to know how old she was, just like he didn't need to know what she truly looked like.

The Agent paused in front of her, as if he was sizing her up. "You okay? You look a little..."

"It's eczema. Bad case of it," she lied. "Just something that popped up kind of sudden-like."

Looking a little suspicious, the Agent took a step backward. "Gloria" knew she'd have to do some fancy talking to get him to go inside with her. Come hell or high water, the kid was going to listen to what she had to say. It wasn't like her to keep on the run, switching skins and identities like they were credit cards. If she couldn't get to this asshole herself, the least she could do was make damn sure the FBI knew who the real killer was.

"Look, Agent Buchanan. I know you're tired, but why not come inside and get a nice hot cup of coffee. You remember Shelly, don't you?" Thank the ravens Gloria blubbered like a baby when she smashed her teeth out with a tire iron, telling her everything she needed to know, right before she cast her spell. Shelly was *useless.*

"How did you know about Shelly?" Agent Buchanan's voice wavered.

*Bingo.* "Everybody knows about you and Shelly, especially with you being a new East Texas University graduate and all. How'd you get on this case anyway?"

The Agent looked down at his feet, mumbling something underneath his breath.

"What was that Agent Buchanan?" She couldn't help but feel a little sympathy toward the Agent. Why, he looked like he just woke up and threw on the first wrinkle-free suit of clothes he could find. What a baby.

"Nothing, Gloria. I guess you recognize me after all," the kid brightened. "You had me scared there for a second. Hard to know for sure who's who anymore, what with that band of Skinwalkers roving around killing people."

*Uh-oh, that didn't sound good.* Apparently the dead Deputy and this kid knew each other in real life. That might be a problem, eventually. But how did such a young kid end up working for the FBI? He hadn't seen much; his aura would have indicated that. A thousand questions filled her mind, crawling around like worms in her skull. No matter what skin she chose to wear, the Skinwalker always had a hard time getting used to the fact that she could never pry her sacrifice's memories from their bleeding skull.

"Well, I'm still going to call you 'Agent' if that's all right with you. I guess these murders have everyone a little bit spooked now, don't they?"

Agent Buchanan smiled widely and bobbed his head. Opening the door to Mom's Diner, the false Gloria was almost grateful for the bright fluorescent lighting that flooded her as she walked in. She tried to cover up her rotting skin as best she could, but she knew she didn't have much time until the skin was useless.

A plump, rosy-cheeked waitress approached them. "Your usual table, Glo?"

The Skinwalker tried not to say too much to the waitress and shot her a disapproving look. Luckily, Agent Buchanan was happy to see the love of his life. Picking her up, he spun Shelly around a few times and gave her a big kiss on the cheek. Shelly squealed, "Not now, I'm working. What will your Daddy say?"

*Daddy. Hmmm... Maybe that's how this kid got his job.* The Skinwalker tried to sneak past the couple, but stopped herself. Shelly wasn't helping her figure out which booth was her "favorite" one.

"Are you feeling all right?" Shelly asked her, giving her a knowing smile.

The Skinwalker smirked, thinking how funny it was that little bits of the truth end up seeping into normal conversation. "No, Shelly. I think it's just a bad reaction to some medicine I'm on." She padded her oversized purse for added effect. "Have everything a girl needs to feel better, right here."

Shelly immediately swatted Agent Buchanan aside and rushed over to her. "Well, here. Let me help you to your table. Then I'm hoping you can finish telling Agent Buchanan here what you started to tell me earlier."

*Don't over-think this, just play along.* "Well, Shelly... that's why I'm here..." she started to say, but Shelly had already rushed off to grab something for their table.

The Skinwalker took a long, hard look at Agent Buchanan and gestured for him to sit down. *So far, so good.*

"All right, Gloria. I'll hear what you have to say, but remember—I'm not really an Agent yet. This is just my Dad's way of playing nice."

It took all of her resolve not to growl at the kid. Whoever his father was, he probably pegged a Skinwalker as the murderer the first time he saw the poorly-skinned bodies.

"Oh, and you can keep calling me 'Agent.' I like that," he grinned as if they shared a private joke. "Now, I understand that you couldn't just go down to the Station with your story, but why Ma's Diner?"

More excuses. she wanted to tell the kid to cut the crap before she hexed him and started pulling out his eye teeth with a set of pliers. Instead she told him, "I thought it would make you feel a little better if you got the chance to see your fiancée."

The Agent threw his hands over the peeling flesh of her lips and shushed her. "Shhhh! Gloria! My dad doesn't even know yet."

She wondered if the kid ever had a moment of his life where he stared Death right in the face. If he knew what she knew...well, they wouldn't be having this conversation if he did.

"I think, *Agent Buchanan*, in the interest of time you'll want to hear my story. Homecoming's just around the corner and there's a lot of scared folk in town."

The young FBI Agent—if she could even call him that—sat back in the booth, his cheeks flushed red. "No, I guess you're right. It's not every day you stumble across a group of bodies without their skins on."

"Gloria" forced the anger that was rising from her belly back down just a little bit. The kid was wasting her time, and it was quite possible he was setting some kind of a trap—for *her*. Luckily, she still had more than a few tricks up her experienced sleeve.

"That's right, Agent. Now, I just want to make sure you get the details right before you go off and hurt yourself. This won't take but a few minutes."

The kid looked "Gloria" straight in the eye, as if to tell her that she had his full attention. For a second she allowed herself to feel sorry for the kid. He was good-looking enough; his rusty brown hair had that "I-slept-too-late-today" look and his eyes were the color of a summer sky. It was a shame he had to die.

"You and I both know that there have been two bodies found so far back in those woods. I think you're going to find two more tonight, and I'm pretty sure I know where they are."

The kid snapped. "Why are you telling me this, Gloria? You know I can't—"

Huh, two can play that game. "Agent Buchanan, just listen to me. You have the wrong—"

"My name is *Phil*, Gloria," the kid shouted. "Are you playing with me? You know I just help my dad out on the weekends."

Oh shit. Her instincts were right. She *was* talking to the wrong Buchanan. Her mind raced at lightning speeds, trying to come up with some sort of reason why he picked up the phone at the agency. Damn, he must have had some connection to Gloria she wasn't aware of.

"Then help me, Phil. Go back and tell that dad of yours where and when to look for the bodies." By the moon, her skin itched something fierce. She tried not to scratch it, but it was no use. Shoving her hands underneath the table, she peeled the flesh off from her fingers bit by bit.

Phil regarded her with pity. "Look, Gloria. I know you lost your job and all, so if you have some sort of a message for Dad, I'll help you out."

"Gloria" tried not to smile too happily at the kid. He really didn't know what he was getting himself into.

"—but you have to promise me you won't tell my dad about Shelly." Phil looked positively panicked that Agent Buchanan Sr. would do something drastic if he found out the kid was going to marry a waitress.

Phil leaned in to whisper across their metal table. "She's pregnant."

The Skinwalker tried not to laugh. If he knew the truth about Shelly he'd probably piss his pants. "Fine, you've got yourself a deal."

"Well, not sure if you know this, but Larry and Carlito were both professors at East Texas University together. The strange part was that they were moonlighting as..."

"Coffee and pie?" Shelly offered them, placing down two steaming cups and a couple of plates.

"Thanks, Shelly. Can you come back later?" Phil asked her politely.

"Sure thing, honey," she said to him, exchanging a knowing look with "Gloria" before she walked away. "I'm going to start cleaning up early since the place is empty."

"Anyway, the two professors were dabbling in the occult. Blood magic. Larry must have gotten greedy, killed Carlito and then decided to sacrifice all his buddies for some big ritual." The Skinwalker waited for Phil's inevitable reaction. *One... Two... Three...*

But he didn't give her one. Phil grabbed his coffee, took a big swig of it, and put it down in front of her.

"They know, Gloria," he said, staring at the fleshy, cherry pie in front of him. "but they're not buying it. Dad doesn't believe in that blood magic shit."

"Morons," she said out loud. "Then what *do* they believe?"

"He thinks Larry was planning some Homecoming stunt to scare folks. Like walking out on the field wearing a referee's skin," Phil sighed dejectedly. "Look, I know you're trying to help, but there's no demon there—only a twisted mind."

*Twisted?* She wanted to tell him who the real Skinwalkers were in Pinebox. She wanted to scream at him that a Skinwalker didn't take a rusted knife to their victims, missing whole patches of beautiful skin and hair in the process. She wanted to tell him that what she did was reasonable and *necessary* in a world overrun with stupid people who had forgotten their ancestors.

Of course, she didn't bother telling him the truth. Instead, she ran her tongue on the inside of her mouth to make sure the teeth she had stolen weren't rotting out of her gums yet, and then she bit down on her own tongue—*hard*—to taste her own blood. It was her ass on the line here. She didn't give a damn about Larry's victims.

"That's part of what I'm trying to tell you, Phil. I don't think Larry is a Skinwalker. You may have the right man, but you've got the wrong kind of villain."

She pulled out a small voice recorder from her pocket. "This interview was recorded a few days ago." She mentally added "when the *real* Deputy Gloria Waddell was alive." Hopefully the kid had enough sense in his head to realize Larry was something other than a Skinwalker. He was sick.

> OFFICER WADDELL: Larry? Larry now I'm just going to sit down right across from you here and put this little voice recorder right in front of me, okay?
>
> PROFESSOR LARRY: You think I did this? Huh, Gloria?
>
> OFFICER WADDELL: (*whispering*) Shelly, why don't you get us a cup of coffee and some of that pie I like.
>
> SHELLY: Sure thing, Honey.
>
> OFFICER WADDELL: Now then, Larry. We've known each other a long time, haven't we?
>
> PROFESSOR LARRY: (sobs quietly) Yes, Gloria. Yeah, we have.
>
> OFFICER WADDELL: Do you trust me to do right by you, Larry? That I'll do everything I can to help you?
>
> PROFESSOR LARRY: I suppose so.
>
> OFFICER WADDELL: (uncomfortable pause) What's that supposed to mean, Larry? You still think I'm going to arrest you today?
>
> PROFESSOR LARRY: You can't appreciate what I've done, Gloria.
>
> OFFICER WADDELL: Well, why don't you go ahead and tell me what it is I don't appreciate, okay?
>
> SHELLY: (clinking of dishes) Coffee and rhubarb pie.
>
> PROFESSOR LARRY: I'm doing the right thing, Gloria. I swear it.
>
> OFFICER WADDELL: (clears throat) Thank you, Shelly. You know that's why it's my favorite. Tastes like blueberries, don't it?

PROFESSOR LARRY: Blueberries? You're talking about fruit and I'm trying to tell you what it's like to reveal a man's soul.

OFFICER WADDELL: Never mind. Just speak clearly and slowly into the recorder, and we'll see if we can't sort this mess out.

PROFESSOR LARRY: You don't deserve to hear what I have to say.

OFFICER WADDELL: Now, Larry... I think you ought to reconsider that last statement.

PROFESSOR LARRY: No, don't listen to her! Just...

OFFICER WADDELL: If your friends are dead, where are the bodies now?

PROFESSOR LARRY: (meekly) I didn't kill them. I freed them and in turn, they gave me the power I needed for the upcoming ritual.

OFFICER WADDELL: I wasn't asking you if you killed them, I just want to know where the bodies are.

PROFESSOR LARRY: (coughs) I don't know.

OFFICER WADDELL: Last chance, Larry. Where'd you put the bodies? Their skins?

PROFESSOR LARRY: You were always so narrow-minded, Gloria. This isn't for me, don't you understand? This wasn't "my" doing.

OFFICER WADDELL: Well, whose is it then?

PROFESSOR LARRY: My enemies.

The Skinwalker shifted her hands underneath the cool, metal table, waiting for the recorder's automatic *click*. The skin she had been wearing for too long was rotting faster by the minute, revealing oozing sores that were staining the inside of her jacket.

*Time to play the sympathy card.*

"I think he got to me, Phil."

It took Phil more than a moment to respond. "Yeah, I suspected as much when you said you were…sick. You don't look so good, Gloria."

By the ravens how she wished more people were as naive as this young pup. "There were five of them altogether, weren't there? Five targets, not four."

Phil's eyes opened so wide she thought that just for a second, she could almost see their red, pulsing capillaries. "Yeah, well. My dad found Hank and Carlito back in the woods when he was hunting that first day..."

She detected that Phil's voice was tainted with sadness and regret. "Gloria" was sad, too. Sad their lives were wasted because some idiot professor started playing around with black magic. "The skins were torn right off of their bodies, but the faces were left on. After Frank and Jose turned up missing, we feared the worst. It wasn't until after the ransom note that we thought for sure you'd be next, since you and Larry used to have a thing…"

*Ransom note. Tricky.* "Gloria" tried to act shocked. Finally, things had started to make sense to her. The deputy had escaped from Larry and stumbled across her path in the woods. If it wasn't for the real Gloria slowing her down, the Skinwalker would've already caught up to the professor.

"Yeah Phil, I can't lie to you. I'm afraid my body isn't long for this world," she told the kid truthfully. "Let me do the right thing here, please?'

Phil absentmindedly poked at his pie. "It doesn't matter, you know. Skinwalker or warlock, they've gone to arrest him. Hell, he practically signed his own confession in that note."

Sure, stick an insane, master of the occult in a cement box with iron bars. Good plan. "If he really was a Skinwalker, how would you catch him?" she asked, not really wanting to hear his response.

"Dad has his ways."

"Isn't it obvious what Larry is doing to you?" she continued, praying to the Coyote god that her borrowed skin would stay intact just long enough for her to get her point across. "Don't you think he just might be capable of blood magic? Maybe he's just biding his time, waiting for all of you to make a mistake."

Shelly busted out with laughter, pointing at Phil as if he just told her a funny joke. The Skinwalker tried to ignore her; she'd already read the girl's aura weeks ago.

"What's so funny, Shell?" Phil took out his cell phone and started dialing.

"Nothing, honey," she said, smiling sweetly.

*Time to change the subject.* "Think about it, Phil. Your dad's in trouble because he can't see the big picture here. There's no way that Larry's doing this for a little revenge, not with Homecoming around the corner." She coughed, spitting a bloody, yellow tooth into her hands.

Holding the phone up to his ear, Phil made a gesture to "Gloria" telling her to wait. It was obvious to the Skinwalker that he was avoiding her cold, icy glare.

*Shit.* She felt the skin on her cheek starting to peel more noticeably, exposing a brown, oozing sore. Not much longer now until her true form came out. She didn't want that to happen here, not in the middle of a quaint, little diner. She needed room to breathe, time to think.

"Hey, earth to Gloria? I just text messaged my dad. He'll be here in about an hour."

*Damn.* That was the last thing she wanted to happen.

"You sure you don't want me to call an ambulance?" Shelly asked, coming up behind her.

Her skin was peeling off in rubbery ribbons now, leaving behind trails of pus-filled sores. "I might be contagious," she coughed, hoping to scare the daylights out him. "Phil, why don't you run and give this tape to your dad?"

Worry lines appeared in the kid's forehead. "You sure about that?"

"Get the sonuvabitch that did this to me, Agent," she rasped, clawing at his oversized suit for added sympathy. "Make sure your dad knows how dangerous Larry is."

"I will, Gloria." Phil said, without looking at her. "Shelly, think you can stay with Gloria until we get Larry to reverse whatever the hell he did?"

Her voice full of fake adoration for the young hero, Shelly agreed to watch over the "cursed" deputy. "Sure thing, Phil. I'll stay right here."

Phil half-jogged to the front door, double-checking the rest of the diner to make sure no one else was in it. "Lock up behind me. I know it's half an hour until closing time."

Walking carefully over to her fiancee, the cheerful waitress kissed Phil on the cheek and watched as he ran back to his car.

"Cute, Shelly. You both just look so cute together, don't you?" the Skinwalker said as she pulled something out of her over-sized purse. "I don't suppose you'd want to sit here and have a chat with me now that he's gone."

Shelly turned off half the lights in the diner and grabbed a chair in front of the Skinwalker. "How long will it take the rest of that crap to fall off?"

"Not long," the she replied, relieved that the kid left before the process was finished. "Eczema and curses, can you believe that kid?"

"Ugh, how long do I have to keep up the *I'm-so-in-love-with-you* act?" Shelly pouted, fascinated with the decaying skin that was literally falling off of the Skinwalker's body. "And when are you going to teach me this stuff?"

Taking off her clothes, the Skinwalker pushed the dead skin right off of her body and laughed. "I told you, as soon as the real murderer has been bought and paid for, I'll teach you everything I know."

"I've been thinking about what you said, about Larry trying to look like he was a Skinwalker. Why would he do that?"

"Gloria" coughed up another tooth and spat blood on the floor. "Think about it, Shelly. What's harder to find: one man's face, or a Skinwalker's?"

"Guess you have a point there," Shelly responded softly.

Gathering pieces of decayed skin and hair into a pile, Shelly started to pick up while the Skinwalker went to work. The skin "Gloria" had been carrying with her in her purse was fresh -- not more than a day or two old -- and would work nicely for all intended purposes. The skin molded to her body. Little by little the Skinwalker started to feel like herself again -- with the exceptions of a few sores and bruises that would heal within a few days.

"Oh, you're *real* good at this, you know that?" Shelly laughed and clapped her hands with glee. "Now I hope you didn't eat any of my pie, because there's a reason why that crust is so good."

It was the Skinwalker's turn to laugh. "Thanks for cleaning up, Shelly. Next I'll have to try the chili, eh? Now please hurry up and find me some clothes. I think I left some with you behind the counter."

"Okay, *Mom*," Shelly emphasized as she looked for the Skinwalker's new clothes.

*BAM! BAM!*

The front door to Mom's Diner rattled and shook. Phil stood with his face pressed against the glass, banging on the door.

"He's gone, you hear me?" Phil shouted futilely in the locked diner. "Shelly, is Gloria all right?"

The Skinwalker rummaged around in the bag she was carrying and snapped her fingers. "Shelly, bring me those clothes." Taking out a few incisors, the Skinwalker jammed the teeth into her head while the waitress tossed a dress over the counter, rushed over to the door and let Phil in.

"He's gone. Larry–" Phil gasped as he tried to catch his breath. "He escaped. My dad told me there was blood everywhere. You were right, he was trying to summon something."

The Skinwalker did her best to look confused. The woman whose skin she was wearing would have no idea that Pinebox was being turned upside to find a dangerous warlock masquerading as a college professor. "What's this about dear, old Larry?"

Playing her part, Shelly walked over to Phil and took his hand. Tears streamed down her face as she told Phil about Gloria. "She said she wanted to be left alone, Phil. I don't think she… I don't think she…"

Phil's arms wrapped around Shelly's waist as she buried her face in his chest. Then, belated understanding dawned across his face and he began backing away with Shelly in tow. "She's a… I couldn't figure out why…" he sputtered. "My Dad was right about the signs. He told me…"

Shelly tried to stomp on Phil's feet, but missed. Phil shoved his girlfriend back and yelled. "What the fuck are you doing? I'm trying to save us!"

"Mom" stood up and made her way toward the kid, trying to mumble something about a lover's spat. "Now, now you two…"

"Get away from me, you bitch!" Phil screamed at the Skinwalker and shoved her down to the floor.

Chuckling, the Skinwalker deftly swung her legs around and knocked the kid on his ass. She might look like an eighty-year old woman, but true Skinwalkers were stronger than the faces they stole.

Shelly stomped on Phil's groin and taunted him. "Don't they train you how to fight in Agent School?"

*No more time to play.* Chanting a string of words, the Skinwalker caused Phil's body to freeze in place.

"His body won't move where it is," the Skinwalker started to explain. "Be a good time to sharpen the knives."

Shelly pouted as she locked the door to the diner and dimmed the lights. "I'm grateful for this lesson, but I thought you said this would only happen after Larry got what was coming to him?"

The Skinwalker's eyes gleamed in the diner's shadows. "Maybe we should do this outside, Shelly," she whispered. "Near the trees."

"Why?" Shelly asked, waving her fingers in front of Phil's frozen stare. "I mean, this is very poetic and all, especially after Phil cheated on me but…"

The Skinwalker hesitated, wondering if she shouldn't just kill Shelly now for being incredibly stupid. Phil hadn't cheated on her—his aura would have indicated that.

"Well, what do you think?" Shelly asked, impatiently.

Staring out of the diner's windows into the abandoned street, the Skinwalker smiled before adjusting her new tooth. "The wind can help us find Professor Larry. Now get your things together. Can't leave a bit of bone or hair or skin behind."

"Cool, just let me finish rolling up these skins into some pie and then we can go." Shelly stuck her tongue out at Phil and said, "Serves you right for being an asshole. Now I get to feel what it's like to be you."

The Skinwalker allowed her protégée to have a little bit of fun. It wasn't every night she got to teach an apprentice how to skin her enemies. Truth be told she needed the practice, especially if Larry was on his way to kill Gloria.

In a rare moment of honesty, the Skinwalker called back to Shelly, "I've never skinned a fake Skinwalker before. Won't that be fun?" She could hear the girl laughing from the kitchen. A few moments later, Shelly brought out two pieces of cherry pie slathered in whipped cream and two cups of Tex-Mex chili.

"Gah, how can you eat that stuff?" the Skinwalker asked, more than a little perturbed that she'd willingly eat her discarded skins.

"My mother always told me to *waste not, want not*," Shelly admitted, shoving a huge forkful of pie into her mouth. "Besides, we're going to need our strength if we end up going after Larry."

The Skinwalker racked her brain to see if she could figure out where the wily professor might be hiding. "Let me guess, your dad told you he's on his way here. Right, Phil?"

Although his body was frozen on the ground, the Skinwalker was pretty adept at telling when her sacrifices were trying to tell her something. Or, at least she thought she was. "I'll take that as a *yes*," she told him. "Shelly, guess I'm going to have to teach you the first step to becoming a Skinwalker sooner rather than later. When Professor Larry comes barging through here, I want you to do exactly as I say. Now, bring me my knives."

"Will do, boss."

****

*Monica Valentinelli splits her time between writing, working as an online marketer, and filling the role of project manager for the horror and dark fantasy webzine flamesrising.com. As a freelance writer for the gaming industry, Monica has over a dozen game and game fiction credits to her name including: Worlds of the Dead by Eden Studios, an award-winning fiction piece entitled Promises, Promises for Promethean by White Wolf, and her recent novella Twin Designs which was part of the collection Tales of the Seven Dogs Society for the game Aletheia by Abstract Nova Press. To read more about Monica, visit her urban fantasy novel series located at violetwar.com or her blog located at mlvwrites.com.*

# ~The Evil Within~

*by Derek Gunn*

"What do you have, Lou?" Deputy Matt Lester asked and pulled his jacket closed against the chill as he tried to balance his notebook and search for a pen at the same time. He hated the damn morgue; it was always so cold and smelt of disinfectant and decay. Although, it did have one attraction worth coming for.

Louise Frazier looked up over her black-rimmed glasses and a smile crossed her drawn face, pushing back the tiredness and transforming her stern countenance in an instant.

"Well hello there, Deputy," her eyes widened as she regarded the Deputy. The damned fluorescent lights were flickering again but Lester fancied he could see their reflections dance playfully in her brown eyes. He liked her eyes. There was something warm and trusting about them that had struck him the first time they had met, and never failed to make him nervous since.

Louise Frazier was the best thing the town had for a coroner. She was, in fact, a very capable professor of Biology at ETU, but she had crossed the Department Head, Bethany Moore, in two very fundamental ways. She was far prettier and was well-liked in the community, and she had been assigned to help the county while they sourced their own coroner. She had done so well in the last two years that the county had, unofficially, stopped looking for a coroner and were quite happy to let Frazier continue until she either gave up or was transferred. Frazier, too, seemed to have fitted in quite happily into her extra-curricular role, so it was a win-win situation for everyone. Lester sighed with pleasure as Frazier walked around the cadaver in front of her and approached him. *Academia's loss is very much our gain*, he thought as he watched her hips sway.

Lester dropped his pen and gratefully dropped to the floor as he felt his face grow hot despite the coldness of the room. Moore had very kindly designated a room at ETU for use as the town's morgue since '94 when the old one had been destroyed along with the old Police Station.

"How's my favorite Deputy?" Frazier brushed a stray hair back into place and Lester managed a shy chuckle as he held up his errant pen like a trophy.

"I'm fine, thanks Lou." She had insisted that her friends called her Lou, never Louise. He had only been a Deputy for seven months now, though he had served a full tour in Afghanistan before that, but somehow he always felt like a damned teenager around her. He had arrived in Pinebox about a month ago but had had cause to visit her more than he would have thought normal for such a small town.

There were an awful lot of disappearances and strange deaths in Pinebox—an inordinate amount, though no-one else seemed to be overly concerned.

Frazier had a pixie face that was dominated by her amazing wide eyes. Her hair, always tied back severely, was auburn; the colour of a burnt spring morning sky, and every time he saw her it seemed determined to untangle and fall free. To date, though, it hadn't succeeded and Lester found himself day-dreaming on more than one occasion wondering what she would look like with it down.

"I suppose you're here because of that," she nodded her head towards the body behind her and pouted endearingly, "and I thought you were coming to see me."

"Well," he began and blushed again. Jesus, how he would love to have the courage to ask this woman out. He had never been good with girls and Louise Frazier was certainly no girl. She was all woman and even a tour in Afghanistan had not prepared him for her. What if she rejected him? He'd lose her friendship, and he didn't have too many friends in this town yet. He just couldn't risk it.

"I'm afraid so," he finally managed and curled his notepad so tightly it cracked. She raised her eyebrows, pushed her glasses back into place and retreated back behind the body. Damn, he thought as he followed her reluctantly over to the table. Another opportunity lost.

"Well," she began, all business now that her glasses were back in place. "I'm not sure what I can tell you." She pulled the sheet from the body and Lester paled and felt bile rise in his throat.

"Jesus." He choked as the smell hit him. It was rank. It reminded him of a patrol he had been on once during his tour. They had missed their pickup behind enemy lines and their platoon sergeant had broken his leg. It had taken a week to get back to camp and by that time the Sergeant's leg had become badly infected by gangrene. It smelt just like this. Putrescent. Decayed.

"It is quite gruesome, isn't it?" She smiled but the earlier sparkle was gone now.

Lester looked down at the body. It reminded him of a mummy he had seen in a history book some years ago. The skin was blackened, as though burnt, and stretched tightly over the bones. But the remaining flesh was still wet, not dried out like he had expected. In places the skin had been torn and whitened bone jutted through. The dead girl's body had collapsed in on itself, suggesting great age, but the hair around its skull was still fresh. The face was the worst though. The skin around the mouth was so stretched that Lester paled as he imagined what could have terrified this woman so badly as to freeze her features into such a rictus.

"I'm not sure what we can do here, Lou," he finally managed after swallowing hard. "We're not really set up for 'Cold Cases'. There's too many new ones without opening the vaults."

"Oh, this isn't a cold case," she shrugged as she consulted her folder. "According to dental records this is Amy Dooling."

"But Amy just went missing last month," Lester spluttered. "What can do that..." he paused as he swallowed again, "...to someone in a few weeks?"

Frazier looked at Lester and shrugged. "What can I say, Matt? Dental records don't lie. This is Amy Dooling."

He remained quiet as he examined the corpse again. It didn't make any sense. "Any ideas what could have done this?" Lester scrambled for his pad and tried to write some notes on his ruined notebook.

"I have no idea I'm afraid," she moved closer to the body and drew his attention to the desiccated face. "You see here?"

Lester took a deep breath and leaned in to see better.

"There are five strange welts positioned around the face that might..." she looked up into Lester's eyes for emphasis, "...might be consistent with a large hand."

"You mean someone did this to her?"

"I didn't say that," she added quickly.

Lester paled as he imagined what she was implying. "Have you ever seen anything like this before?"

Frazier paused for a moment and then shrugged as if coming to a decision. "There was a case two years ago, back when I had just started doing this," she swept her hand around the room and Lester nodded for her to continue.

"Anyway, I was new in town and new to this role so I wasn't quite sure what was expected of me. A body came in." She paused again as if ordering her thoughts. "It was worse than this one. It had been discovered over by the swamp and the local wildlife had got at it. Anyway, I did some tests and presented my findings but nobody came back to me and the body was listed as another unsolved case."

"There are a lot of those," Lester interrupted.

"There certainly are," she agreed with a sigh.

"Did your tests come back with anything interesting?"

"Well," she spent another moment looking very carefully at Lester and he felt uncomfortable under her glare. "Can I trust you, Deputy Matt Lester?"

He was shocked. Why would she have to ask?

"Of course," he stammered.

"You're not stupid, Matt, I can see that. But you are naïve. You must have noticed that this isn't a normal town."

Lester paused as he slowly looked up from his notepad into her eyes. "Yes," he dropped his eyes again and looked at the body between them.

"There seems to be two types of people in this town. Those who ignore the situation and get on with their lives and those who try to do something about it. The question is," she paused. "Which one are you?" She left the question hanging in the air and Lester looked again at the welts on the woman's face. "Are you prepared to do anything about it or will you let it slide like the rest of your colleagues?"

Lester tore his eyes from the terror-stricken corpse and looked up at her. He knew that this was a defining moment in their relationship. He would have to be a fool not to have noticed the amount of strange occurrences in this town, even if he was a rookie.

He had broached the subject with some of his colleagues but none had commented beyond generalities. He had wanted to talk to Sheriff Anderson about it, but he had been called away soon after he had arrived and had only returned yesterday. He got the impression, though, that that the good Sheriff liked things simple. A dead body was a dead body. Report on it, write it up, and file it. Lester had still not decided what to do about it.

On one hand he was used to taking orders. The army had drilled that into him and he was comfortable following his superior's lead. But this was different. People were dying in this town and no-one was doing anything about it. Why? How many had to die to convince the Sheriff and his officers that there was something not quite right in their town? Couldn't they see that something was wrong? He wanted to do something but what could he do on his own? He wasn't even sure he wanted the job. With his military experience he could have joined a more metropolitan force in Houston or Dallas.

It would all be sorted out when the Sheriff met him later today for his one month review. Until then he continued to feel isolated. It was like people living in California. They knew that someday the big earthquake might very well kill them all but they pushed the fear aside and got on with life. But this wasn't a positive state-of-mind. This was like pulling the covers over your head and hoping it would all go away. Was Lou more like him than he had thought? Could he have found a kindred spirit?

"I am not of the same mind as my colleagues," he offered and suddenly found himself able to meet Frazier's glare without embarrassment.

She looked at him for another moment and then nodded and her smile returned. The room seemed to brighten with it and he felt a weight lift from him.

"Good man," she said. "I knew I was right about you." She crossed to a filing cabinet on the other side of the room. "This is the report I did before." She flipped open the folder and began to shuffle through the pages. "The victim showed signs of salt, iron and magnesium deficiency."

Lester pursed his lips and cocked his head to the side. "In English for the poor grunt if you don't mind."

"Oh," she smiled distractedly and then put down the report and gave him her full attention. "These are minerals that the body needs to survive. There are large amounts of each in a healthy body, but this one," she held up the report, "and that one over there, had none. The bodies have been drained of these minerals completely."

"And that's bad?"

"You can see what it does when these minerals are sucked out of the body."

"Is that what happened? Someone sucked the body dry? Could that be what the marks are?"

Frazier shrugged.

"Like a vampire?" Lester insisted.

They looked at each other, each still unsure how far they could go. There was a tension in the room that was almost claustrophobic and it disturbed him. He had never been uncomfortable with Louise Frazier before, at least not when he was thinking with his brain rather than from between his legs.

"Yes, Matt," she sighed as the last of her suspicion melted away. "Just like a vampire."

"Okay, but, just so we're clear," he held her eyes with the intensity of his glare. "The blood, was it missing as well?"

"No, the blood was still there, though without the minerals it wasn't exactly blood anymore."

"Okay, so, like a vampire but I don't have to go around looking for a tall guy in a cape?"

"No," she laughed again and the tension in the room disappeared. "We're not looking for Dracula. But something is sucking the life from these girls and it's not normal."

"How often does it happen?"

"I really don't know," she sighed. "I have only seen one body like it before but, like I said, it was found over by the swamp and there could be hundreds over there that the wildlife got to first or have already slipped beneath the surface. There are enough disappearances around here for this to be a regular thing, though."

Lester doodled on his pad as he took in what she was saying. "If this is some kind of feeding," he paused as he looked at the body and tried to order his thoughts, "would there be any sign, something that someone with an abundance of these minerals, might be recognisable by?"

"I'm not sure," she looked off into the ceiling in thought. "These minerals are so tied into health that I suppose it would act almost like a huge injection of life-force. They should look really healthy, almost glowing I suppose."

"So I just have to lock up the healthy people then."

She stuck her tongue out at him and continued despite his mock-hurt expression. "They should also be able to heal very quickly and be quite strong." She paused and then snapped her fingers. "They might have a slight yellowing of the eyes from the magnesium, but nothing that you'd see at a distance."

"Okay," Lester sighed as he flipped his book closed.

"Where are you going now?" Frazier asked as she pulled the sheet back over the body.

"To do some research and see if I can't find out how long our friend has been doing this."

****

It was hot when Deputy Lester walked back to his cruiser, but he shivered regardless. As he settled himself in the car, gingerly placing his butt on the scorching seat, he noticed a number of students walking and laughing as they travelled between the buildings of the university. They seemed so relaxed, completely oblivious to the horrors that were preying on them.

The squawk of the radio in the car brought him back to his senses and he lifted the unit as the students disappeared inside.

"This is Lester," he responded.

"Hey, Mark, oh shi... Deputy Lester,"

Lester smiled as he pictured Sandy Robinson back in the station. They were short-handed at the moment with a flu epidemic and the Sheriff had brought in his sister's eldest daughter to handle calls and radio traffic. She was a lovely girl but hadn't quite gotten the hang of the correct radio procedure and call signs yet. He could imagine the scowl of disapproval she was getting from Sheriff Anderson at this very moment.

"What have you got for me?"

"Eh, Sheriff requests a 10-106, no, a 10-19, damn, can you make your way back please?" Lester laughed.

"On my way."

****

Lester was anxious about his meeting with the Sheriff. There was so much he wanted to talk about but he had no idea how to approach a virtual stranger about his concerns. How do you tell a Sheriff that he isn't doing his job? It was nearly four in the afternoon, but the heat and humidity were stifling as he pulled himself from his cruiser and hurried across the street. He sighed in relief as he opened the door and was bathed in cool, conditioned air.

"Hey, Mark," Sandy Robinson perked up immediately. "Uncle ... Sheriff Anderson," she corrected with a wink, "is in his office if you want to go on in."

Lester nodded somewhat distractedly, knocked on the office door and entered. Butch Anderson sat in his chair looking at the ceiling as he finished a phone conversation. The man nodded at him and motioned for him to sit. He was a big man with broad shoulders that would not look out of place on a football field. He stood six foot three in his boots, though he was beginning to develop a somewhat rounded belly. His hair was receding but, as he almost always wore his hat, few people knew this. His face was craggy from his ever-present scowl, in fact the only time Lester had seen a hint of any lighter emotion on his stony-faced visage was when he was talking to his niece.

The Sheriff leaned forward and placed the phone in its cradle.

"How did it go?" He leaned back again and Lester winced as he heard the chair creak alarmingly.

"Lou identified the body as an Amy Dooling," Lester took out his ruined notepad and flicked to the relevant page. "She went missing a month or so ago."

Anderson nodded and pursed his lips. "I know her father," he sighed as he picked up a pencil and ran it though his fingers.

Lester could see the look in the Sheriff's eyes and he didn't like it at all. He had seen that look in Afghanistan in the field hospitals. It was the look of resignation, the look of a man who had come to the end of his ability to cope.

"Sheriff?" Lester crumpled his notebook again as he struggled to formulate his thoughts.

Anderson seemed miles away.

"Sheriff," Lester repeated. "I know I'm new here but I've been looking into the number of missing people. No-one here seems to care..."

Anderson looked up at him as if he already knew what he was going to say. The pencil in his hand snapped and the sound was like a shot in the small office. A deep red flushed his face and Lester felt his knees go weak at the thought of being bawled out, but then Anderson seemed to deflate.

"Son," he began as he brought the two ends of the broken pencil together. "I know you mean well but there are a few things you need to understand."

Lester leaned forward and Anderson threw the broken pieces of pencil onto the desk with a sigh. "Hell, son, you aren't stupid. It doesn't take long in this town to see that we have more than our fair share of problems." Lester nodded and, for a moment, there was a spark in the Sheriff's eyes, as if something long dead had begun to smoulder.

"You know, I was a lot like you when I came here." He looked out the window as if lost in thought. Just when Lester thought he was going to have to interrupt, Anderson continued.

"I'm not blind, son. I know there's something eating away at this town. Something rotten. But, God forgive me, I've never been able to get to the source." He sighed as he picked up a new pencil and shifted his attention back to his hands as he continued. "I've spent years investigating deaths and disappearances that made no sense at all to any normal-thinking man. I've even put down a few critters that were best laid to rest in secret, if you know what I mean."

He looked back into Lester's eyes. "What I'm trying to say, son, is that you shouldn't confuse acceptance with not caring. Every officer on my force cares more than you know. But you'll burn out if you chase every missing person and grieve for every death. There are just too many."

Lester felt a deep sadness fill him. Jesus, how has he coped with this for so long? Lester had assumed that the Sheriff, while nice enough, was just incompetent. How else could you explain the number of missing people? But this was worse. Anderson was the last line against an evil that threatened to swallow the entire town. Maybe it was only his dedication, and that of his officers, that had kept the number of victims as low as it was.

"All you can do is concentrate on the living and together, hopefully, we'll keep as many safe as we can."

"Isn't there anything else we can do?" Lester's voice came out as a hushed whisper.

"If you have any suggestions, I'm open to them," Anderson threw down the pencil. "But I'll warn you, it's been like this for as long as the town has been here."

"Why do they stay?" Lester looked out the window at the people walking past, seemingly carefree and unaware of the evil around them.

"Many were born here. And those that came later usually came with family," he sighed. "It's hard to uproot those you love, especially where there's no proof. This is home. Some of us stay to fight back as best we can, others find a way to ignore the danger and continue on regardless." He chuckled. "Maybe we're all mad. Well, son. What do you think? Do you want to quit? No hard feelings."

Lester nearly blurted out an instant refusal, but stopped himself. He should think this through. This wasn't a normal town. He didn't owe these people anything. It seems as if the Sheriff usually recruited anybody he needed locally. It had been a surprise when he got the job. In his first month, though, he had come to know a lot of these people, and he liked them. He had become a Deputy to help others and he couldn't think of a place that needed help more than Pinebox.

"I think I'll stay, Sheriff." He announced with a finality that elicited a raised eyebrow form the Sheriff. "It looks like you need all the help you can get."

A faint smile crossed Anderson's face. "Glad to have you on board, son." He leaned back in his chair as if a great weight had been lifted from him. "Did you bring back Amy's effects? I'll take them out to her father."

"No, I didn't. Sorry," Lester felt his face grow hot. He should have remembered that. "I'll take a run out now and pick them up. I'll see if Lou has anything more for me at the same time."

****

Lester pulled the cruiser almost to the door of the College building. As he turned off the engine, he accidentally dropped his coffee cup onto the floor. He was leaning down to retrieve the cup when something slammed into the roof of the cruiser. The noise was incredible but his training took over. He slapped the door release and he launched himself out onto the grass. He rolled once, snatching at his gun and coming up with the weapon levelled at his cruiser. There was a body spread-eagled across the roof, its sightless eyes staring at him as he checked the surrounding area. There was no-one around. The roof had been dented but not as badly as it should have. The body was lighter than a normal human carcass should be. It had been drained similar to Amy Dooling. He shuddered as he saw the familiar blackening of the skin but this time the process had not been completed as fully. He could still see patches of pink skin and raw suppurating flesh that still oozed blood. The girl's face was terribly distorted and her jaw was impossibly open and locked into a silent scream.

He pulled his attention away from her face with great difficulty and scanned the roof of the building above. The sun seared into his eyes and he fumbled for his sunglasses as he blinked to clear his vision. Nothing. Why would the killer be so blatant? Was this a direct challenge to him or did the killer really not care what he did?

He ran towards the building's entrance, snatching at the door and startling three students who looked at his weapon uncertainly. He brushed past them and ran towards the stairs. *What if the killer takes the elevator?* Ignoring the thought he ran up the stairs, taking three at a time. His heart thumped in his chest. Shit! He should have called for backup before rushing into this blind. He faltered as he considered going back but adrenaline surged through him and gave him a courage that drowned out reason.

The building was ten floors and by the seventh Lester was struggling. His breath was ragged and he had already holstered his weapon to allow him to grip the banisters and pull himself up the steps.

By the time he reached the top he had to stop at the door and allow himself to recover. There was no point rushing headlong into danger and falling on his face in exhaustion. His knees wobbled slightly and he was a little light-headed from the adrenaline but he sucked in a deep breath, drew his weapon and placed his hand on the door. It was probably a waste of time. The killer would be long gone. He turned the handle and pushed the door open.

****

"It's about time."

The voice startled him and he whirled towards it in shock. His training clicked in though and he brought his gun up in a smooth motion and trained it on the figure in front of him.

"Jesus," he sighed in relief as he recognised Louise Frazier He lowered his gun. "You scared the shit out of me, Lou. Did you see anybody on your way up?"

"No, it was all clear," she replied distractedly. "What are you doing back?"

Lester felt his heart begin to slow as the initial danger receded. "Butch wants Amy's effects."

"Don't let him catch you calling him that." Frazier smiled as she moved over to the edge and looked over at his cruiser below. "Have a look at this, Matt."

Lester's heard the change in her voice and felt his heart begin to thump a little faster as he started over towards her. Jesus. He was going to have to take up jogging or something. He had let himself go far too much since leaving the army.

"You know," she began as she reached out and gripped his arm lightly. "The body is an amazing thing." He caught a faint odour on the air before a stiff breeze snatched it away. It brought with it a memory of apples rotting in an orchard at the end of summer. "The chemicals that were released into your body to carry you up those stairs saturate every muscle, did you know that?" She smiled at him. "They leave an intoxicating tingle."

"What?" Lester felt his heart begin to thump again. What a strange thing to say. Had he heard her correctly? He fumbled with his sunglasses to see her more closely but the sun was so bright that his eyes began to water. He blinked and a small tear trickled down his cheek. Suddenly her face moved in front of the sun casting a shadow over him and allowing him to see clearly. He looked directly into her eyes.

"Oh, come on now, Deputy." She gripped him tighter and he felt as tough his arm would break. "You don't think I could let you loose to investigate these deaths, now do you? I have such a good thing going on here. I mean, they actually send the bodies to me first for analysis. And then follow up on whatever theories I give them." She pouted. "Why couldn't you be more like the others? We could have had a little fun, you and I." She traced her finger along his chin and he flinched away as realization finally hit him.

"You..."

"Oh you're cute alright. Just not that bright," she smiled and he could see the slight yellow tint in the corner of her eyes.

"How... the eyes..." he stammered.

"The fluorescent lights hide the discoloration in the lab," she shrugged. "And there are always sunglasses for outside. God bless Texas weather eh?" She laughed, but this time there was nothing pleasant about it.

He tried to pull away but her grip was far too strong.

"It's a shame to waste such a fine specimen." Lester saw her raise her hand. There was a wet cracking sound, like bone breaking. He had heard it before at the field hospital when his Sergeant's leg had been reset. Her fingers seemed to lengthen as the digits changed, distorted. A scream started deep in his throat but never made it to his mouth. He felt something wet slide against his face and then his brain felt like it was melting. His vision dimmed as the pain took over. He felt himself slump against Frazier and then darkness rushed up to meet him. From somewhere he thought he could hear laughter but its cold, emotionless timbre did nothing to comfort him as he slid into oblivion.

****

*Derek Gunn is the author of the post-apocalyptic thriller series, Vampire Apocalypse, widely praised on both sides of the Atlantic and published by US genre press Black Death Books. The first two books in the series are A World Torn Asunder and Descent into Chaos. The third book, Fallout, is due out in 2009. A World Torn Asunder is currently in development as a major movie.*

*Derek has two additional books coming out in 2009: The Estuary, from Permuted Press (US), and The HMS Swift Chronicles, from Ghostwriter Publications (UK). Derek lives in Dublin, Ireland with his wife and three children. Visit his website at derekgunn.com.*

# ~Stigmatized Property~

*by Jess Hartley*

Moisture hung heavy in the air. She could taste it, gritty on her tongue, as she swung open the car door and stepped out into the sauna that was downtown Pinebox. Before she could turn back to lock the car, the sweat was already gathering along her spine, even under the crisp layers of baby blue linen of her favorite work suit. By the time she'd finished and turned towards the office, she was inwardly cursing the heat in general and Pinebox in particular, with a silent internal monologue her clients would have never believed possible of her.

The sun weighed down on her, although it was not even 8 am. An ungodly hour to be doing business, but these days you did whatever it took to get a sale, even if that meant pretending to that you were happy to meet the client at your office at an hour you'd normally still be home in bed.

The sign on the storefront window read "Loblolly Realtors, Suzanne Marie Whitcomb, CRS." The company name was in the block font they required their franchise holders to use, but for her own name she'd chosen an elegant cursive style. The letters flowed one to the next, as if she'd written them there herself on the window in delicate gold-leaf ink. It added a touch of class and personality to the window, she thought.

She unlocked the door, swinging it open carefully to minimize the harsh jangle of brass bells she'd attached to alert her to visitors. Stepping inside the building's dark interior, she hurriedly punched in the security code and stilled the alarm's incessant beeping. The warning set her nerves on edge every time she had to deal with it. She paused as the beeps fell silent, but the quiet did nothing to settle the goose-bumps spreading across her arms and down her spine.

The air inside the building was cold and damp. Thick walls, cavernous high ceilings, and an utter lack of windows on all but the south-facing wall kept it that way throughout the year regardless of the temperature outside. She hated it, hated the clammy feeling and the smell of "old" that permeated the building. But Wade had negotiated an excellent rate on the lease, and she still had more than a year left on the terms of the contract so it would be at least that long before she could even consider moving out of the office and away from this one-horse town. Maybe longer, if business didn't pick up. Didn't want to move when houses were selling, couldn't move when they weren't. It was a catch-22 predicament that had kept her here ever since Wade had convinced her to move back to his hometown.

They'd been able to get the owner to agree to a jaw-droppingly low monthly rent, in exchange for a signed multi-year lease. He was a mechanic, not a landlord by trade, and after he had inherited the building he had so many short-term rentals in the place that he jumped at the chance to settle into a long-term, no-hassle bargain. She and Wade had managed the other small office spaces that branched off of the lobby in the ancient building, taking care of the monthly rents for the landlord in exchange for a kickback on their own rent. But one by one, the other business shut down or moved away, and finding new renters became first difficult and then impossible. For months now, her office had been the only one occupied.

She hurried over to the light switches. Her footsteps echoed on the dusty hardwood floors, boards creaking with each step. She held her breath and flipped up all three switches, hoping the lights weren't feeling persnickety. In buildings this old, sometimes even the basic amenities were a crap shoot. This time, however, the overheads flickered on, sending a wash of yellowed light throughout the lobby, pushing back the shadows that she'd felt creeping up on her. She sighed, straightened her shoulders and walked further into the building towards her office space.

Up until a few months ago, she'd come in and find her office already open, coffee brewed, phones answered, and business begun. But with the market dropping, she'd had to let Kristin, her "office manager," go. Since then she'd been handling everything herself. Of course, she told the ladies at Pinebox Professional Women that she preferred it that way. "If you want something done right, do it yourself." But, especially on early mornings, she missed coming in to an already bustling office.

Shoving those thoughts aside, Suzanne busied herself opening the office. Every light in the place on, and damn the rising costs of electricity. The front desk, which used to house Kristin and the bulk of the office's paperwork, was now mostly vacant, so it wasn't difficult to tidy. She checked the clock, and then spent a few extra minutes adjusting the pair of cow-hide upholstered chairs in her private office, trying to achieve the perfect angle and proximity to create an air of elegance and professionalism between them and her own leather-ledger desk. She'd moved them in after Wade had died, trying to make better use of the office space that had once housed both of their desks. Despite the larger chairs and multiple attempts at re-arranging, the room still felt too big. The corner where Wade's desk had once stood was glaringly empty.

Her thoughts were interrupted by a cavalcade of brass bells, somehow brighter and more appealing now, announcing her client's arrival. With a final nervous glance around her office, she turned to face the client she couldn't really afford to let slip away.

"Good morning! You must be…" She started before was all of the way out of the office, and as she caught a first glance of her new client, her mind filled in the sentence in a myriad of inappropriate fashions.

*"Incredibly handsome"* was the first thing that flashed across her mind as she took in his chiseled features and bright blue eyes.

*"Not from around here"* followed, a heartbeat after. His hair, silvered at the temples, had obviously been cut by someone with more skill than Ms. Jenkins of Jenkins' Beauty and Beyond. But even more telling were his natural features. The exotic angles of his face, aquiline nose and craggy brow certainly had something other than Texan origins. They spoke of the Mediterranean, Suzanne decided quickly. Of Greco-Roman statues she'd studied in art history classes back in college, or the handsome heroes on the covers of romance novels.

Finally, uncomfortably, another thought slipped quickly into the forefront of her mind. "*Filthy rich*," she thought, as pragmatics overrode more emotional assessments. Her gaze darted from his impeccably polished leather shoes, up perfectly pressed slacks and across the tailored lines of his button down shirt, taking in the obvious quality of the crisp garment complete with French cuffs and discrete gold links at each wrist. This man looked like he could afford to buy any house in Pinebox out of petty cash – and she was just the woman to sell it to him.

She stuttered, her unspoken thoughts garbling the introduction she'd planned and practiced to the otherwise empty room before his arrival. He smiled, a disarming flash of alabaster against the craggy gold of his skin. He reached forward, extending a hand.

"Alistor… Alistor Strega."

She accepted his hand and his name, repeating the latter as if it were a mantra that would help steel her against the unaccustomed reactions she was having to his presence.

"And you must be Mrs. Whitcomb. A pleasure to meet you in person at last. The photograph on your advertisements do not do you justice."

He pronounced it "ad VERT is mints," and the lyrical play of the word on his tongue distracted her once again. She found herself pronouncing it silently in her head, rolling the soft syllables around as if she could taste them, buttery sweet, with each repetition.

"Mrs. Whitcomb?"

Suzanne startled, wondered how long she'd stood there staring at him with her hand wrapped in his. She pumped his arm enthusiastically.

"Please, call me Suzanne. Technically, it's Ms. Whitcomb. I'm a widow. That is… Whitcomb is my maiden name, but I've always used it. Business, you know. Independence, equality…"

*You're babbling.* Her inner voice took on a dour and disapproving tone.

"I'm so sorry, Mr Strega. I was just…" She gasped and glanced up as the overhead lights in the office flickered momentarily.

Strega's hand tightened on hers, as if in reaction to the second of darkness.

"Oh, sorry about that. It's the building. Original wiring, I think. The landlord keeps promising to… Strega, that's a lovely name. Is it Greek?"

Apparently undaunted by her ramble, Strega shook his head, reclaimed his hand, and allowed her to usher him back into her office. "Italian, actually. I was born on the island of Poveglia, near Venice. Perhaps you've heard of it?"

Suzanne nodded, enthusiastically. "Poveglia… of course…" She struggled for some frame of reference. "Aren't they famous for their cheese?"

Strega smiled, chuckling softly. "Something like that."

"I love Italian food," she heard herself saying. "Sometimes my late husband and I would drive all the way to Houston to visit the Olive Pit."

*Oh, you haven't forgotten that entirely in your hormone rush?*

She blushed at her internal monologue, and frowned as she realized how mundane her comments must sound to him. "It's not much. But, it's as close as you can get to real Italian out here."

He nodded graciously, but declined further comment.

Gesturing to the chair closest to her desk, she welcomed him into her office. "Have a seat. Can I get you something to drink? Water? Coffee?"

"No, no, I'm fine. But thank you very much for asking." He settled into the chair, folding long legs gracefully. She imagined that was how a stag would find repose, or a majestic elk. Blushing, she moved around the desk and settled herself into her own chair.

"Have you had a chance to look around Pinebox yet, Mr. Strega?"

He shook his head. "No. I arrived late last evening, and haven't had a chance to see much of town."

"You're staying at the Pine Hotel?" Of course he was. The only other options in town were the Timber Ridge Motel or one of the park models that the trailer trash tried to rent out to unwary vacationers. The "historic" Pine might not be much to look at, but it was still the best option in town.

He nodded, but didn't elaborate. Suzanne took the hint and pulled out the folder she'd been working on since he'd called a week before.

"Before we get started, there's some preliminary paperwork. Just formalities, really. This one says that I'll be your agent, and gives me the authority to call other agents and gather information if necessary, on your behalf. This one informs you of Texas state laws regarding the rights and responsibilities for home buyers. And, this one is a state-mandated warning about mortgage fraud and how to avoid it." She paused, thoughtfully. "Have you begun pre-qualification proceedings with your mortgage lender of choice?"

Strega paused in signing the papers she'd dealt out before him. "No. No, I haven't."

"Would you like me to introduce you to Marlene, down at Ravens State Bank? We have very good luck getting approvals through them, they're very familiar with the..."

"That won't be necessary." Strega hadn't looked up from the forms, but his pen tip floated in mid-air above the one he'd been preparing to sign.

*He's planning on paying cash.*

Suzanne frowned as her own lack of forethought. Of course, with a man of his obvious wealth, that was an option.

"If you are planning on paying cash, we'll just need to be sure to include proof of funding at the time of offer. It's just a reassurance to the seller that..."

"Of course. That will not be a problem." He lowered the pen tip to the heavy black signature line on the final form, and inwardly Suzanne sighed in relief.

*He's not hooked yet. You still have to find him the right house.*

Suzanne straightened in her seat, taking the pile of papers back and neatly organizing them into her client's folder. "Have you given any thought to what type of home you're looking for? How many bedrooms? Do you and your wife have children still at home?"

"I'm not married, Ms. Whitcomb. And no, no children."

*Suzanne. Shame on you.*

Frowning at being called to task by her own thoughts, Suzanne grabbed a pad and pen and began taking notes as Strega went on, describing his price range and what sort of a place he was looking for.

"Three bedrooms, I think. Unless it already has a den or office. My current home is around two thousand square feet, so somewhere in that range would be best. I prefer historic homes, rather than newer construction. A yard, or at least a little elbow room."

Suzanne began compiling a mental list of the homes for sale that met her client's needs, hoping the professional process would drive out the scolding thoughts that had begun to intrude upon her.

"In that price range, there are multiple options on the market right now. You're very lucky, actually. With the uncertainty about the economy and the word "recession" hanging in everyone's ears, sellers are very motivated to work with prospective buyers, and there's a glut of available homes."

"I'd begun doing some research myself. There's a place I came across. I believe it was on West Church Road?"

Suzanne thought deeply. "Church... Church..."

*Across from the Old Cemetary...*

"Oh, yes… lovely place, two story Victorian, seventeen hundred square feet, not including the fully finished basement. Three bedroom, two bath. Just over two acres of lot, and well within your price range. It's across from the Shepherd Cemetary, too, so your neighbors are quiet." Suzanne chuckled at her own joke, then looked up when Strega didn't join in.

"A cemetery?" Strega stiffened slightly, but nodded. "How… interesting. Well, I suppose it wouldn't hurt to have a look."

She hadn't pegged him as one of those superstitious types, but every client had their foibles, and she had not gotten where she was by trying to row upstream against her customer's ingrained character flaws. "Good, good. We'll mark that one down to take a look at, then. Let's see what else we have that might work…" She pulled a city map out and laid it on the desk between them. "Homes in this area to the north are mostly newer. The older places have, unfortunately, mostly been divided up into multi-family dwellings, and are being rented out to college students. There's couple of places up there, but the prices are high for the value, and all of them would need to be converted back into single-family dwellings. It's doable, but..."

Strega nodded thoughtfully, and continued to do so as she pointed out the neighborhoods around town and the features which made each a good or bad fit for him. She knew the streets and buildings of Pinebox like the back of her hand, and within a matter of minutes she had put together a list of a half-dozen homes that might suit Strega's needs.

"If you'd like, you can leave your vehicle here and I'll take you around to see these. We can discuss what you like or don't like about each place on the way to the next. That will help me help you find the perfect match for you."

*Maybe that's not such a good idea. I mean, you don't' really know this fella. What if he's some kind of a…*

"That would be fine, thank you." Strega's words cut off the worrisome nagging in the back of her mind. Within moments, she had escorted him out of the building, and they were on their way.

****

"This one is lovely. A real value for the price, and the sellers are quite motivated."

As they walked up the steps, Suzanne gave the house an assessing once-over. The bushes were overgrown, and the flowers dead. Nothing that couldn't be replaced or fixed, but bargaining points none the less. It had good bones, but looked like someone had been haphazard with maintenance of late. Still, she'd shown her client a half dozen houses so far, and none of them had been quite what he was looking for. This one wasn't the most expensive on the list, but the seller's agent was offering a better-than-average percentage to any agent who brought in a buyer. And she could certainly use the extra cash.

"The roof is newer, and it comes with all the appliances. Gas heat, and air conditioning…" She continued extolling the unit's virtues as she punched in the lockbox code and retrieved the key from the little brass mechanism hanging from the house's front doorknob.

"Why are the owners so… motivated?" Strega asked, as he waited for her to unlock the door.

The question she'd hoped he wouldn't ask. Still, there it was, hanging between them and now she had to answer.

"Are you familiar with the term "Stigmatized Property, Mr. Strega?"

"No, not specifically. Stigmata? The house bleeds from its hands?"

Suzanne laughed, but paused when Strega didn't join her in appreciating what she had assumed was his joke. She opened the door and escorted him into the foyer, closing the door behind them.

"There are certain types of property which, according to state law, a seller must disclose as potentially stigmatized… meaning they may not be appealing for some sellers because of certain… factors…"

She chose her next words carefully. "The good news is, this is neither a former methamphetamine lab, nor is it in gang territory. The former owners were not murdered here, nor does it rest on a former Indian burial ground." She bit her lip, remembering his reaction in the office to the house across from the cemetery.

"But…" Strega turned away from the Victorian staircase and looked at her, waiting for the shoe to drop.

"But… And this is really very silly. Legally, there's no way to prove it, so the fact that it's still on the lawbooks at all is a throwback to older and more… superstitious times, at best…"

He waited, head tilted slightly.

"You see. The house has a reputation. That is, there are stories. Some of the people who have lived here say that… The house is, supposedly… haunted. Mind you, nothing bad has ever happened here, at least nothing provable… But the locals do talk, and…"

He shut his eyes for a moment, and Suzanne felt her heart sink as she pictured the profitable sale fading off into the sunset.

Before she could speak, however, he opened them again and smiled. "There's no ghost here."

"Well, of course not… I mean, you and I are logical individuals. We know there's no such thing as…"

"If there were, I would feel it, and I do not, so… no ghost."

Suzanne stopped in her tracks, mouth slightly open. She could feel her jaw flex back and forth just a bit as her mind whirled in neutral. "I… that is…" There was simply nothing she could think of to say that didn't sound either idiotic or contradictory, and if there was one thing she'd learned in her years as a realtor, it was that the customer was always right. Even if they were crazy. Especially if they were rich and crazy. Double so if they were rich, handsome and crazy. And, apparently, hers was all three.

Strega turned away from her and walked further into the house. He continued to talk, his voice echoing in the nearly empty rooms, and Suzanne was forced to hurry to catch up with him.

"It's a family thing, you see… My mother could see them. Had been able to since she was a child, according to my grandmother. Nana would find her in her room, conversing away with someone who had died long ago. Nana was more like me, and could only sense them when she tried to do so. A blessing, really. Being able to see the dead as clearly as the living was a burden which took a harsh toll on my dear mother."

"How… interesting…" Suzanne's mind continued to spin as she tried to make sense of the things Strega was saying.

"All of us tend to… how would you say it? Disturb, perhaps… Yes, disturb is a good word… the otherwise peaceful spirits of those who once lived. One or two, we can even influence. Drive them away or control their actions. More than that, though, and it's a bit overwhelming. That's why the house we discussed earlier… the one across from the cemetery? It wouldn't have been a good fit. I try not to spend any more time in locations where large quantities of ghosts might gather than necessary. It can be quite… challenging… to deal with."

"I… see…" Suzanne didn't see, not at all. She'd helped clients buy and sell stigmatized properties before. In any town as old as Pinebox, there were a good portion of the older homes that had stories of some sort attached to them. Especially back before hospitals and doctors' offices were prevalent, folks tended to die in their homes, and she doubted there was probably a house in town more than 60 years old that didn't have some sort of ghost story attached to it. She'd met those who believed and those who didn't, but never someone who spoke about such things with the sheer nonchalance that Strega was.

"The fireplace is exquisite," he said, moving past her back into the parlor. "Is it original?"

Happy for a change of topic, Suzanne nodded enthusiastically. "Yes, as a matter of fact, it is. As are the hardwood floors, although they've been refinished."

Resting one hand on the heavy oak mantle, Strega turned to her and flashed his alabaster grin her direction. "Ms. Whitcomb, I believe we've found my new home. Can I take you out to dinner to discuss the offer?"

*****

"Now, I'll just fax the offer over to the seller's agent, and, hopefully, we'll have a response by morning." Suzanne neatened the paperwork for the offer and put the cover sheet on top.

"Thank you for all your help today, Suzanne." Strega reached across the desk and patted her hand. The gesture, while brief and casual, sent goose bumps up her arm.

*Oh, it's Suzanne is it now? What happened to Ms. Whitcomb?*

"Of course. That's what I'm here for, isn't it? I like to say that the best business partners are good friends."

Overhead, the lights flickered again. When they came back on, they were dim, not half as bright as normal. The finicky wiring had gotten worse that evening, crackling and snapping when she'd first turned them on. Her computer hadn't wanted to boot up, either, and she'd had to write out the offer all long hand rather than fill out the form on the computer and print it like she normally did. There was an electric buzz overhead and Susan made a mental note to call the landlord and insist he send out an electrician the next morning.

"Do you need anything else from me, then?" Apparently unshaken by the electrical chaos, Strega's voice was like honeyed whiskey – sweet and rough, with just enough texture. Suzanne wasn't certain whether it was the tone or the red wine they'd shared over dinner, but she felt a flush rise in her cheeks.

*Don't you dare answer that question, Suzanne Marie Whitcomb.* Her inner voice was gruff and low, holding a threatening tone that sent a shiver down her spine.

She shook her head to clear it, and stood to move around the desk to shake his hand. "No… no, I'll call you as soon as I hear something back. With this market and the generous nature of your offer, it should be well received."

"Thank you, then."

"The pleasure was all mine, I assure you."

He left her with the warm imprint of his hand wrapped around hers. The bright jangle of the front door bells signaled his departure, and she sank back into her chair, flushed with an inner glow that she hadn't felt since Wade passed away.

"Oh, so you do remember me?"

For a moment, she thought Strega had come back into the building. She turned towards the door and then realized that the voice was coming not from the front lobby, but from the far corner of her office.

She turned towards the space that used to house Wade's desk. The dimmed lights flickered again, and the shadows in the corner seemed to writhe in response. She blinked, rubbing at her eyes to clear them. When she looked again, he was standing there, leaning against the wall.

"...Wade?"

He looked good. Not like he had before his death, all yellowed skin and bones, hunched over and struggling for breath. No, this was Wade as he was when she'd met him, tall and strong. His eyes were dark and shining, beneath the brim of the cowboy hat he'd always worn. The only thing missing was his smile. His mouth was set in a solid straight line, jaw clenched and brow furrowed.

"You can see me now, can you? I guess that's one thing I can thank him for."

Suzanne clutched the arms of her chair. "W...Wade?"

"Who else would it be? Has it been so long you don't even remember me any more?" He took a step forward and the lights overhead dimmed further, spreading a deep shadow across the office. Suzanne swallowed hard and tried to breathe, but it was as if the darker the room became, the thicker the air was. It caught in her nose, her throat, her lungs, like a cold, murky fog.

"But you're..." She couldn't bring herself to say the word.

"Yeah, yeah. I know. I'm dead. It's not like you think, though. I didn't go away. I've never been far from you. I promised you I wouldn't, and I've been true to my word."

She nodded, but as he took another step forward, she found herself pushing back in her chair to keep a distance between them. She came up short, the back of her chair pressed against the lateral file behind her desk. There was no where else for her to go.

"Now, why'd you want to go and do that? I'm not going to hurt you, Suzi."

Her nickname sent a chill down her spine. He'd called her that, from the first day they'd met. Now, though, it just felt wrong.

"Wade, you... you've gotta go... You..."

"Oh, I will, Suzi. I can't stay long. It's hard being here, even with the boost your new friend gave me. See, I know you kind of set your hat on that gent, but he understands. He knows how bad I've been missing you, and you me. He understands."

Suzanne started to protest, but he cut her words short.

"No, none of that... There'll be time enough for that..."

She blinked, trying to make sense of his words.

Wade smiled then, but it wasn't the smile she knew. This one was hard and cold, and it didn't reach his eyes. He took another step towards her, and she held her breath as the icy shadows around him danced across her skin.

"See, the thing is, Suzi, you and I have been apart too long. We promised to be together forever, and... well, the way I figure it, forever's not up yet. Strega, he knows that too. Knows we belong together."

She pushed back in her chair, trying to put more space between them. When it wouldn't yield any further, she pressed herself hard against the chair-back, as if flattening herself might give her a millimeter or two more of room. The gesture pushed all the air from her lungs, so when he began to reach for her, there wasn't even enough there to fuel a last scream.

Then the lights flickered out entirely, and there was only darkness in the office they'd once shared.

****

"Excuse me, please? Are you Mister Fielding?"

"Hang on. I'll be right down." The greasy-haired man finished wiping the window he'd just scraped, clearing the last of the gold paint flakes off of his squeegee with a dirty rag. He climbed down the step-ladder and gave the stranger a cursory glance before nodding curtly. "Yeah, I'm Fielding."

"I was wondering if I might speak with you about the building? I understand you own it?"

Fielding sat down the bucket he'd been cleaning the window with, and wiped his hands on the thighs of his jeans as he shrugged. "I'm listening."

"I understand you've been having some trouble getting occupants, since... the unfortunate incident with Ms. Whitcomb."

The mechanic shrugged again noncommittally, shoving both hands deep into his pants pockets.

Strega went on, undaunted. "Since, from what I understand, it's been empty or nearly so, for a year or more, I thought perhaps you'd consider selling it to me. I'm considering moving my business here, and would like to make you an offer on the building."

Fielding frowned, coughing up some phlegm which he spit on the floor near Strega's impeccably shined shoe. "Folks say it's haunted, you know."

Strega chuckled deeply. "Somehow, Mister Fielding, I don't think that will be a problem. I will just consider that a part of its charm... Now, can I buy you lunch while we discuss the matter?"

The bright jangle of brass bells echoed in the empty lobby as the two men departed. And, as the door shut behind them, the antique yellow lights flickered angrily overhead.

****

*Jess Hartley has the good fortune to work as a freelance novelist, writer, editor and developer in the gaming industry. She started working with White Wolf Games in 2003, when she penned the Exalted novel, In Northern Twilight. Since then, she has written content for more than 30 game projects including products for the World of Darkness core game line, Vampire: The Masquerade, Werewolf: The Forsaken, Mage: The Awakening, Promethean: The Created, Changeling: The Lost, Hunter: The Vigil, Geist: The Sin-Eaters, Exalted (Second Edition), and Scion.*

*Jess dwells in a state of contentment (and occasionally denial) with her family and a menagerie of other interesting creatures. She's an active member of The Camarilla and the Society for Creative Anachronism, and participates in a plethora of other strange and curious pastimes which often make her neighbors and acquaintances scratch their heads in confusion.*

*More information about Jess can be found at her website, jesshartley.com.*

# ~The Witch of Linda Lane~

*by Ed Wetterman*

Mom said Mrs. Jones was just a sweet old lady, but all of us kids knew better. Especially after what she did to my friends. Of course, no one believed us. We were just kids, and adults are too busy with business and bills to listen to kids. Well, except for old Leonard. He believed us, but no one believed him.

Mrs. Jones had lived forever in the old A-frame ranch house near the railroad tracks. It was yellow with dingy white trim, and the paint peeled so badly that it almost looked like some animal with long, sharp claws had decided to use it as a scratching post.

And cats. She had lots of cats. The place reeked of cat piss and that old, musky smell of someone who had lived too long.

Just before the Fall Festival, we were riding our bikes down the hill on Linda Lane. The last house at the bottom of the cul de sac was Mrs. Jones's, and her circle concrete driveway was exactly at the bottom of the hill. The Three Amigos, that's Tommy, Jimmy, and me, would cruise down the hill just as fast as we could, racing the wind and each other. At the bottom we would have to hit our brakes just as we left the pavement for the concrete of her driveway. Of course this left bike marks, but we didn't think anything of it at the time. Then we would lean our bikes and whip around the circle as fast as we could to build up speed for the ride back to the top of the hill.

Tommy was my best friend. We did everything together. We even shared the same birthday, April 11th, and we both turned twelve years old that year. We played in little league on the Giants, attended the same class in Pinebox Middle School, and his parents took me on a vacation with them the previous summer to Little Rock, Arkansas. We went to a diamond mine and dug for two hours. We found a small one. Tommy and I decided we would be co-owners of it forever. Every week we would pass it back and forth between us. I keep it on my dresser now, right next to the frog aquarium. I can't bear to touch it anymore. I just can't.

On our seventh race down, it was Jimmy Berry in the lead, followed by Tommy and me. I usually was last. My bike wasn't a racer like theirs, but mine was the best trick bike. We raced full speed down the hill, the mailboxes flying by. As Jimmy pulled out in front, he yelled, "Hell Yeah!"

As we hit the small bump leading from the pavement to the concrete of her drive, old Mrs. Jones herself appeared in the doorway. Her wrinkled old face looked like an angry Halloween mask, but I couldn't hear what she was saying over the loud hum of bike tires over asphalt. She held something in her left hand and at first I thought she was just waving a stick at us like crazy old people do.

One second we were riding the wind, and the next Jimmy's front brakes locked up. Right in front of us, he flipped over the handlebars and swam through the air like a rag doll. When he hit the old lady's concrete driveway, his head sounded like a watermelon thrown at the ground. Tommy and I laid long, black skid marks while our friend's body scraped forward, rolling and tumbling.

No, he wasn't wearing a bike helmet.

How his mother screamed when she got to the scene. The police had covered his body beneath some kind of dark blanket. What I remember the most is the blood. It seeped onto the concrete drive and slowly spreaded onto the grass.

That was the first time Tommy tried to tell the other adults about Mrs. Jones. He swore she had held a wand and cast a spell to cause the accident. Of course the police didn't believe him. No one did. I'm not even sure I did, yet. But then as the body of our friend was being lifted from the pavement, she smiled at me. She was missing several of her front teeth, and her smile grossed me out, but it was the *idea* of the smile at that horrible time that repulsed and scared the crap out of me.

Of course no one else saw her do it, but after that I knew her evil secret. She had cast a spell. She had killed Jimmy. She was a witch.

Something had to be done.

Tommy and me were not allowed to play together for a week after the "accident," although we did attend the funeral together. I felt so sorry for Jimmy's mother. She didn't talk to anyone. She just sat there and cried, staring straight forward but not really seeing anything.

We couldn't believe that Mrs. Jones came to the funeral. She wore a black dress with a white shawl, though her thick, curly grey hair still popped up like some sort of mop.

Tommy glared at her, but I was afraid to even look at her. At the end of the funeral, everyone began to file by the coffin. Mrs. Jones suddenly appeared right behind us. She placed her hand on Tommy's shoulder. "Sorry about your friend." Her words were soft in volume, but to me it sounded like she spoke with the voice of a hundred small stones rubbing together. I jumped in sudden fright.

Tommy turned quickly around and slapped her hand from his shoulder. "I know you, you old witch. I know what you did." His face turned red in anger and I thought he was going to attack her then.

Tommy's father grabbed him and hauled him away from her. He was yelling at Tommy, and Tommy was yelling at Mrs. Jones. The entire procession seemed to fall into anarchy as some were crying, some were shocked, and others turning away from the bizarre scene.

Only Mrs. Jones didn't seem as if Tommy's outburst had bothered her. She glanced at me, and moved to the coffin. She looked in on the corpse and placed a yellow rose into it next to Jimmy's husk. She then moved to Jimmy's mother and they whispered to each other.

I realized I was shaking. The idea of having come so close to her turned my legs to rubber. Mom whispered something in my ear and pulled me away to the car.

As we left, I saw that I wasn't the only one who was afraid of Mrs. Jones. Leonard was a strange man, maybe in his late twenties or early thirties. He was a giant, with huge muscles, but his face was almost childish. Dad said he was touched—you know, not right in the head. He worked as a handyman around town, usually mowing yards and working on people's gardens. His pudgy face usually carried a smile, but right then he seemed frozen in fear. He was staring at Mrs. Jones, and as I walked past him I caught the smell of urine. Looking down, I saw a dark patch spread across the front of his pants and down his thighs.

No one else had noticed it yet, but I did. I knew that Leonard knew the truth about Mrs. Jones. I knew she scared him, too.

****

Finally, Tommy and I got together again in the middle school cafeteria during lunch and I told him about Leonard. We agreed to find him and ask him about the witch. We didn't call her Mrs. Jones anymore. She was just "the witch" to us, and we swore to get even with her. Now I wish we had just left her alone.

We spent the next few weeks riding our bikes after school and on weekends looking for Leonard. We didn't know where he lived and we couldn't find him in the phonebook. We figured if we rode around long enough, we would spot him eventually.

Finally, one Saturday evening, we saw him. He was working in the Lowe's garden down on Oak Street. The Lowes were rich and they had a huge mansion with lots of gardens. We rode up the driveway and parked our bikes behind Mr. Lowe's Mercedes and walked over to Leonard.

When he caught sight of us, Leonard stopped weeding and stood up in his very dirty, blue overalls. He took off his leatherwork gloves and smiled his goofy smile at us. "Howdy boys." He waved.

Tommy took the lead, and I was happy to let him. "Mr. Leonard, we need to ask you some questions."

Leonard stood there smiling. "Sure, I got time for a rest anyway. You should rest occasionally. Daddy said if you don't take time to rest, you could work yourself to death. My daddy was a wise man. Yessir." He led us to the shade of an old cedar tree and sat down.

Tommy looked at me but I just shrugged. He began, "Um, Mr. Leonard. What do you know about Mrs. Jones?"

Leonard stared at Tommy blankly for a moment, then stood to his feet. "Well that's enough rest, I think. I should get back to work. Work won't do itself."

Tommy stood as well, "Mr. Leonard, please. Talk to us." Tommy grabbed Leonard by the forearm. "She killed my friend Jimmy. You know she did. No one will believe us. We need to talk to you about her."

Leonard stood there looking from Tommy to me and back. "I…I really shouldn't. You don't want to make a witch angry. She can find out. She always does."

I looked at Tommy, but he seemed at a loss for words. "Um…" I began, and stumbled again before the words finally came. "How do you know it, Leonard? How do you know she is a witch?"

Leonard gave me a puzzled look, "I'm really not supposed to talk about it. Not after what she did to me and my dad. No, I really shouldn't. Promised him, you know, that I wouldn't. He said loose lips sink ships. That's what he told me, but then again, she killed him right after that. Right in front of me. She killed him and took my mind. Yes, she did."

Tommy punched me in the arm as if to say, I told you so. I absently rubbed the arm and focused on Leonard. The big man was crying.

"I'm sorry Leonard. About your dad," I said.

Leonard nodded and sobbed, "I'm not supposed to talk about that. Daddy told me not to talk about it."

Tommy leaned forward and placed his hand on Leonard's. I found this kind of shocking and something I would never have expected of my best friend. "It's okay Leonard. We are going to take care of her once and for all. I promise."

Leonard's face turned hopeful. "Are you a witch hunter too?"

Tommy glanced at me, then back to Leonard, "Sure we are."

"So you are like my daddy then. You know how to fight em?" A broad smile crossed Leonard's face. "I've been waiting for the chance, ya know. For what she did to my daddy and me."

Tommy nodded and smiled. "Yeah, we want to fight her, but no, we don't know how."

Leonard's mouth worked as if he was chewing cud, then said "My daddy did, but it didn't help him. She won in the end. Maybe we should leave her alone."

Tommy gripped Leonard's hand in his. "No, Leonard. We can't let her hurt anyone else. Your daddy would want you to help us. Can you? Help us?"

Leonard's face pinched up as he thought it over. You could practically hear rusty gears turning in his head. Finally, he nodded. "Yeah. I guess he would. Come to my house tonight and I'll show you his stuff."

The front door of the Lowe's home opened then and Dr. Lowe looked out.

"I've gotta get back to work now." Leonard stood and began walking back to the garden with a wave to Dr. Lowe, who smiled and closed the door.

"Hey Leonard." Tommy again caught at the hulk's arm. "We don't know where you live."

Leonard put on his gloves. "I live at 313 Edward Street." He smiled. "See ya'll tonight." He moved back to the garden humming some song that sounded like the theme song from Rocky.

Tommy was very proud of what he had done and learned. I, on the other hand, felt as if my stomach had clamped into a tight-knotted ball. Tommy and I agreed to meet over by the old railroad station at midnight. Edward Street wasn't far from there and we both knew we would have to sneak out of our homes.

That night, waiting for midnight, was impossible torture. It felt like I was sick and the world just sort of moved past me. I wanted to sleep, but knew if I did I wouldn't wake up in time to meet Tommy and I couldn't let him down.

The more I thought about our situation, the more scared I became. Mrs. Jones was a real witch. She had killed people, including my friend Jimmy and Leonard's father, and somehow had retarded Leonard. What would she do to us? I didn't want to end up like Leonard. I *really* didn't want to end up like Jimmy, with my blood seeping out from under a blanket onto her driveway.

Finally, my alarm clock flashed 11:48 in big, red letters. Time to go. My father had screwed the windows down several years earlier, so I would have to to sneak out my room and past my parent's bedroom, go down the hall to the dining room, then slip out the sliding door to the backyard. The front door made a loud squeaking noise, so I couldn't go out that way. Once outside, it would be nothing to hop the fence and follow the highline to the railroad tracks only a few blocks away.

I slowly got out of my bed and arranged my pillows to look as if I was sleeping beneath the blankets, then put on my jeans and sneakers. Next came the dangerous part. Opening my door might wake up my parents and then I'd be caught. I slowly pulled the door open, but the air conditioner caused some suction which turned into a sharp whistle through the cracked door.

My heart pounded. I knew I was busted. I stood there in the open doorway for what seemed like eternity, waiting for some sign that my parents had awoken and were coming to check on me. Nothing happened except the air conditioner kicked off, which made the house even quieter.

Finally I started down the hall and past my parent's room. When I heard my dad still snoring like a lumberjack, my heart slowed its pounding in my ears. In the dining room, I pulled up the wooden stick my parents used to lock the sliding door in place. Just when it seemed like I was home free, disaster struck. I accidentally banged the stick against a chair leg and dropped with a loud clack onto our wooden floor. Immediately I heard my mother say, "Ray. Someone's in the house!"

Busted. I had two choices. I could stand there and face the music, or get out now, meet with Tommy, and face the music later.

I dashed out the door and across the yard. I had leapt the fence and was running full tilt down the highline when I heard mom yelling my name, but I didn't stop. Tommy needed me.

I arrived at the railroad tracks, with my heart pounding, the blood rushing through my head, and breathing hard. I bent over to catch my breath and looked for Tommy. I didn't see him.

"Damn." I muttered. I was sure then that I would catch hell and Tommy wasn't even going to make it.

I sat on the cold metal tracks and waited. About five minutes later I heard something moving in the bushes to my left. I stood up and wished I could see in the dark like a superhero. Had Mrs. Jones found me, or had she summoned something to tear me limb from limb and eat my heart? Then something moaned, a low guttural sound. I picked up a rock and threw it into the bushes.

"Missed me." Tommy laughed and rolled out from the bushes. "Dude, I scared the shit out of ya."

"Real nice, Tommy. Thanks man." I felt both embarrassed and relieved. Tommy walked over and slapped my back.

"Sorry man, I just couldn't resist."

I really wanted to deck him, but instead I sighed, "Screw it. Let's just get going."

Soon we were making our way down the tracks towards Edward Street. I told Tommy I had been busted and would probably be grounded for a while. He laughed and told me that he had stopped to grab some cold pizza out of his icebox before sneaking out. His father was a drunk who had passed out hours before.

"Check it out." Tommy lifted his shirt and I could see his daddy's .38 snubnose pistol.

"Tommy, you shouldn't have taken that." I had been raised around guns and went to deer camps with my dad. I knew what damage a bullet could do.

"Hey, if we need it you won't be bitching." Tommy dropped his shirt over the gun barrel.

"Just be sure you don't pull the trigger when you're pulling it out of your pants. You'll probably blow your dick off." I was trying to be funny, but neither of us laughed. The more I thought about it and Mrs. Jones, the happier I was that he had the gun.

As we came to Edward Street we spotted a Pinebox police car and hid under a pink crepe myrtle. Of course there was also a fire ant bed and as soon as the car turned the corner we were both dancing and waving the ants off our bodies.

Just a few minutes later we were standing in front of Leonard's home. It was very small and old, and the porch was leaning as if ready to collapse. Tommy led the way up the steps and I cautiously followed, looking over my shoulder down the street. Looking for that police car. I wondered if my parents had called them. What if there was an All Points Bulletin on us? That gun would really get us in trouble then, and it wasn't like anyone would believe us. I took a deep breath and turned back to the front door. Tommy knocked, and after a long wait the door opened to reveal a large, half naked Leonard. He stood there wearing white boxers with a smiley face on the front, and nothing else.

I was surprised at his upper body muscles. I hoped I would grow some of my own someday. It would be cool to look that tough.

Leonard smiled his goofy smile and waved us inside. "I didn't think you guys were gonna make it."

Tommy entered first, "We just had to wait till our parents went to sleep."

The inside of the house was packed with stuff. Junk was piled everywhere. I had never seen a house like that. There were two paths through the knickknacks, clothing, and collectables, one of which we used to follow Leonard into his bedroom.

"I got the stuff for ya." He bent under his bed and pulled out a large black, leather chest with a silver lock. He said the combination out loud, "64, 42, 12," and opened the lock.

Inside the case was a small black book, a bag of iron nails, a machete with a wooden handle, and three old fashioned scissors like my grandmother always used when sewing. Leonard reached inside and pulled out the book, then sat on the bed next to the chest.

"This was my daddy's. I can read some of it, but some is in a weird language." He flipped through the pages and I could see many hand drawn pictures, bizarre markings, and lots of writing.

He handed the book to Tommy, who took the book and immediately began flipping through it. There was a section in the back marked Witches and my heart stopped. Tommy began skimming the page.

"It says here we can kill her with iron, or by cutting her head off, burning the body, and burying the head in sancty…sancti…."

"Sanctified ground. You know like a cemetery," I helped. Tommy looked at me and nodded. I had been helping him with his reading for years.

"Okay, so when do we do it?" Tommy asked.

I shrugged. "Man I don't know if we can do it. I mean *kill* her? Cut off her head, burn the body, bury the head…that's…I dunno man. I don't know if I could do something like that."

Leonard nodded. "I've thought about it many times, but she scares me."

Tommy glanced from me to Leonard. "Me too, but we can't let her just keep getting away with murder. If we don't stop her, how many other people will die? How many other kids like Jimmy? We gotta do this, man. We gotta."

I kept remembering Jimmy's head and the sound it made hitting the concrete. The red blood on the green grass. The witch's smile. "Yeah, I guess we do."

"Do we go tonight?" Tommy looked directly at me once more.

"No. That would be bad. Her powers are greater at night." Leonard spoke up.

"Did you learn that from your father?" Tommy asked.

Leonard shook his head. "Nope. Saw that on an episode of Supernatural Hunters." He smiled broadly. "That's a great show, and the good guys always win."

Tommy and I laughed at that.

"Okay, so…tomorrow then?" Tommy asked.

I hoped so, but I knew my parents were going to have a complete fit over me running off in the middle of the night.

"Maybe. It depends on my parents. They may not let me out tomorrow."

Tommy nodded. "Okay, we'll put this off for a while. Lay low, but we need to keep an eye on the witch." We all nodded in agreement. Tommy took the book, the nails, and the scissors, but left the machete. They offered it to me, but I refused. I knew I was in enough trouble as it was. Adding a big knife to my problems wasn't going to help.

I should have known it would all come to a bad ending when Tommy said that we should "keep an eye on the witch." I wish I had thought it through. My parents grounded me for two months and my mother threatened to take me to a doctor to get to the bottom of my delinquent behavior.

My response: "Yeah mom, I'm a real axe murderer!"

That didn't go over too well.

She smothered me the next week. She would walk me into school all the way to my first period English class, speak with my teacher regarding any "changes" in my behavior, then would pick me up immediately after school, take me straight home, and hover over me as I completed my homework. She did allow me to watch television in the living room, but I couldn't play any games, talk on the phone, or go anywhere.

My father decided to put in an alarm system, so my days of sneaking out of the house were done. It seemed everything that was fun in life was over. Of course our plans to take out the witch were put on hold.

Well, my plans anyway. See, true to Tommy's word, he and Leonard started watching the witch's dingy yellow house. I warned him to stay away from her, but Tommy was committed. Jimmy's murder sat like a rock in his stomach. He said he was in for the "whole hog," which means he wouldn't quit or wait for anything.

The next Friday night, Tommy decided to sneak behind the witch's home and peek in the back windows. Of course he didn't tell me his plan. He knew I would have pleaded with him not to do it.

I would have begged him. I'm sure that's why he didn't tell me about his plan.

I found out about it when his mother arrived late Saturday night to ask if Tommy had come to visit. She was upset and had already contacted the police. I think she knew. Mother's intuition. Tommy was gone. A few minutes later, so was she. She had gone to scour Pinebox to find him. I knew she wouldn't.

I knew.

I slipped into my mother's room and used her cell phone to call Leonard. When he answered the phone he was crying and just kept repeating, "She got him, she got him, she got him."

I asked him to tell me what happened, but he was too upset. "She's got to die. She got him, and now she's gotta die. Just like my dad, but she's gotta die. She got him, and now she's gotta die." That's when he hung up.

It was like watching a car wreck in slow motion on TV. Jimmy's head thumped and skidded on the witch's driveway. Something bad had happened to Tommy. Now poor, touched Leonard was going to do something stupid, like a one more car driving right into that wreck. I had to stop him. I didn't see any other choice. I had to turn to my parents for help, even though I knew they would never believe me.

I told them everything. The looks on their faces went from concern to fright. I knew they were worried that something else might have happened to me. We had had the sex talk and the "there are bad people who want to hurt you" talk, and of course that's what my dad asked me about.

I lost it. For the first time in my life, I cussed at my parents. "No, damn it. Listen to me! I'm not fucking making this shit up. You *have* to believe me. Something's happened to Tommy, and now my friend Leonard is going to the bitch's home, and she's probably going to kill him too."

Yeah. That went over well.

Eventually, my dad called the police. They came to the house, and I told them everything and begged them to stop Leonard.

They were too late. When the police arrived at the witch's home, they found her headless corpse in the kitchen.

They also found Leonard holding the bloody machete in his right hand and the witch's head in his left. I heard that Leonard had been looking into her dead eyes and asking, "Why did you do it?"

They sent Leonard to jail and he was found guilty of murder and placed in prison for 45 years. I was asked lots of questions by the police and reporters, but that was the end of it. At the witch's home they found Tommy's clothes. They were hidden in her garden behind a large gardenia bush, but they never found him.

Most in town believed Leonard did it.

I knew better.

A week after Leonard was arrested, I skipped school during lunch and walked all the way over to the witch's home. I snuck into the garden to look for Tommy. I never found him either, but I did find a large green toad. I took it home with me.

Was it Tommy? I don't know.

Is she really dead? I don't know.

I hope so.

I do know that someone has to do the work that Leonard and Tommy were trying to do. The work that killed Leonard's daddy. They say there's a serial killer around these parts, but they wouldn't call it murder if they could handle the truth. I'm a witch hunter. I find them and I kill them.

I kill them.

****

*Ed Wetterman is a history teacher, game designer, writer, native Texan, genealogist, fisherman, Assistant Scout Master, Christian, husband, and father of two. His reading tastes lean toward fantasy, horror, science fiction, history, and role-playing games. He enjoys driving a big truck, shooting guns, camping, writing, and hanging out with his geeky friends. He helped found 12 to Midnight in 2003 and wrote Last Rites of the Black Guard, Green's Guide to Ghosts, Innana's Kiss, Fear Effects. He has also contributed to Bloodlines, the upcoming Realms of Cthulhu by Reality Blurs, and has written several short stories and articles. He and Preston DuBose are currently working on ETU: Degrees of Horror, a plot point role-playing game for the Savage Worlds system.*

# ~Blood-Born~

*by Charles Rice*

Drug seeking?!?"

Jack stared at the nurse in disbelief, her disapproving scowl having little effect on him. He was many things. A guy who cheated on his girlfriend, got busted and got dumped? Sure. A guy who got fired for unauthorized computer use at work? Sure. But drugs?

After the shock wore off, Jack tried again, "Look, I've never used drugs in my life it's just, I'm in pain and I..."

The nurse looked down at the clipboard in front of her, pursing her lips with disgust, "You've been here looking for pain meds four times in the last seven months and when I called Nacogdoches and Lufkin E.R.s, it seems you make the rounds to them when you get turned away here."

"But I..."

Jack looked down as the nurse pressed something into his hand. For a moment a wave of relief washed over him. Sometimes the nurses would lecture him but give him a 'scrip anyway. Relief turned to embarrassment, however, as he turned over the small business card in his hand:

**Sober Living**

*Inpatient and outpatient treatment for drug, alcohol and gambling addiction.*

1616 Pandora St.

Pinebox, TX

Call 555-8921 to schedule an appointment.

*Sponsored by the Safe Health Foundation.*

By the time Jack finished looking at the card, the nurse had retreated into an employee only area guarded by a huge, scowling security guard.

Jack had never been much of a fighter and was usually the first one to walk away. Plus, the guard had 5 inches and 50 pounds on him. Yet, something about him—in fact *everything* about him, from the way he looked to the smell of his cheap cologne—set Jack off in that one moment.

"Don't you walk away from me," he shouted at the retreating nurse.

He met the now-advancing guard in stride, catching him by the throat and throwing him down in a single motion. It was nothing like what he'd seen in movies or the occasional mixed-martial arts match on pay per view. There was no skill, no finesse. Just raw power fueled by the rage inside him.

He tried the door into the back. It was locked.

Without hesitation, he moved over to the admittance counter and jumped through the little window there. As he went through the window he felt something sharp cut into his side. The pain flared up instantly, fueling his anger even more.

Behind him, a police officer who had come in with his partner was yelling something. Jack couldn't care less. Someone was going to listen to him.

"Listen to me you stuck up, little- ahh!!!"

Suddenly, Jack was on the ground, snarling and writhing impotently at the stunned nurse. Every muscle in his body was cramped and flexing involuntarily as the electricity from the Taser shot through his body.

****

Jack's first sensation on returning to consciousness was the return of the pain that had been growing inside him for months. It was like his skeleton had started growing again while his skin and organs stayed the same size. He stared at the ceiling, writhing in agony. It took him a few minutes to figure out where he was. Someone spit on him and he realized he was in a holding cell. The pain flared up again. It was terrible. He wished the darkness would claim him again. Eventually it did.

****

Jack's next return to consciousness was pain free for the first time in ages. For a moment he didn't realize where he was. Slowly, awareness crept in. It was the smell that finally made it click. He was in a hospital of some sort, strapped down to an antiseptically white mattress and wearing nothing but a hospital gown. As his confusion grew, he began to struggle against the leather restraints that held him to the bed. Finally a nurse and a doctor in puke green scrubs came running in.

The doctor was a Japanese man in his 40's with a worn, weathered face. He was impassively calm in the face of Jack's frantic strains against the straps that held him immobile on the bed,

"Nurse, give me that sedative I prepared earlier." Almost immediately after the needle jabbed into Jack's arm, his movements became smaller, more languorous, as if he'd been coated in honey.

When Jack stopped struggling entirely, the doctor smiled down at him. "Jack? Can you hear me? I'm Doctor Kim. You gave the E.R. a bit of a scare back there, Mr. Compton. You know, you really should have told the nurses a bit more about your medical history. If they knew you'd had leukemia, they might not have been so quick to dismiss your complaints of bone pain. We took a blood sample and have sent it to oncology. We're also monitoring these bruises you have, to see if they heal normally or if your cancer has returned. Do you understand what I'm saying?"

Jack nodded, swallowing several times as he tried to summon his speech back from wherever it had retreated during the night. In his confused state, all he could think of was how lined and weathered the man's face was. He looked like he could sleep for a week and still not be rested. Jack's voice was raspy and barely audible, "You look tired."

The doctor laughed, which only made the comfortable wrinkles lining his face more pronounced, "Occupational hazard I'm afraid. You're at the Safe Health Foundation Free Clinic. Do you remember being brought here?"

Jack shook his head as much as to clear the cobwebs as in answer. "The drug rehab place? Fuck. That nurse really wanted me to come here."

The doctor looked matter of fact, "No, this is a free clinic for indigent patients. Sober living is a separate clinic funded by the same endowment. Now I see from your records that you had a bone marrow transplant three years ago. Have you been in remission since then?"

Jack nodded. He knew what the doctor was driving at. It's not like he wasn't aware of what "phantom bone pain" could mean. But he wasn't going through chemo again. He wanted pain meds, and other than that his cancer could do whatever the hell it wanted for whatever time he had left.

The doctor nodded and took a pen out, writing something on Jack's chart. Jack had spent a lot of time in hospitals during his life. Too much. He knew the procedures almost as well as this guy.

"Any symptoms besides bone pain? Any fever?" Jack nodded.

"Night sweats? Chills?" Jack nodded again.

"Bleeding gums?" Another nod.

"Malaise?"

Jack frowned. Whatever the doctor had given him had kicked into high gear, "What?"

"Fatigue?"

Jack nodded again.

He'd determined weeks ago not to mention his cancer to any more doctors. He just wanted help for his pain. But here he was singing like a canary to this guy. Stupid drugs.

The doctor said something else but Jack couldn't make it out. It was like they were on boats drifting in opposite directions. Still, the doctor's questions and his answers prompted one last thought before he slipped back into unconsciousness, a thought he tried to vocalize but had no idea if he did or not.

"Fuck."

That seemed to sum things up.

****

Doctor Kim looked down at Jack. As they talked he saw that the sedative was taking full effect. Still, he wanted as much information as he could get. "Any diarrhea?"

Jack stirred a little and murmured, "Fuck."

The doctor frowned. He didn't really care for that kind of language and heard it far too often in the the clinic. "Is that a yes, Mr. Compton?"

No answer. His patient was now fully unconscious. Oh well.

Dr. Kim left the room by an adjoining door next to a large mirror. In his drugged state, Jack hadn't noticed the large mirror. If he had, he'd have known it was not a feature common in hospital rooms. Especially not those given to guys like Jack, who had no insurance.

Doctor Kim winced as the man in the room reached into his dark suit jacket and pulled out a pack of cigarettes. Another thing the doctor hated. Another thing he was having to get used to.

"So how is our wayward lamb doing? Or should I say wolf?" The man spoke in a cloud of exhaled smoke.

Doctor Kim shrugged, looking through the window at Jack as he slept fitfully. "He's progressing. A little slower than the others. But he seems on the same track, strength and aggression increasing at geometric rates. Eventually he'll be uncontrollable. The process was slower this time because of his illness, I think."

The suit looked thoughtful as he stared at Jack through his own reflection. "Well, maybe we need to move away from tests on soldiers and more toward men like Jack. Terminals. If nothing else, I'd think they'll be grateful for a new lease on life."

****

Dr. Kim's beeper sounded, waking him from the deep sleep that he'd instantly fallen into upon laying down in an empty room. Operating on instinct, he looked at his beeper, then his watch. He'd been asleep for almost an hour. Not bad. In the waiting area, he saw one of the security guards, his arm badly broken. The bone was piercing skin and blood spurting from the opening.

Though he moved quickly, Kim had the same outwardly relaxed attitude he always had, stopping the bleeding, giving the guard a sedative and prepping him for the surgery that Kim would do himself in moments. After getting the guard squared away, he turned to the head nurse while he was scrubbing. "What happened?"

Like him, the nurse had seen just about everything, but she looked a little rattled. "It was Compton. He went berserk. Tore right through his restraints, then did that to the guard on his way out. It was unreal."

****

Something silently called to Jack in an appeal that wouldn't be ignored, even from his hospital bed. The guard never saw what was coming. He just wished that the cop who "tased" him had been there too. He'd have ripped his throat out. Somehow, the image in his mind of doing that, of the screams of pain, the spray of hot, wet blood wasn't in the least disturbing to Jack. In fact, he relished in it.

He shivered as the night air cut through his hospital gown. He did not want to delay, but taking a momentary diversion to get some clothes seemed like a good idea. After savagely beating some street punk, he was back on his way, following a silent call. Quickly, the sidewalks ended and before he knew it he was deep in the Big Thicket. By the light of the moon, it seemed primordial, like a forest that had never been touched by man and never could be. It stirred something deep inside him.

Without warning, he came into a clearing and stood face to face with the last person he expected to see—his uncle, Tim Compton.

"Thanks for coming, Jack. We need to talk."

Definitely a dream. Jack's uncle was a distant relation in many ways. He never came to any of the family functions. The last time Jack had seen him was during the transplant procedure. His uncle had been the closest matching donor. Uncle Tim had not even visited him as his cancer went into remission, even though Jack had asked for him. Before that, it had probably been ten years since Jack had seen him.

"Uncle Tim? What's going on? How is this happening?"

Tim smiled, an expression that wasn't comforting at all on his face. "I called you. Not verbally though. What's happening to you, I can explain it because I'm the cause. You're turning into something Jack. Something like me. A werewolf."

Jack laughed. Whatever Dr. Kim had given him, it was definitely some good stuff. Maybe it was time do a little drug seeking after all.

Right before Jack's eyes, Uncle Tim disappeared and was replaced by something inhuman. It was horrible. Jack's heart pounded like a hammer against his chest. His mind screamed to run but, his body did just the opposite, leaping at the thing that had been his uncle with a savage snarl.

The thing seemed to laugh as it slammed Jack into the ground with a force that both stunned him and convinced him beyond all doubt, all reason, that this was no dream. Just as suddenly, his uncle was back in place of the thing, effortlessly pinning him to the ground.

"You're family. I have no regrets doing what I did. It saved your life. But you traded one disease for another, like a junkie trading heroin addiction for a methadone addiction. You were too far gone for medicine, but one of the benefits of our condition is immunity to things like cancer. But now you need to understand what's happening to you."

After seeing that he was listening, Tim released his nephew, moving off of him to kneel beside him on the ground.

Jack shook his head to clear it and moved to his knees opposite his uncle. His head spun. "Wait. You're saying…I'm going to turn into a thing like you? And this is the reason my cancer went away?"

Tim shook his head. "The disease is like a virus. It exists only to perpetuate itself, through us. It won't allow anything else to get in the way of that. Over time, the virus gains more control. Influences your behavior so you'll spread it to new hosts."

Jack suddenly felt his anger rising again. "And you knew this would happen?"

Tim held his hands out in front of him, palms facing Jack. The movement somehow eased the anger that had been building up inside Jack. "I wouldn't wish this on anyone. Letting the cancer get you would have been better. No, you won't end up like me. It's too late for me but I've learned something—something that can help you keep control…if it's done soon enough."

****

The two men sat in Tim's car, drinking the Brazen Hussy beer they'd bought at Speedy Pete's. With a flash of guilt, Jack remembered his escape from the clinic. "So, what about the guard? I broke his arm but—"

Tim tossed his empty into a dumpster and reached for another of the bottles with the bikini-clad model. "He's not infected. His blood would have to come in contact with your blood, saliva, or DNA. Also, if he was infected, you'd already know."

Jack digested that thought for a moment, "What is that anyway?"

Tim shrugged and took another long drink, "It's instinct. How do you know when you find a woman attractive? It's not a conscious thing. It just is. There are going to be things you know that others won't. You're not an animal and you're not a man. You're something else. Better in some ways."

"Will I... am I immortal now or something?"

Tim laughed, throwing another bottle into the dumpster, "No, you've been watching too many vampire movies. You're going to live a natural lifespan, except that you won't be affected by disease for most of your life. Except the virus. Every full moon it will go into overdrive, multiplying itself. Affecting your behavior more and more. Trust me, it's not like in the movies. Most of us turn into mindless killers 12 times a year. Like me."

Tim sat silently drinking for a moment before finishing the thought Jack knew was coming. "Which is something else we need to talk about. After I do this thing, to help *you*, I want you to end this for *me*."

Jack nodded. Like in the clinic, he'd just known.

****

Jack sat in his car on a hill in the dark, looking out over the Big Thicket. It had been almost a month since that pain and the life-changing realization that accompanied it. Something had been nagging at his gut every night since then, a louder and louder call to slip out of his bed into the night. This was the first night he'd let himself leave the house. He'd dreaded a call from his uncle at first but now he was desperate for him to get in touch. He was like an addict recovering cold turkey, pacing the floor of his cramped apartment, then clawing at his own arms, just trying to make it to sunrise again. Finally, he had compromised with himself and driven outside of town. As the largest full moon Jack could ever remember seeing rose up into the sky, he lost control. He was out of the car, running into the night.

Jack felt like he was chasing the moon. He had never run so fast. He wasn't aware anything could cover ground like this through such thick undergrowth. The sound of his heart pounding in his ears was a drumbeat urging him on. Finally he lost control entirely and howled at the moon. Within seconds another howl echoed through the forest, answering him. He turned without missing a beat, moving toward the howl, releasing another of his own, moving toward the answer.

Finally Jack emerged into a clearing. It formed a perfect, empty sphere in the center of the piney forest. The moon was directly overhead. In the center of the clearing, directly under the moon, stood some sort of altar. It seemed to catch the moonlight and hold it, releasing it in a soft glow of its own that cast an unearthly nimbus around the clearing.

Within moments, Jack's uncle emerged from deeper within the forest. He was gripped by the same transformation as the last time the pair met in the Thicket. The creature who was Tim looked up at the moon and howled. Within moments another cry echoed through the forest. Jack hadn't realized until that moment that there was a third wolf in the forest.

Tim shuddered and shook, like a dog trying to get dry. After a few moments he began to transform back into a man, more slowly than he had during their earlier meeting. He walked over to Jack, his clothes torn and ripped from his transformation and his run through the forest.

"All right, my contact is going to be here shortly with a package. This is the moment you decide how badly you want to be free. It's not going to be easy. Take this rifle. You do remember how to use one of these, right?"

Jack looked at the weapon and nodded. It was a typical hunting rifle, unusual only for the starlight scope. Tim continued, "Go back into the tree line and wait until my contact gets here. If things go the way I think they will, I want you ready to back me up. Put a silver bullet in him, but don't kill him."

Another howl filled the eerily quiet forest again, closer this time. Tim gave Jack a shove toward the tree line, "Go, go now!"

Jack had barely stepped into the darkness when another creature like his uncle burst through into the clearing. It snarled and snapped as Tim relaxed his grip on humanity and gave way once again to the primal raging inside him.

Jack couldn't really make out what they were saying. It sounded like speech under a layer of guttural snarls and growls. The discussion ended abruptly and the two creatures jumped on each other with tooth and claw. Jack brought the rifle up to his shoulder and watched through the sight. In the eerie moonlight he couldn't really tell his uncle from the other creature, so he just watched.

The battle was like nothing he had seen before. It was a raw, savage fight for survival. The battle raged back and forth as Jack watched through the starlight scope, waiting for a clear shot. As quickly as it had begun, it seemed the contest had been decided. One creature lay prone on his back, the other in a dominant position. Jack cursed under his breath and prepared to charge from cover when a voice he recognized as Tim cried out, "Now!"

Without thinking, Jack brought the rifle back to his shoulder as the thing on top looked right at him. Jack fired once. The gunshot and sick crack of a bullet striking soft flesh were so close together that they were one sound; a sound that stilled every other sound in the forest, it seemed.

By the time Jack reached the center of the clearing, Tim had reverted to human and lifted the dying creature on the altar. Jack's uncle bled from dozens of wounds, but his grip was firm as he pressed a knife into Jack's hand. Its blade caught the light the same way as the weird altar.

"I told you not to kill him! We don't have much time. He'll be dead in seconds. You have to finish him, with that, before that bullet does."

Jack barely hesitated before driving the knife into the twitching thing with all his strength. When the knife tip pushed through flesh to strike solid alter, Jack felt the ever-building background buzz of rage drain away from him like a lightening rod redirecting nature's wrath. The altar changed colors from pure white to red. Cautiously, he pulled the knife away and it too was red.

Tim staggered and almost fell, drawing Jack's attention away from the altar and what he had just done.

"We need to get you to a hospital."

Tim forced himself upright, then pushed the thing off the altar, "No. I told you I was going to save you from this. There's only one way. We've known of this place; known that if one of us kills another here, it slows the illness. It gives us a little humanity back. There were rumors of a knife, but nobody knew where it was until it showed up in Russia. Yuri had his own plans for tonight. It's the final piece of the puzzle. Kill two of our kind here, with that, and you can be free. Forever."

Jack just watched in disbelief as Tim lay down on the altar, "No way in hell."

"Trust me, it's better for both of us."

"No way!"

Moving with supernatural speed and strength, Tim grabbed Jack's wrist and forced the weird red blade over his own chest.

"Listen to me. This is big. Bigger than Area 51. Bigger than JFK. Bigger than any one government. Someone is trying to make perfect soldiers. What's going to happen when they get it right? Stop it. Stop us."

Jack struggled in vain as his uncle pulled his wrist inexorably downward and forced the knife through his own chest. The older man gasped in renewed pain, but finished the deed. Under him, the altar went black as obsidian. Blood rattled from his lips, spraying onto Jack's shirt. For a moment Jack thought it was finally over, then Tim's eyes opened again, "The Safe Health Foundation. They--."

And just like that, Jack knew he was finally gone. He had to stay with him for several more minutes as he pried his wrist free from the vice-like grip that held him, even in death. For the longest time he stood frozen, rifle in one hand, knife in the other, unable to look away. Finally he stumbled over something and spilled over backwards, breaking the spell the place had over him. He turned and ran for all he was worth back in the direction of his car.

****

## Ninth Girl Missing

PINEBOX, TX- Police continue to work around the clock with no results as the "Pinebox Strangler" case continues to go unsolved. Three girls have been found while five remain unaccounted for. Police Chief Jacob Miner reiterated his refusal to comment on an ongoing investigation. He also refused to speculate whether this latest missing girl is the ninth of the strangler's victims, noting that many ETU students have gone home until the current crisis is over.

****

Jack looked at the headline from the window of his idling car. He took his hand off the rifle laying across his lap long enough to give the bloodhound sitting next to him a reassuring pat.. His companion restlessly sampled the air from the passenger window and whined. Somehow, like him, it knew.

"Soon, girl. First the wolf, then Safe Health."

****

*Chuck Rice is an author and board game designer who has written for Vigilance Press, RPGObjects, Green Ronin, Mongoose, Empty Room Studios and Mystic Eye Games.*

# ~Guitar Zero~

*By Shane Lacy Hensley*

Freddie fingered the keys like his life depended on it. Fast and furious. The notes screamed down the screen. Had the plastic guitar in his hands been real, his fingers would be bleeding. But it wasn't—it was a souped-up, plastic *Guitar Hero* controller he'd opened up and "improved." Freddie was always improving things. Countless "warez" he'd pirated were, admittedly, better after he'd opened up their guts and rearranged their innards a bit.

But sometimes Freddie's "improvements" got him in trouble.

Tonight they would get him killed.

****

It was a cold Tuesday morning at East Texas University in Pinebox, Texas. The overnight lows in the 40s drove students to their jackets and sweaters. Cal Griffis was the first one in. He usually was. It wasn't that he was an early riser—he just didn't sleep much. Nights were spent delving dungeons in the latest massively multiplayer online game, or scoring headshots in the "kewlest" next-gen shooter on his game console. He'd stay up until one or two in the morning on his games, then get up and moving again by 7 a.m.

Cal was a video-game junkie, but that was an acceptable flaw in a computer science major.

This morning he juggled a large coffee on top of his textbook while trying to jiggle open the stubborn lock to the computer lab with his other. Cal's thick glasses started falling off as he did so, and the heavy bag on his shoulder that held his screamin' laptop started to slip as well.

Disaster struck. The laptop strap slid off the shoulders of his ill-fitting denim jacket, hitting the crook of his elbow with considerable force. The textbook in his hand up-ended and sent steaming hot mocha latte all over Cal and the lab door.

A moment later, Cal's glasses slid off his face and landed lenses-down in the mess.

Cal said something his mother wouldn't be proud of.

Near blind and covered from crotch to toe in sticky coffee (Cal liked it sweet, so it was extra syrupy), he entered the lab. He couldn't see, but he knew something was wrong. There was an acrid smell—even stronger than the latte—as if something electronic were overheating.

He could barely make out a black blob slumped at one of the desks.

"Freddie? That you? Wake up, man."

Cal crossed to the restroom and grabbed a handful of paper towels, then headed back toward the scene of his disaster. "Dude. You fell asleep here again." Cal stepped toward the coffee and heard a sickening crunch—his glasses.

Another expletive. "It's gonna be one of those days. That's the second pair this year."

A string of expletives followed as Cal cleaned, but Freddie didn't stir. He remained motionless five minutes later when Cal finally finished.

The college junior went back into the bathroom and rinsed off his glasses. He put them on his face and sighed heavily as he saw twin cracks up both lenses. He could just make out his thin face, stubbly chin, moppy black hair, and piercing blue eyes beyond them.

"Come on, Freddie. Get up. I've made enough noise here to wake the dead."

Cal exited the bathroom and turned on his desktop. It would take a few minutes to boot. He walked to Freddie's desk and tapped him on the shoulder. "Hey man. Wake up. You okay?"

Freddie wasn't okay. Cal shook him and gasped in horror as his cohort's chair rolled backward and Freddie fell awkwardly on the tile floor. There was a disturbing crunch as his skull bounced and Cal elicited his second to last expletive of the morning.

"Freddie!" Cal leaned over and grabbed his sometimes-friend to help him up—certain the fall would wake him—but recoiled quickly. Even through his shattered glasses he could tell Freddie was gone. His eye sockets were two charred holes and his lips were burned black with bright red bloodlines in the dark cracks.

Cal issued his last expletive of the day and called the campus police.

****

Cal sat numbly after calling campus security. As he stared at the horrific visage of his fellow student, he eventually noticed the hacked guitar still strapped to his corpse. It was a *Guitar Hero* controller. Cal couldn't imagine why Freddie would have been playing it here rather than at home on his massive television and surround sound system. Cal stood, looked around a bit nervously to see if the campus police were here yet, then stepped over to Freddie's desk. The monitor was burnt out and the guitar was plugged into one of the PC's USB ports. Another USB cable ran to Freddie's distinctive hard drive.

"Big Mac," was legendary. It was a custom job with a terabyte of storage and enough porn, warez, and pirated apps to get Freddie a lifetime of fines. Cal stared at it. Eve couldn't have wanted the apple more than he wanted to see what was on that drive. He looked around nervously one more time, grabbed Big Mac, and stuffed it into his own bag.

****

"You say you found him like this?" Jim Styles was ETU's newest member of campus security. He was sharp, efficient, and could stare a hole through a tank.

Cal nodded. 'Yeah, I…I spilled coffee coming in and didn't really notice him until I was done cleaning up. Then I broke my glasses and couldn't really see. When he didn't wake up to all my racket I checked on him and…"

"You didn't notice him sprawled out all over the floor?"

"No. I mean, he wasn't. He was slumped at his desk. He fell back when I tried to wake him."

"So you touched him?"

"Yeah, I just told you. To wake him up."

James took off his ETU security baseball hat and creased the brim. His steel-gray eyes never moved from Cal. "So you touched the body, and you did a little cleaning here."

"Yes. I mean…what?"

"Where are the paper towels you cleaned up with?"

"I flushed them."

James put his hat back on his jet-black hair. "Convenient."

"What?"

"Convenient. You've concocted an alibi for having touched the victim, and you obviously did a little cleaning. Both the floor and yourself. You sure you were cleaning coffee and not blood?"

"Are you insane? I told you what happened. For God's sake I called you!"

"Look, I may not be a computer science wiz like you genius college boys, but I know these controllers can't transmit an electric shock. This kid's obviously been fried, and that fifty-dollar chunk of plastic didn't do it."

Cal fell back into his chair and stared incredulously. He'd never dreamed of being a suspect.

"I've already called the Pinebox police. They'll be here in a minute. If you wanna go ahead and tell me what *really* happened here, I'll tell Butch to go easy on you."

Cal shook his head. A student was dead and this ladder-climber was looking for a collar.

"I'll wait and talk to my lawyer."

"Only the guilty need lawyers, Griffis."

****

Cal left the lab amid a sea of lights from police and photographers. It was lunchtime, and even though he wasn't really hungry, instincts took over and he headed toward Mom's Diner.

*What the hell were you doing, Freddie?* Cal asked himself. Styles might have been a self-serving creep, but he was right about the controller not being able to deliver that kind of shock. Besides barely carrying six volts, it never would have jumped the plastic casing into Freddie.

Ten minutes later Cal stared vacantly at a Reuben, fries, and Coke. He ate two fries before he realized the morning's events had stolen his appetite. Cal stared down at his laptop. *What was Freddie working on?*

Cal looked around. He was in the corner of the diner with his back to the wall. No one would see what he was doing. He dragged the heavy laptop out, booted up, and looked down with some unknown trepidation at Big Mac.

Cal was smart. He knew the hard drive was evidence. He didn't think he'd have any real trouble proving he didn't kill Freddie's—he was truly innocent and there was no evidence to the contrary—but stealing Big Mac would definitely look suspicious.

But he had to know what was going on. He glanced about nervously once again, then ducked down under the table to plug the drive's power supply into a nearby wall socket. On the way back up he banged his head—causing everyone in the place to turn and look at him. Cal smiled, adjusted his still-cracked glasses, and looked away unconvincingly.

Anxiety rose inside him like mercury in a thermometer. He felt like everyone was watching, but he knew they weren't. Not really. To most of the other patrons he was just another nerdy college kid with a laptop, instant messaging friends about parties. Cal took a bite of the Reuben and washed it down with a gulp of Coke so everyone would stop looking, but the ice stuck together at the back of the glass and broke loose all at once—slamming into Cal's mouth and splashing loudly out onto his shirt.

The other patrons looked his way again. A friendly waitress by the name of Norma Jean headed over with a rag. The spill wasn't too bad, but Cal felt butterflies well up in his stomach. "I got it!" he said to Norma Jean as she mopped up the spill on the table. Cal tilted the laptop lid down—even though there was nothing to see—and helped the waitress by using the napkins on the table to sop up the spill.

As he finished, Norma Jean stood up and cocked her head. "You okay, sug? You seem kinda antsy."

Cal nearly choked. He managed a "n'yme awright" and smiled.

Norma smiled back. Cal thought she looked just like a young Flo from the old *Alice* show. "I'll bring you another soda, hon. Don't worry 'bout the mess. It happens."

"I'm fine—still got half a glass—thanks..." He was terrified she'd see his stolen evidence, even though he knew there wasn't a chance in hell she'd even know what it was or where it came from.

"No, hon, I'll top you off. Just a minute."

Cal shook his head but she was already off with the glass. He waited nervously, not daring to open up the laptop until Norma Jean had come and gone again.

"There you are," she smiled. A new glass of fizzing soda sat before him—but Norma Jean didn't leave. "You're a regular. Calvin, right? I 'member from your debit card. Gotta take care of our regs."

She knew his name. This was getting worse every second. He could see her talking to ETU's newest supercop James Styles. *"Why yes, sir. Calvin Griffis sat right there in that booth with the dead boy's hard drive. A hard drive full of pirated software, I might add. Little sonovabitch spilled soda all over hisself he was so nervous."*

But Norma Jean just smiled and moved on to another customer.

****

He turned on Big Mac. The lights in the diner dimmed. The rest of the patrons glanced up at the ceiling. Cal blinked twice. *That shouldn't have happened.*

The drive's autorun booted, and of course, asked for a password.

Cal stared at the screen. He hadn't considered that. Freddie was years ahead of everyone else on campus—of course he would have protected his data. *Damn. I've stolen evidence in a MURDER investigation and I can't even open it.*

Cal put his head down on the table and closed his eyes. "Can this day really be happening?" he muttered.

"I know! Isn't it crazy?"

Cal jumped up in shock as Tricia Plumber slid in opposite him. She was an English lit major with a strong preference for skinny, brainy types. Cal was both, and the two had been dating for nearly a year now.

"You heard about Freddie, right?" Tricia stuffed a couple of Cal's fries into her mouth.

Cal nodded. She was as beautiful to him as ever. Even in his current state he managed to notice her long stringy blonde hair, horn-rimmed glasses, and perky nose with the little green jewel on the side.

"I was walking by the computer lab when I saw all the cops. Someone said he was murdered by one of the students!"

"He wasn't murdered!" Cal said all-too-quickly.

Tricia cocked her head.

"I mean, maybe he was, but whoever said that doesn't know what they're talking about."

"How do you know?"

"'Cause I was there, Trish! I walked into the freakin' lab this morning and found him."

Tricia frowned. A rarity for her. "I'm sorry, Cal. What happened to him?"

"I have no freaking idea. He was just slumped at his desk."

"I heard someone bashed his head in…that there was blood all around the door." Tricia frowned.

Cal sighed. "No, his head…got hurt…after I touched him. And the blood at the door was coffee."

"The killer spilled his coffee?"

"It was MY coffee!"

"So…"

Cal sighed. "I spilled my coffee, then I went into the lab, got some paper towels, and cleaned it up. Freddie was slumped over his desk and I tried to wake him, but he fell backward and cracked his skull."

"And that killed him?"

"No, he was already dead."

"How do you know?"

Cal paused and looked away. "Because his eyes were burned out…"

****

Tricia ordered a salad and Diet Coke from Norma Jean, who knew her name too. Everyone paid with debit or credit cards these days, Cal thought. Technology ruled their lives.

"So…he was electrocuted?"

Cal nodded. "Something like that. He was playing *Guitar Hero* at his station. I think he'd modded the game or something. You know how he was."

"Frabjous."

"Huh?"

"Frabjous. Freddie said it sometimes when he was being sarcastic for 'fabulous.' It's a nonsense word from *Jabberwocky.*"

Cal stuffed the last bite of his Reuben in his mouth and opened up his laptop lid. The window for Big Mac was still on the screen waiting for the password. Cal typed "FRABJOUS…"

The window opened onto the contents. It took a full 43 seconds to populate the half-terabyte of information stored inside.

"What's that?" Tricia looked around the laptop screen.

"Freddie's hard drive."

"Big Mac? Why…why do you have Big Mac?"

Cal ignored her as he scanned through the list of programs. "I…borrowed it."

Tricia stared at him, realizing the truth. "From the lab? From the crime scene?"

Cal said nothing.

"Oh, Cal. You're gonna get in trouble."

"Maybe. But I gotta know what Freddie was working on. Whatever he did killed him. You think the Pinebox police are gonna know what to do with Big Mac? They'll spend a year alone on the porn…"

Tricia stole another of his fries and frowned. "So what's on there?"

"Mostly…stolen games. The Adobe suite. A couple thousand PDFs from the library of the University of Zurich. Windows *10?* Damn. Er, we probably shouldn't look at that folder…"

"Is one of the games *Guitar Hero?*"

"Er….let's see. Yeah. Looks like he ported a console version to PC. It'll take me a while to figure out how he did it."

"My Spidey Sense is buzzing here, Cool Guy."

Cal looked around. "Yeah, mine too. Lemme look this over for a few hours. Come by tonight?"

"Yeah. I'll come by after my late class. See you tonight." Tricia stood and left, leaving Cal to pay. He packed up his laptop, unplugged Big Mac, and waved his treasonous debit card at Norma Jean.

****

Cal was obsessed. He entered his apartment, drew the shades, and locked the door with the chain. He set his laptop on his small dining table and hooked up Big Mac's USB cable. He powered up the PC, then flipped the switch on Big Mac. As before, the lights dimmed.

*Must be a coincidence,* Cal thought. *Pinebox must be having power issues.* In the back of his mind, he knew better.

Cal sat down and navigated back to the *Guitar Hero* folder, then double-clicked on an icon that read "*Guitar Zero.*" Freddie had a strange sense of humor.

A loud guitar screech screamed from the Alienware's capable speakers. Cal jumped back so hard he tipped his four-legged chair over and fell onto the floor.

The astonished student looked around nervously—though of course no one would pay attention to such a sound in a busy student apartment complex like this—and got back into his chair.

The screen read:

NO GUITAR=NO ROCKAGE!

(Please connect your controller.)

*Crap.* Calvin looked at his own wireless *Guitar Hero* controller. That wouldn't work. He had an old wired one, but it was an X-Box 360 connector. He'd have to do some work to make it work with USB.

*Maybe Freddie stored his notes on Big Mac,* Cal thought. He went back to the hard drive's root and did a search on "*guitar*.*" Strangely, he found just such a Windows NotePad .txt file in the Zurich library directory.

*Now why would you store there instead of in the GH folder, Freddie?* Cal asked himself. He opened the doc and was relieved as he realized he could follow Freddie's hack to make the console controller work with the PC.

An hour later, Cal hooked in.

Another loud guitar screech.

READY TO ROCK?

(Hit A to begin.)

Cal tapped the green fret key and was utterly disappointed. It looked like the normal *Guitar Hero.* He scrolled through the song list. Nothing special. Freddie hadn't even unlocked the bonus songs.

*Damn.*

Cal played through a quick set of *Iron Man* on Expert and saw nothing special there either.

*What did you do, Freddie?*

He flipped to the Bands screen. *Ah...* There was one band profile saved on Big Mac—a band called "Frabjous Day." Cal selected it.

Another guitar screech.

CONTINUE TOUR?

*(A to continue. B to go back.)*

Cal hit A again and waited while the screen said "Loading..."

Freddie's avatar looked just like him. Tall and thin, stringy hair, glasses, and a weak little mustache that never really filled out. Cal knew the first Guitar Hero didn't have customizable avatars, so Freddie had likely lifted and inserted the code from one of the sequels. That sounded easy, but Cal knew how tough it really was, and how amazing Freddie had actually been.

The set was like something he'd never seen before. The stage looked like it was in Hell. The set had a fire motif and was painted in reds, oranges, and yellows. A blazing sign at the back proclaimed this virtual club "The Purgatorium."

LET US ROCK…

That message had been spoken, not displayed on the screen. It was a booming voice, yet not jarring. Somehow loud and subtle at the same time. Almost…oiled. Cal noticed the lights had dimmed again as well.

DIFFICULTY?

Cal selected a new level Freddie had obviously added called "HELLACIOUS."

ARE YOU SURE? said the voice again.

He hit the A button. Yes.

ARE YOU SURE…CALVIN?

Calvin scooted back in his chair.

The computer had just said his name.

Calvin stood up and backed away.

****

Calvin Griffis sat on the second-hand couch in his dark apartment and stared at the glowing screen of his laptop. Sometimes applications scanned other files for a user name. It was easy enough to do. The author tag on a Word doc, a Windows Live ID, or any number of other files would have his name in them somewhere. The program was as often as not to grab the wrong piece of data, but if it got it right, it was impressive. Magic. It was programmer magic. Freddie liked to say that. He was the Criss Angel of computers sometimes, pulling off impossible tricks with clever manipulations and lucky guesses.

But this had *said* Cal's name, hadn't it? He couldn't be sure—the guitar shriek *had* obscured it a bit. It was attached to his laptop—maybe it recognized something in the registry. And as for the voice it could be an advanced speech synthesis program—maybe that's what Cal was really working on and *Guitar Hero* was just where he was going to show off his magic. Several video game companies were coming in a couple of weeks for a career day—maybe that's what Freddie was working on.

It all sounded so plausible.

But deep in his heart, Calvin knew he was rationalizing.

*All right. Let's play.*

Calvin stepped up and hit the A button. Yes.

The game started in the usual way. The camera flew around the crowd, the set, and then Freddie's avatar as the song warmed up and the fans cheered.

Only it wasn't Freddie's avatar anymore. It had changed. It was a tall, thin, male with moppy black hair and glasses. *Broken* glasses.

Calvin felt very cold. A shiver went up his spine. He felt panic coming on. He would have run but the song started and his fingers instinctively started to play. It wasn't a song he'd heard of, some heavy metal garbage called *Prelude of the Damned.* The rhythm had obviously been sampled from some other song Calvin had heard because he got into the groove fast—which was good because it wasn't a particularly easy song.

Three minutes and 37 seconds later he'd managed to hit 87% of the notes. Not bad, all things considered.

NEXT STAGE. ARE YOU READY TO ROCK?

Calvin timidly tapped A. There had been no voice this time.

The screen changed:

CHOOSE YOUR REWARD

A drop-down list appeared. Calvin tapped down through them slowly. They read:

WEALTH
FAME
HEALTH
HAPPINESS
BABES
PROGRAMMING GOD

Cal rationalized again. Freddie had programmed in a new reward system. The first five made sense for a rock game—the last one was more than a bit suspicious. Calvin selected it.

Another loud guitar screech—this one more exotic and fantastic than before.

ARE YOU SURE, CALVIN?

The voice again...

Calvin steeled himself. This was all Freddie magic. And Freddie wouldn't need it anymore. Maybe Calvin could lift the code for himself. Guessing the user's name was a fun party trick, but that smooth speech processing was worth millions.

Calvin tapped A...

****

The song was called *The Deal.* It was a composition of the damned. It started out low and wailing, but quickly built into a screaming frenzy of notes flying down the screen. Calvin hit as many as he could, banging the plastic strum bar to the beat while struggling to finger the trickier chords.

It was exciting. It was frightening. It was Hell.

Calvin played for ten minutes and the song had barely started. Thirty minutes more and his fingers started to cramp—but he knew he couldn't quit. He couldn't say why—he really couldn't even think about it—he just *knew* he had to get to the end. He had to finish *The Deal.*

Tiny tendrils of smoke rose from the laptop as Calvin played. The fan was working overtime and the heat warning was flashing on the taskbar.

****

Calvin's stomach rumbled. A long note in the song allowed him to glance at the clock. Half past seven. He'd been playing for four hours straight. His fingers had gone numb an hour ago.

*Ding dong.*

The doorbell. Trisha.

"Calvin? You home?"

Calvin couldn't answer. If he lost his concentration...well...he wasn't sure what would happen. Just like he wasn't sure what would happen if he quit. But he knew it would be bad.

"Calvin? I can hear you in there—are you playing *that* game?"

No answer.

"Freddie's game?" she prodded.

Still no answer. Trisha walked to the window and peered in. She could make out Calvin's back and the red glow from the laptop, but little else. "Calvin? Pause it and let me in!"

Pause...of course. Calvin waited for another long note then risked a stab at the Start button on the controller that usually paused the game. Nothing. The notes on the screen seemed to come even faster than before.

THERE IS NO PAUSE, CALVIN.

The voice. Calvin's blood ran cold. This was real.

HAVE YOU EVER HEARD THE SONG "THE DEVIL WENT DOWN TO GEORGIA, CALVIN?

Calvin nodded, dumbfounded.

IT WAS A TRUE STORY.

YOUR FRIEND FREDERICK THOUGHT HE COULD OUTPLAY ME AS WELL.

"This isn't happening," he mumbled.

"CALVIN!" Trisha screamed, pounding on the door. She twisted the handle—and it opened—but the chain was in place. "Let me in! Something's wrong, I know it!"

Calvin looked back at Trisha pleadingly. She screamed. His eyes were smoldering! "CALVIN!!!"

The game screeched. Calvin missed a half-dozen notes and the Applause Meter plummeted.

I WOULDN'T LET THE CROWD DOWN, CALVIN.

Cal re-focused. This was complete and utter madness, but he was in it now and quitting would be bad. Damn bad. He dug in, fingering the keys as if his life depended on it. No, my *soul,* he corrected himself.

Trisha was frantic. She kicked at the door, but the liberal arts didn't focus on physical education and it held firm. "Stop, Calvin! Turn if off! Your eyes…"

"Can't, Trish. Can't, baby. I hacked it…now I gotta pay the devil his due…"

Trisha kicked and screamed and cried but the damn door wouldn't budge.

****

"Will that be all, sir?"

The executive nodded and looked out the window of his private jet. Flyover country. There was nothing important down there between LA and New York. Just a lot of dust and fat ugly people who shopped at Wal-Mart.

And Pinebox. Damned Pinebox. Where Hell broke loose daily.

He picked up his cell phone and dialed his wife. "Hey, baby. How's rehab?"

"It sucks. I wanna come home."

"You will. Soon. I got that thing with Microsoft on Sunday, then I'll fly down and pick you up. We'll do Maui or something for a couple weeks. Get away from it all. 'K?"

His wife sniffed. "'K, baby. I wish I could be there to see the look on their faces when you smack them with the hostile takeover."

"Heh. Yeah. They know it's coming though." The executive looked at the stewardess as she started undoing her blouse. "Anyway, gotta run, baby. Got some business to attend to. See you Sunday."

Calvin Griffis, programming god, leaned back in his leather seat and smiled.

****

*Shane is a writer, designer, and video game developer in the sunny state of Arizona. He's best known for creating Deadlands: the Weird West and a host of other game systems and worlds. The powers that be blessed him with a wonderful wife, Michelle, and two incredible boys, Caden and Ronan.*

# Mother

*by Trey Gorden*

As usual, Art set himself apart from the crowd by hurting himself. When his shift ended at Durgeson Concrete and Gravel, he walked out of the north building with everyone else. Most people managed to get in their cars without incident, and a few crossed the tracks on foot, glanced both ways at Old Railroad Street, and then hustled across to a small, abandoned lot—also without making idiots of themselves. Art, as usual, was in this second group. Today, as folks waved their goodbyes and high-stepped through the unmown grass to their own houses, Art tripped on a crawdad mound and landed on a pile of bricks hidden by a serrated tangle of blackberry vines. The sight of the chunky guy in the red hunting vest wallowing around in the brambles brought snorts and cackles from the others. Two of them came over to help him out, but they weren't gracious about it.

"Damn, Crane," was all Mark Bicknell had said as he and Ed Lowrey walked away.

Art kept turning the moment over in his mind as he trudged west along the road to the Indian Summer Trailer Park. When he got to number 12, he took his mail from the mailbox, climbed the stairs, and opened the door with a lone key on a long leather lanyard. He flipped through his envelopes as he smacked the light on and kicked the door closed. Nothing indicated that he'd won anything. He remembered Mother's favorite old proverb, "Sweety, if you want something bad enough, you'll make it happen." Well, he sure wanted to win something, but it wasn't happening. He tossed the hunting vest onto the couch with his keys, dropped the mail onto the pile that concealed the trashcan, and headed straight to the bathroom, closing the door behind him.

Somewhere outside, a woman shouted something unintelligible as a door slammed and a truck started up with a roar. Art's phone rang.

"Ah, crap!" A shuffling, jingling sound came from behind the bathroom door.

The phone rang. "Gaht," and then a strangled, "damnit!"

Again, the phone rang. More scuffling. The ice maker in the freezer made a "ker-chunk" and dumped a load.

The bathroom door burst open as the phone rang again. Dragging his pants from one pasty ankle—his beige briefs, wadded at the waistband, crookedly in place—Art lurched for the phone, barked his shin on the coffee table, stumbled, and, with an airy grunt, bounced off the couch, banged his cheek on the end table, and hit the floor to a ringing cheer from the phone.

Obligingly, the answering machine took the call.

"Hi. This is Art Crane," he was saying.

He didn't move—just lay there.

"I'm unable to take your call right now, but if you'll leave your name, number, and a brief message, I'll be sure to get back with you."

His shin was starting to throb. He decided not to check to see if his cheek was swelling up. Yep. It was swelling up.

"Art, you slacker! Pick up the phone!"

Lenny.

"This is Lenny. I bet you ain't home yet." His voice dropped to a moan, "Or maybe you got a little bit o' company. Is that it? You got a lady over there?"

Lenny.

"Tell you what, if you want to come over and watch T.V., I got beer." Lenny hung up the phone.

Art lay on the floor, relieved to be alone. If Lenny had seen what just happened, Art would have had to watch him laugh with peanuts in his mouth.

Rachel wasn't going to call. He was sure of that—been sure of it for a long time, but somehow, whenever he heard the phone ring . . .

He sat up and cradled his forehead in his left hand. With his right, he felt his cheek. It felt like a baby rat: a soft, hairless, throbbing baby rat. He could see the bruise starting red on his shin, glazed with a little blood slick and bracketed with thin, rolled-up bits of white skin.

"I'm cursed," he grumbled.

****

For a moment, the sound of gravel crunching under tires drowned out the pulsing of crickets and frogs. A two-tone brown Buick Regal glided to a stop beside an oil-topped road just outside of town, its engine already still, its headlights already dark.

A big, hairless man with shoulders like a viola and a gut like a washtub emerged from the driver's side and plodded around the hood of the car to the passenger door. If any of the people back in Pinebox had seen him, they would have commented to their friends that he looked "shady," though they certainly would have waited until he was out of earshot.

But if the man who opened the passenger door looked shady, he was a ray of sunshine beside the fellow who got out of the car next. He was no closer to five feet than his friend was to pretty, and he walked with a stiff-legged shuffle across the small gravel area toward an opening in the dark line of the woods. He wore a baseball cap on his bulbous head and filthy clothes that were several sizes too big. He carried what looked like a shiny metal cane.

Without a word, the big man followed him to a couple of muddy wheel ruts and together they walked along in silence between dark walls of trees until they came to a house in a clearing. The house looked not only deserted, but surprised and confused, as if its master had just driven away leaving it chained in the yard with nothing but a bowl of kibble and some scraps of scattered junk. The two silent figures ambled into the yard and headed up onto the porch. The house didn't shrink away in fear or run to the end of its chain, barking in desperate bluster. Of course, that should have been the first clue that these two fellas weren't from around here. As any East Texan knows, it's the ones that don't bark that you have to watch out for. They're the ones most likely to bite. Was there a faint growl deep in its throat? The short one in the baseball cap paused for a moment, as if listening. Then, with a hiccup of fire and a spray of glass and splintered boards, the house, its two guests, and most of the junk in the yard leapt into the surrounding woods in handy, party-size bites.

****

Art dropped into the surly embrace of his brown couch, propped his feet up on the coffee table, and hit the remote.

Boong. The T.V. screen shimmered for a moment, and then showed Art a picture of Mother's car. ". . . was known to have been hurt in last night's blast. A two-tone brown, 1983 Buick Regal with expired plates, license number U81-OIC, was found abandoned near the scene, off the Pinebox Cutoff Road. The Golan County Sheriff's Department is asking anyone with knowledge of who or what might have caused the explosion to call their hotline at 1-800-555-4357, that's 1-800-555-HELP."

"Shocking. Thank you, Will. And now, on East Texas News at Nine, we take you to . . ."

Art stared at the television, hardly registering the knock at the door. It had been Mother's car. There was no mistaking the license number; he and his sister had made too many jokes about it. Jokes about it before Mother disappeared. They had been ten years old. He had to find her. Find who? Which her?

Another knock. "Open the door, Art. You gonna leave me out here all night? The beer's getting warm."

Art opened the door. Lenny pushed his way in and rushed straight for the fridge clutching a plastic grocery bag with the unmistakable profile of a six-pack of cans.

"Lenny, don't stick those in the freezer. They'll just blow up."

"They gotta stay cold. We'll drink 'em before they pop."

Lenny shut the freezer door and smiled at Art, showing off his discolored front tooth. Then his smile plunged into a slack-jawed O. "Aw, man. What happened to your face?"

"Why don't you call first or something?"

"Aw, hell, I knew you was home. I was on my way back from work and thought I'd drop by."

"And everyone in Travis Nursing Home knows, these are two Pinebox sisters with plenty of funk … in their spunk. I'm Amanda Payton—East Texas News."

Art turned off the television. In the silence, Lenny took two cans of Brazen Hussy out of the freezer and handed one to Art, who opened it automatically and took a long pull.

"You got gas in your truck, Lenny? We need to take a drive."

****

The Pinebox Cutoff Road wound through the dense woods of the Big Thicket: a black-tarred tunnel through overhanging branches and steep banks as high as the windows of Lenny's lop-sided truck. The headlights lit the leaves from the bottom and threw exposed roots and clumps of rust-colored pine straw into sharp relief. Art wasn't sure what they were looking for. He had told Lenny about the news story and about Mother's car. That was all.

"The police'll have towed that old Buick off by now," Lenny had assured him.

Art didn't say anything. His heart was pounding in his chest and his head was like a bar fight, with thoughts of "Turn around and go home" scuffling with thoughts of "All over. Frickin' Rachel! This could be all over." Lenny sat silent behind the wheel, munching on peanuts.

Suddenly, on the left, a yellow stripe in the trees. "Lenny, pull …!"

"I see it. Hang on." Lenny slowed the truck down. In the headlights they saw a gravel pull-out and a narrow opening in the woods, cordoned off with yellow tape. POLICE LINE DO NOT CROSS.

Lenny pulled onto the patch of gravel and shut off the engine, then sat looking out the windshield, saying nothing. After listening to the bar fight for a few moments more, Art opened the door and slid slowly from the truck with a crunch of gravel.

The old Buick, as Lenny had predicted, was gone. Art walked around the hood of the truck, into the headlights, and cast a giant shadow on the line of yellow tape. The tape cordoned off a little dirt side road that led into the trees. Art craned his neck and tried to see what was down there, but his shadow plunged everything into darkness.

He heard Lenny rolling down the window. "Maybe you'd better come back tomorrow, when you can see. Aw, man! Do not go in there! Damnit, Art!"

Art had ducked under the tape and taken a few steps down the road. As he moved away from the truck his boxy shadow shrank a bit, but still blocked out most of what was ahead of him. "Len, why don't you turn off your headlights for a second?" Darkness.

"Art?"

As his eyes adjusted, Art thought he could see a grey spot up ahead where it might not be so dark. Hard to tell. He heard Lenny get out of the truck. "Art, that's a police line. You're not supposed to cross that."

Art took a few more steps down the road. His eyes were adjusting slowly, but it wasn't making much difference. Lenny was beside him now, still holding his tubular, cellophane package of peanuts. "Why didn't we bring flashlights?"

They picked their way along the muddy wheel ruts until the darkness swallowed up the truck behind them. They had just started to make out a clearing up ahead where there was a little moonlight, and to notice the smell of wet ash, when they heard a rustling back in the trees to the right. Art froze, his hair prickling on his scalp. As he turned toward the sound, something large smashed into him from behind, knocking him into the dark ooze in the deep ruts. He heard himself scream a high, girlish sound, as he clutched and kicked at the darkness. Something passed over him: tall, lanky, flailing arms and legs in a desperate panic.

Lenny.

Art sat up and spun around in the muddy rut to face the source of the rustling. He strained his eyes and ears, trying to get some idea of the threat.

He heard Lenny's hoarse whisper from the clearing. "You all right?" Art didn't answer; he just peered into the darkness, trying not to breathe. "Sorry 'bout that, buddy. Did you hear that?"

Trying to stand up, Art pushed his hands into the mud. He felt something hard and smooth under his fingers and grasped it as he stood. It felt like a bar of light metal, good for a club, maybe. Taking it with him, he scrambled toward Lenny's dim outline in the grey gloom of the clearing, glancing over his shoulder in the direction of the noise.

Lenny's peanut package crackled in the silence as he tipped a few more nuts into his open mouth. "Probably just an armadillo," His whisper was casual, but he looked ready to bolt again. Big help. The two of them stood in silence, staring into the black wall of darkness that was the tree line. After a while, Lenny whispered again. "This wasn't your mama's house, was it?"

"Mother's been dead for twenty-one years." Art stepped backward, away from the trees, and felt something wrap around his foot. He tried to pull away, lost his balance, pivoted sideways, and fell onto a pile of something hard and sharp that clattered and shifted beneath him.

Lenny laughed. Even without looking at him, Art could tell he had a mouthful of peanuts. The knot on Art's cheek throbbed.

Art pulled his leg out of the twisted mass of wire, picked himself up off the pile of broken boards, and looked around. In the darkness they could just make out a broad, shallow heap of charred remnants that filled the clearing and reeked of wet ash.

"What are we doing out here, Art?"

Art looked at Lenny's shadowy outline in the darkness. He didn't like Lenny very much. He talked constantly, and Art couldn't remember Lenny ever saying anything interesting. He'd always hung out with Lenny because Lenny hung out with him. Yet he'd brought this poor guy out to a dark, stinky hole in the woods on what was probably a dangerous and pointless trip. Shame and self-pity tried to get his attention, but fear wouldn't shut up and let them talk. Lenny was the best friend he had.

"I'm looking for my Mother … Mother's grave." Art stammered, "My sister wants me to do it."

"I didn't know you had a sister. What's her name?"

"Rachel."

Lenny sat down on a section of broken brick chimney and took another mouthful of peanuts. "You don't know where your mama's buried?"

"I guess I never got around to looking."

"I've known you for a long time, man. You've never mentioned this before."

"Well … My sister and I don't get along. I haven't seen her in a long time."

"On account of you ain't found your mama's grave?"

"Yeah." Art could hear Lenny chewing peanuts with his mouth open. "We lost Mother when we were ten, and . . ."

From the same spot as before, Art heard a rustling, like something sliding through the leaves. It lasted for about a second, and then it stopped. Lenny rose slowly from the shattered chimney while Art hoisted his metal bar, blood pumping in his ears. There it was again, moving through the woods with painful sluggishness toward the road they'd come up. Art realized he was standing on another pile of boards and something that might have been sheetrock. His right leg was starting to shake.

Something made a squishing sound as it stepped into the mud on the road. Too dark to see. The shaking in his leg threatened to throw him off balance. He sprang forward, raising the metal bar over his head. The sheetrock under his feet slid back and pitched him forward. He felt his right armpit connect with something that ripped his skin and wrenched him around to land with his left shoulder and thigh on the pile of rubble underneath.

"Art!" But Lenny didn't move. Art could see him silhouetted, faint against the cloudy sky, craning his neck to peer down the road. After a short silence, Lenny bent his knees and squatted over to where Art lay clutching his armpit. "You all right, buddy?"

"Yeah, I think so."

"Come on. We gotta get out of here."

"What was that thing, Len? Is it still there? Where did it go?"

"I don't know. I think you scared it off with your little ballet dance."

The walk back to the truck was slow going, Art still clutching his metal bar. Lenny had picked up a board and was carrying it like it was Excalibur. They picked their way back to the truck, straining their senses for the slightest sign of movement.

Art's armpit hurt worse than all his other injuries combined, and when they got back to the truck and turned on the dome light, they discovered it was still bleeding. Art balled his shirt up under his arm to staunch the blood, exposing his pale, doughy chest. But the real show stopper was the metal bar.

"What is that thing, man?" Lenny asked.

"How should I know?" It was a long silver tube, bent over at one end like a candy cane. The other end had what looked like a smooth lens. "Let's take it back to my place and check it out."

Lenny started up the truck, flipped on the headlights, and screamed. A tiny, naked, grayish-white figure, its body covered in angry red welts, stood in the headlights. In its hands it clutched a large, hairless, disembodied arm.

Lenny continued to scream as he yanked the gearshift and stomped on the gas. Gravel and dust flew forward, obscuring the small figure, as the truck lurched backward, bounced across the road, and crunched into a tree. Lenny, still screaming, jammed the shifter into drive and roared back down the road toward town.

"Ohhhh, God!" Lenny sobbed. "Please, Lord, please deliver us from all unholy demons and other creatures of darkness. Amen. Ohhhh, God!"

"What was wrong with its head?" asked Art.

"I think part of it was missing. Ohhhhh!"

Art's heart was pounding again. When he closed his eyes, all he could see was the tiny, scarred figure holding … "Whose arm … Lenny! Pull yourself together. Breathe." Lenny stopped moaning and started a rhythmic, open-mouthed panting. Art continued. "Was that an arm? It was holding?"

Lenny didn't answer. As they neared the city limits of Pinebox, he closed his mouth and drove the rest of the way to Art's trailer with a fixed, distant stare. As soon as they walked in, Lenny went straight to the freezer, opened it, and screamed again. The cans had frozen and burst open, spraying beer all over the inside of the freezer.

****

The metal rod lay on the coffee table among the old beer cans and dirty plates. Art, bloody shirt replaced with a washcloth and duct tape, had been thinking hard ever since Lenny had stopped screaming in the truck. He had to come clean. "Sorry, Len. I shouldn't have mixed you up in this... crazy... it's a curse."

"Aw, it's all right. I'm starting to think that little fella was just a possum. I reckon one of them could hold their tail like that. And us all tired, we could have thought that was an arm."

"No. I mean it. It's a curse. I'm cursed."

"Aw! Now don't start getting..."

"Lenny, Rachel put a curse on me, when we were sixteen—that I had to find Mother's grave or live with the curse. That's why stuff always goes wrong for me... why I'm always hurting myself."

"A curse." Lenny didn't sound convinced.

"Rachel and I are twins. When we were ten, Mother died... you know... just... didn't come home. We didn't know what to do. We just, you know, found ways to live. We kept going to school and doing the same stuff we always did, and when we needed a grownup we just, well, we just found a way. Eventually we stopped all that stuff, school and stuff, and things got hard, but we were always able to... Mother used to say, 'If you want something bad enough, you'll make it happen.' Well, we were able to make things happen."

"Make things happen?"

"Rachel was always better at that stuff than I was. She got to where she could do things on purpose. It was just sort of—well—kind of like luck."

Lenny's face had taken on the look of someone who was watching someone else pluck a nose hair. "You trying to tell me, magic?"

"No! No. It's nothing like that. Magic is all, you know." Art moved his hands back and forth and wiggled his fingers. "This is more," he dropped his hands in his lap, "you know."

Lenny didn't look like he knew.

"Rachel always thought it was important that we find Mother's grave; you know, so we could pay our last respects. We never even got a chance to say goodbye. I could see her point, but I also didn't see how ... well, you know, what if she's ... what if we find her and she's not really ... how would we live with that?"

"Aw, shit, Art."

"So, on our sixteenth birthday, Rachel and I are camping in this old house outside of town. She had started the same old conversation again about finding Mother's grave, and I wasn't interested. She was getting pretty mad. And so she whaps me on the foot, and the hand, and all manner of spots and curses me. Something like, 'By this foot,' and 'by this hand,' and 'by this . . .' whatever, 'will you be betrayed until you see Mother's grave,' or some such crap. So. I'm cursed."

The phone rang.

"It's almost four in the morning," said Lenny.

Art, for once in fifteen years, didn't jump up to try to get it. As the phone rang over and over, he sat and looked at it.

The answering machine clicked on. "Arthur," the whisper was unmistakable, "Arthur."

Rachel.

"What did you do!" She rasped this last out with painful force. "Don't move until I get there."

Lenny stared at Art, eyes wide. "What are we gonna do?"

"Let's go find Mother's car."

****

The auto impound for the Golan County Sheriff's Department was behind a high, barbed-wire-topped cyclone fence at the end of an alley.

Art and Lenny stood at the end of the alley, staring at the cyclone fence. Art clutched the metal bar. Mother's car faced them, with the passenger door open and the dome light on. Someone was crouched down in the front seat, rummaging around.

Art yanked on the padlock that held the gate shut, his eyes darting around the alley and across the fence, looking for some way in.

"Art, quit it! What if it's a cop searching the car?" Lenny jerked Art's arm, pulling him off balance. Art's left sneaker caught on his right and he stumbled sideways onto the ground, whacking the metal bar on the side of a dumpster with a ringing clang. His armpit lit up with pain as the makeshift bandage pulled away from the wound.

Art and Lenny froze and looked back at the old Buick. Art saw a head rise momentarily to peer out the windshield, then disappear again. After a moment, the passenger door closed with a thump. The dome light went dark and Art could see a small figure in shabby, outsized clothes standing on the asphalt beside the car. Even in the darkness, Art could see that this was the same small, pale figure they had seen in the headlights of Lenny's truck. Perched on top of its spindly neck was a bulbous head. Maybe it was the darkness, but the left side of its head seemed less ruined than he remembered from earlier in the evening. Its large, avocado-shaped right eye, peering into the darkness toward Art and Lenny, caught the faint light from the night sky and reflected it back like a glistening black slug. Its hands still clutched the same large, hairless, disembodied arm.

With a click and a creak, the door leading into the sheriff's office opened and two people stepped out as overhead floodlights burst the darkness. The first was a stocky man in a grey cowboy hat. The shirt of his uniform was rumpled over his ample belly, and he walked with a jingling swagger. The other glided along behind him, a tall, regal woman in a flowing dress and large jewelry.

"Oh, sh—!" Art seemed to shrink into the soiled pavement.

"What's the matter? Who's that?"

"Rachel!"

Rachel screamed. The sheriff stepped back, bumping into her and nearly knocking her down. "Freeze!" he yelled as he fumbled with his sidearm, finally jerking it free of its holster and pointing it at the intruder on the far side of the car.

An elderly woman in a baseball cap and filthy clothes stood where the small figure had been, a large, hairless arm clutched in her hand.

"Hello, Rachel," the old woman said, walking around the trunk of the car. "I've been looking for you." She was missing an eye and part of the left side of her head. As Lenny studied her features from the shadows, he realized that what he had taken for wrinkles was actually a webwork of faint scars crisscrossing her face. "And I see you've brought your brother." She gestured with the arm toward the cyclone fence.

The sheriff glanced over at Art and Lenny before returning his gaze to the woman with the arm.

"Arthur, give me the imprisoning rod!" The old woman's voice indicated that she expected him to obey.

"Ma'am, do you know this lady?" To his credit, the Sheriff's weapon arm did not move.

"No, Sheriff Anderson," Rachel replied without taking her eyes off Art. Her voice was husky with her obvious lie, and she had lost some of her regal bearing. "I have no idea who she is."

With a casual flick of her wrist, the old woman cast the large, hairless arm across the intervening fifteen feet or so and caught the Sheriff in the middle of the face.

He went down without firing a shot as she leapt across the top of the Buick and sprinted for the fence.

"Arthur," Rachel screamed. "Stop her!"

Not knowing what else to do, Art sprang to his feet and pointed what he hoped was the business end of the metal rod at the old woman. She stopped suddenly, her face impassive. "Hello, Arthur."

"Mother." Art gave a curt nod.

Lenny looked from Art to Rachel to their mother. He noticed that the scars on the old woman's face were fainter than a moment ago—and was her left eye starting to open?

"So, Mother." Art's tone was casual, "A little late getting back from the store? That Pinebox traffic's a bear." His hand, knuckles white as it clutched the metal bar, was starting to shake.

"Arthur," her voice was gentle. Sadness filled her eyes. "Oh, sweetie. This has been so hard for you. I tried to find her. I tried to stop her. I know how she's hurt you."

"Use the rod, Arthur. End it. If you only knew what she's capable of." Rachel's voice was steady and even, but her face was frozen in fear.

Mother's face softened to a kindly smile. "We used to have such fun, didn't we? How did Rachel learn to be so cruel and you so gentle. You were always my sweet boy. Please put that thing down. Someone could lose an eye." Lenny might have laughed at the joke if not for the fact that, with that, Mother's left eye popped open.

"What are we, Mother?"

Rachel sighed, "Oh, Arthur."

Mother's warm face turned serious. "You two are like the poor fellow your sister murdered with her booby trap," she cocked her head back in the direction of the arm, "but so much more. The clinical term is *servitors*, but that's too demeaning for someone like you, sweetie. You're elite, made to rule worlds in my absence. I always thought your sister would be the strong one, but now I know. I thought you two would be co-regents, but she's not fit to share power with you. She lives or dies at your pleasure. Others, like this one," she glanced at Lenny, "will be your slaves. All you have to do is give me back my imprisoning rod."

Art closed his eyes and the metal bar gave a brief, faint hum. Mother popped like a soap bubble, leaving no trace behind.

Rachel sank to the ground, her mouth open in a long, silent sob. Art stood staring at the place where Mother had been.

"Holy shit," Lenny said, "How . . ."

"If you want something bad enough, you'll make it happen," and then, lowering the metal bar, Art opened the gate with the key he knew would be there and walked over to his sister. "Here." He held the bar out to her.

She looked up at him, reached out, and touched the bar. It dissolved into an oily sludge on the pavement.

"Rachel, why?"

"Arthur, I'm sorry. I knew you didn't have the power to hide yourself, so I had to leave you too weak to be useful. When she and her servitor found me, I laid a trap. When she survived it, I thought she must have gotten to you."

"So, the curse is lifted?" Art asked.

Rachel smiled. "You're free."

Art turned to Lenny. "Come on, buddy. I'll make us some breakfast."

As the two walked away down the alley, Rachel smiled and reached down for the cane-shaped metal bar that was already reforming on the pavement. This was going to be easier than she'd thought.

****

*A native of East Texas, Trey Gorden spent his youth tramping around in the Piney Woods pretending to be, depending on his mood, either Legolas or Nyarlathotep. After living among the misty mountains and damp cafés off the country's upper-left-hand corner for several years, he recently returned to East Texas and is now a graduate student in English at Stephen F. Austin State University in Nacogdoches. He has decided that, if he can't be Legolas or Nyarlathotep, he'll settle for being a college professor.*

# Lovable Creatures

*by Jason L Blair*

The dog mess stuck to her heel something fierce. She'd tried just about everything to get it off—drug her foot across the thick part of the front lawn, shoved it into the sand in Darla's playbox, scraped it against the cement steps leading to her trailer—but it was purt near supernatural in its adhesiveness.

"Figures this'd happen tonight," Luellen swore, prying off her most expensive pair of shoes. She rubbed her feet, feeling no relief from doing so, then set the red suede heels on the coarse welcome mat.

She grabbed a much less glamorous pair from the wire rack, hoping they'd be just as impressive in her date's eyes. Luellen needed this date to go well. It'd been six months since her last, fourteen months since she and Antonio broke up, and about five weeks since the last time she picked up a man for some recreationalizing.

"Bobby, honey!" she called toward the back. Her declaration was met by a garbled moan.

"Bobby!" she called again.

Nothing.

"Robert Anthony Wallis, you get your boo-tay out here right now!" Luellen screamed, checking her face in the reflection of the window.

Her son ambled from the back, half-leaning against the wall along the way.

"Wuh, mama?"

"Honey, I gotta go. I love you, okay? I may be back late. And when I do, I may have a suitor, if everything goes well."

"A suitor?" the thick-necked boy rubbed a wide palm across his face.

"I'll tell you when you're older, Bobby."

"I'm 15," he mumbled. "I know what the damn word means."

"Robert Anthony!" Lou Ellen scolded. "You watch your tongue. Now go on back there and get some sleep. You have school tomorrow."

"I know. I was," the boy turned on his heel and wobbled back to his room.

"Make sure your sister makes the bus this time!" she yelled after him. Her command was answered by a door slam.

****

Henry flipped the coins in his palm like he was a magician performing his act on a Vegas stage and not just some two-bit runner sitting outside a low rent department store in the underknuckle of Texas. He'd seen a lot of a crap places in his time, a lot of which was spent laying down rubber along the Mighty Miss, but this so-called "Pinebox" just reeked of ugly.

His contact said to be there at 10 p.m. sharp and he'd beat the time by fifteen minutes. It was now half-past and no one had showed. Henry was giving it ten more minutes then he was out of there. He'd had just about enough of Tay-Hoss period and this half-horse town wedged inside the armpit of the Devil was just—

Henry swung his head around toward the row of trash cans that lined the western wall. A cat screeched from behind one, then ran toward the loading alley.

"Damn cats," he spat between his teeth. He kept a tire iron in his trunk dedicated to the purpose of changing tires. The one he kept under the passenger seat was for sport. He gave a few practice swings, one of which knocked a stone clear across the parking lot.

"Here, kitty kitty," he called, tapping the iron against his upper leg as he wound his way toward the darkened wall . Henry'd hated cats as long as he could remember. Something about the way they lorded over folks, like their thumbs didn't mean diddly, really scruffed his neck hair.

"Things'll stab you in the neck soon as look at ya," his pappy once told him, "then ask what's for breakfast."

From between two of the trash cans, Henry spotted his quarry. Scrawny thing, a stupid shade of orange, with as much skin showing as hair.

"Hey there, Heathcliff," his voice a friendly hush. "Hey, little fel—"

Henry crashed into the garbage cans, belly first, swearing the whole way down. Anyone who glanced at the short, pudgy man knew he was no dancer, but that tumble was not of his own volition.

"Son of a—" he swung around, iron raised, primed for a fight. There was nothing behind him.

The cat preened itself, unfazed. It stopped licking its paw for a moment to address Henry.

"Mrrow?" it said, cocking its head.

Henry looked around some more. Nothing but moonlight and asphalt.

The cat lowered its gaze. Its mewling turned into a growl.

"Oh, you little rat," Henry looked down at the cat. "Think it's funny, huh?"

"Yes," the cat replied, pouncing onto the man's face.

****

The overnight shift at Speedy Pete's was never what one would call an "exciting time." That was the primary reason that Alby Jensen refused to call it the "graveyard shift."

"Cuz the graveyard's twice as exciting as this place," he told his coworker, Angie Barnett, while sipping a blue raspberry Shaker.

"Yeah, but I sure ain't working there," she shot back, flipping through the pages of the latest celebrity tell-all. "Don't want nothing to do with bodies. Hard enough time putting up with these folks when they're alive."

"Heh."

"Hey now, who's that?" Angie tossed her magazine to the side and eyed the cherry red Mustang rolling up to the pumps. A man in a leather jacket got out and started pumping gas.

Alby saw it in Angie's eyes. He wondered if she'd ever—

"Where's the damn police station?" a short, red-faced man yelled, before the door even closed behind him.

"Pardon me?" Alby turned to face him.

The man was breathing heavy. Blood and pus oozed from around his tan shirt collar.

"The police station! Where is it?"

"Oh, well..." Alby started.

"Oh my God, he's coming in!" Angie jumped as she squealed, overturning a two-pack special and a display of grenade-shaped lighters. She tugged at Alby's shirt. "How do I look?"

"Where's the police station?" Alby pondered, slowly. "Angie, where's the—"

"Hello sir," she called to the Mustang's owner as soon as he opened the door.

Alby rolled his eyes at the man's leather pants and open, Renaissance Faire shirt. He turned his attention back to his customer.

"Okay, you're gonna wanna go left out there, on 96, then keep going 'til you see the car lot. Turn left there. Can't miss it."

The sweaty man limped away eagerly, rushing out the door the best he could.

"Pack of Tarnations," the so-called sexy Mustang man nodded toward Angie as he sauntered up to the counter.

"Right away," she said coyly. Alby noted the extra long glance she held before turning.

"Tarnations, huh?" Alby said. "Kind of a..."

Alby made a swooshy motion with his hand.

"Kind of a what?" the man said gruffly.

"Just, y'know, my grandmother smokes those."

"Yeah?"

"Yeah," Alby said coolly. "Well, at least she did until the throat cancer got her."

The man glared at all five-foot-five of Alby's wiry frame and grunted.

"Make 'em Lights, sweetheart," said the man. A pause and then, "Sorry to hear about your grandmother."

Alby bounced his head a little, picking up Angie's discarded magazine.

"Yeah, thanks," he replied.

"Here you go," Angie handed the cool customer a red and green hard pack.

"How much?" The man winked. "Sweetheart."

"Oh," Angie punched some buttons on the register. "That'll be—"

"Woah," Alby shot up. "Is that bloody guy taking your car?"

****

"Why, yes, I do," Lou Ellen mouthed, watching herself in the rearview mirror. This was her attempt at appearing dainty.

"Yes, I," she watched the motion of her lips and the shapes they made. "Doooooooo. Why, yes, I doooo."

She picked at something in her teeth, removing both hands from the wheel. She caught it again just in time to swing the car away from the guard rail.

"Doooo," she accentuated the syllable, loosening her mouth. "Doooooooooo–"

Something small and furry jumped across the road ahead of her, cutting right through Lou Ellen's view.

"Holy heat!" She squealed, turning to see behind her.

Lou Ellen put her weight on the brake, biting her lip so as not to swear. The rusty brown fastback's bumperless nose almost touched the tarmac as its momentum was pulled out from under it. The rear axle yelped as it touched back down, the underinflated tires on each of its ends threatening to blow.

"Son. Of. A." Lou Ellen didn't say the last part but she certainly thought it.

She put the car in park and shut it off. A glance at the rearview just showed the Piney Woods and the lonely highway behind her.

Lou Ellen stepped cautiously onto the cool tarmac. She surveyed the surrounding area.

"Meow?" said something under her car.

Lou Ellen jumped at the sound.

"Meeeeeeerooooooow?"

A large tabby limped out from under her car, dragging its rear legs behind it.

"Oh my goodness!" Lou Ellen gasped, rushing over to the cat. "Oh you poor thing! Are you okay?"

"Merr...," the creature pathetically answered.

"Oh, look at you," Lou Ellen cupped the creature in her hands. "Oh what did I do? What did I do?"

Luellen brought the injured cat to her chest. It nestled against her heartbeat. The woman inspected the cat's legs.

"Huh," Lou Ellen looked into the cat's eyes. "Your legs are just fine."

The cat smiled the best it could.

"Yeah," it said. "But yours are better."

****

Henry struggled to control the Mustang. His head was too fogged, too flustered to do anything but suggest directions. It was anyone's guess whether his hands would respond. Something low grumbled between his ears.

"Ark, ark, ark," it seemed to say. "Errrgh-guh-googoo."

"Shut up," Henry spat through gritted teeth.

"I eat you," the voice said clearly. "Eat you like potatoes."

"SHUT UP!" Henry yelled, slamming his palm against his temple.

The car drifted into the oncoming lane. Henry pulled it back in line.

All he remembered was a set of glowing orange eyes and the screeching of that damned cat.

Henry mindlessly clawed at his neck.

"Hate cats," he mumbled.

"Cats hate you," the voice rebutted. "Turn left."

Henry's hands turned the wheel of their own volition. He didn't know where he was going—but something inside him did.

****

Alby couldn't help but smile. He didn't really wish this guy serious harm—or for anything to happen to his car—but then again if it had to happen to someone here, well...

"Gimme your keys!" the man turned to Alby, palm out.

"Uh, no?" Alby cocked his brow.

"I can drive!" Angie piped up, her face positively glowing even in the convenience store's sallow overhead light.

Alby looked at her over his glasses like a schoolmarm correcting the slow kid for the third time that day.

"You don't have a car," he said.

Angie shrank back.

Alby looked the man up and down, then dug his keys from his pocket. "Alright, let's go. But I'm driving."

"What about the gas station?" Angie squeaked.

"What about it?" Alby shrugged. "You're here."

Angie cocked her jaw and hip in unison.

"Nuh-uh, I'm coming!" she said, grabbing her jacket from underneath the counter.

Alby rolled his eyes.

"Whatever," he said, walking to the door. "But lock up."

Alby walked the other man outside past the ice box, around the corner, to the dark yellow pickup that was blocking the external restroom. The two got in quickly.

"So what's your name?" Alby asked, slamming his door shut.

"Denny," the man said. "Now can we just go already?"

Alby pumped the clutch and turned the key.

"Alright," Alby said, reversing out of the spot. He cruised around the curb toward the doors. Angie was struggling with the keys.

"Set the alarm!" Alby called from the car.

Denny slapped the dash.

"Jesus! Can we go?!"

"Yeah, yeah," Alby waved his hand. "Don't sweat it."

Angie set the lock code on the flush metal panel. Happy, she turned to the car.

Alby gestured with his thumb.

"Get in the back!"

"Ew," Angie said, climbing over the tailgate. "I'm gonna get tetanus from this heap."

"Yeah, yeah," Alby smirked at Angie's reflection in the rearview mirror.

He then turned toward his passenger's anxious face.

"Well, Denny," Alby smiled, putting the truck into gear. "Let's see how this old beast matches that Mustang of yours!"

****

Lou Ellen blinked a couple times, adjusting to the newly black and white world around her. She smelled something pungent in the air. Dead squirrel, maybe. Something small and fragile. Then, underneath it, she caught another scent. Something sweet, something she wanted. No, something she needed. A strong desire clutched her heart, pulling her back towards the car.

Lou Ellen stumbled across the road, her torso wobbling awkwardly upon her uncooperative hips.

"How do you bipeds do it?" a voice in her head asked, frustrated.

"Wuh-wuwu," Lou Ellen babbled.

She tumbled as her mind filled with a sudden succession of images. Flashes of pyramids and golden chariots. Something shiny dangling in the sky. People from distant places and times. Foreign eyes.

Somehow, Lou Ellen made it back to her car.

"What just happened?" Lou Ellen braced herself against the car door.

"Go, c'mon, we're going," the voice echoed around her skull.

"Where? Where are we going?" Lou Ellen slid down the side of her car. She blinked, trying to fix her vision. It didn't work.

"Get in. Get in the car," the voice became stern, demanding.

Like a marionette with slack strings, Lou Ellen struggled to get to her feet. She managed to open the door and slide onto the seat.

"Take wheel. I drive," the voice commanded.

Lou Ellen had no choice but to comply.

****

The old beast didn't match the Mustang very well at all. Alby struggled against the gasping engine, pushing the inherited heap the best he could. Denny sat impatiently, scanning the environment for any sign of his prized vehicle.

The engine sputtered a bit, threatening sudden death, then roared to full speed. Its unpredictable nature was part of the vehicle's appeal.

"Yeah," Alby said, patting the dash. "You hear those horses?"

"Oh yeah," Denny nodded. "Yeah, this is a machine alright."

Alby's face beamed.

"Hell yeah, it is."

He thumbed a wheel in the center dash and a violent shock of sound assaulted Denny's ears.

"Do you like BOC?" Alby yelled over the music.

Denny turned the volume all the way down. Alby grimaced.

"A simple no, man--"

"There!" Denny yelled, jerking the steering wheel to the left.

"Hey man!" Alby smacked at Denny's hand. "Verbal directions are sufficient, thank you!"

Alby turned past a bakery, easing his yellow contraption down the narrow alleyway.

All two doors and two hundred horses of Denny's muscle machine sat in the grey shadows near the end.

The truck clattered to a stop, drifting a couple extra feet for effect.

Denny jumped out, running over to his beloved 'Stang.

Angie rushed up behind him.

"Wow, great car," Angie said, coyly.

"Damn straight it is," Denny replied.

He knelt down to check for scratches and dings. Alby sauntered over to the passenger side.

"Ah dude," Alby hissed.

Denny shot up.

"What? What do you see?"

"Sorry, man," Alby said, casually. He held up the passenger side mirror.

Denny's eyes went huge.

"SON OF A—"

His words were cut off suddenly by the hissing of a cat and the swearing of a man around the other end of the alleyway.

Denny clenched his fist and marched toward the sound. Someone was getting a whoopin' for what happened to his car.

****

The signs along the highway were a blur. Lou Ellen was far exceeding the speed limit. Figures this, of all nights, would be the one time there wasn't a cop around. Not that there was anything a cop could probably do, she thought. She wasn't even sure she could explain what was happening.

A gurgle in her guts interrupted her thoughts.

"Rrr," the voice said, forcing her to pull over the car.

Lou Ellen let the car idle while she dug around in the loose sand along the highway. She carefully pawed out a bowl-shaped indentation.

"Ah, this'll do," she cooed.

Moments later, feeling quite relieved, Luellen got back in the car. Almost immediately, something annoyed her. She felt confined, constricted. She sat and thought about why she felt that way while she unconsciously unbuttoned her shirt.

****

Henry sat on his haunches in the faint moonlight, licking his stubby, sweaty hand. He didn't know what was compelling him, but he hated it. He didn't realize he tasted so much like salt and vinegar potato chips. Henry hated salt and vinegar potato chips. He was a barbecue man through and through.

He tried desperately to shake his tail and was severely disappointed that he didn't have one. Not even a nub. Henry kicked at the ground, impatient.

"Dude, he's naked," someone yelled from behind him.

Henry jumped, putting his back toward a wall. Bracing against it, he sat back on his legs, hands up in a defensive manner.

"Oh man!" Denny said, cracking his knuckles. "You better not have sat on Greta's seats with your bare ass!"

Denny stomped toward the man. Henry hissed, scratching lamely at the air. Inside, he cursed his short human fingernails.

Denny lifted up a massive fist and bore it down hard. It thudded against Henry's ribs. The man collapsed with a screech.

Denny brought his hand up again, but a flash of light from the side street filled his vision with white. Henry scuttled away on his butt, toward the light.

"My prince!" A feminine voice yelled from somewhere beyond the light.

"Princess!" Henry replied. He did his best to smooth his hair. He must have looked a mess, all fleshy and fat and hairless. Like an overfed pig with mange.

Through the light, a woman stepped, as naked as Henry. Alby nodded approvingly.

The woman crawled toward Henry on her hands and knees.

Denny blinked, clearing the spots from his eyes. He squinted toward the new arrival. Something familiar about her, something he knew.

"Lou Ellen?" Denny called. "Lou Ellen, is that you?"

The woman looked right past the rugged, leather jacketed man. Her eyes were transfixed on her pudgy prize. The two nude figures crawled across the dirty asphalt, finally meeting in the center.

They embraced, moaning painfully as they did so.

Denny stared in disbelief.

"This jackhole not only stole my car—but he just stole my date."

Angie glanced at Denny, then Lou Ellen.

"You're better off," she said, unable to contain her glee. "You know, perhaps it's fate."

"Nah," Denny said, turning around. "Just my bad luck."

"Chicks, man," Alby shrugged. "Who knows, right?"

Angie scowled at them both.

"You two," she said, disgusted. "Ugh."

"Oh God," Alby said, pointing at the two weirdos in the alleyway.

Denny and Angie looked and immediately cringed.

"Oooh," they said in unison.

The headlamps illuminated perfectly a scene everyone of the three witnesses would have prefered to keep in the dark. As Henry and Lou Ellen embraced, their shapes changed. Their pale pink flesh shuffled off, like icing sliding off a wet piece of cake. Underneath, where one would expect muscle and bone was instead a blood-streaked furry mess. Like newborn–

"Kittens," Angie gawked. "This is exactly what it looked like when Mrs. Whiskerson had kittens."

"Wow," Alby nodded, impressed. "That's disgusting."

"Yeah it is," Denny winced. "Yet I can't look away."

It took mere seconds for the remaining facade of humanity to give way to the strange feline hominid forms underneath. Although they retained their former size, that was the only thing human about them. It was hard to tell what color each was, but Angie was pretty sure the female one was a tabby.

The beasts brought their flat fur-lined faces together. Their mouths open; their eyes closed. They made a soft growl—almost like purring.

"What are they doing?" Angie's disgust slurred her words.

"I think they're…kissing," Alby said, agape.

Denny shifted his feet.

"Yeah, um…" he quickly backed toward his car. "I, um, God, screw this!"

Angie watched the Mustang clear the alley, turn right past her down the side street, and fade into the night. Her mouth twisted into a little glum smile.

"There he goes," she said wistfully.

"There he goes." Alby repeated, still caught in the spectacle of the cat things.

"We should get back to work."

"Yeah, I reckon." He nodded, unable to look away.

Angie shoved him, knocking him from his reverie.

"Let's just go," she said.

"Yeah," Alby agreed. "Yeah, I—yeah."

The two got into the yellow truck. Alby backed up, navigating the thin alley the best he could, then turned back onto the main road. They drove in silence.

"So, um," Angie said finally, "What were those things?"

Alby pursed his lips and shook his head.

"What things?"

"Those things!" Angie's eyes went wide. "Those freaky furry things! Those—"

"What," Alby interrupted, emphasizing the words, "Things?"

He looked at her until she got his drift.

"Oh," Angie nodded, feebly.

Alby fixed his eyes on the double yellow line.

"Yeah," Angie said, doing the same. "I guess you're right."

****

Unaware of their surroundings or even the other people who had been there, the monsters withdrew from their extending embrace.

"I've been looking for you forever," Lou Ellen-monster said finally.

"As have I," said Henry-monster.

They held a glassy-eyed gaze for a moment.

"Millennia of incarnations..."

"Thousands of bodies..."

"Finally we are together."

They sighed.

"So," Lou Ellen-monster straightened herself. "Are you ready?"

"I am," Henry agreed, enthusiastically.

"How hungry are you?"

Henry-monster smiled.

"Hungry enough to eat a town."

****

*Jason L Blair has been a writer, editor, graphic designer, layout guy, and game designer for the past ten years. One day, he will get around to figuring out his life. For now, he'll stick to playing video games. His list of credits can be seen at www.hekeba.com. For information on his latest project, visit littlefears.com.*

# ~Off Radio~

*by David Wellington*

We found Frances Bucknell's body down at the railroad siding on Sunday, but couldn't make a positive ID until Tuesday when some kids found her head in a drainage ditch off Cane Bottom Road. In a town like this not even Sheriff Anderson tried holding the information back from the press—there was no point, since gossip moves faster around here than email. Needless to say by lunch time everybody in Pinebox had a pet theory as to how she died.

"Those boys said the head wasn't cut off so much as yanked out by its roots," Tiffany Bishop, the bank teller, said. We'd stopped in for a bite at the little diner on Highway 96, the Sheriff and me, and we couldn't help but overhear the quartet of ladies in a booth right by us discussing the case. Especially since they were staring at us the whole time where we sat at the counter. "That poor girl. She was a student at the university, right?"

"I heard that part of the body was missing. Maybe even consumed." This from Jane Blewer, and when she said it I looked down at my sandwich in despair. They make a fine chicken salad at Mom's Diner, with paprika in the mayonnaise, but suddenly I was not hungry at all. Judging by the volume of their voices they weren't talking to each other. They were talking to us. "I suppose," she went on, confirming my suspicion, "we will be told it was another one of those 'gator attacks you always hear about."

Sheriff Anderson sat up straighter on his stool and swished his coffee around in his mouth like it was mouthwash. He did not respond. I shot Jane Blewer a look that she should have understood, a look that said now is not the time.

Alicia Crowley was next to speak up, though, and she was not the sort to be put off by a meaningful look. "I've never heard of an alligator that would take a girl's head off and carry it four miles into town," she added. The ladies were after something. Did they know I already had a good idea who the killer was? God, I hoped not.

"Gators do funny things, sometimes," I said, trying to defuse the situation. The sheriff sighed deeply—he wasn't enjoying this game. He picked up his sandwich but didn't bite into it, just stared at it for a while. I suppose he knew what was going to have to come next.

Because the fourth woman at the booth was old Ethel Gastock, who saw a ghost one time and hasn't stopped telling people about it since. "It seems to me one of those crimes for which no explanation of a conventional sort will satisfy. Deputy Clark," she said, coming over to touch my arm, "wouldn't you agree?"

I opened my mouth to answer but the sheriff spun around on his stool then and leaned his bright red face close to hers. "Miz Gastock, I am of the opinion that this kind of conjecture is not helpful in an investigation, especially not at this early stage. And I will thank you not to waste the valuable time of my employees."

"She's speaking on behalf of the whole community," Alicia Crowley said, half standing up in her seat. "I think we have a right to know what's going on. Why, any of us could be next."

"At least tell us if there are any leads," Tiffany Bishop pleaded, pulling her friend back down into her seat.

"Well now, I wouldn't know," the Sheriff told her. He looked about ready to pop an artery. I wiped my mouth with my napkin, knowing how this would end. "Seeing as it's out of my jurisdiction."

"They found the body in Golan county," Ethel Gastock exclaimed. "That makes this your business, sir!"

"It sure was, but then the head was found here in town," the sheriff said, with a nasty smile. "Which makes it a matter for the Pinebox Police Department. Come on, Clark." He threw some money on the counter and stormed out into the East Texas sun. I hurried to follow.

I didn't relish what came next but I suppose there are things that ought to be done in this world and there are things that have to be done, whether they ought to or not. When Jane Blewer mentioned that part of Frances Bucknell's body had been eaten, I knew I was looking at one of the latter. I waited till the sheriff had his sunglasses on, then I said, "Butch, I'd like to go off radio for a while. Just for the afternoon, if that's alright."

He looked across his shoulder at me. "You'd like that, huh?" I couldn't see his eyes but I knew he was thinking from the way his mouth went flat. "A kind of personal day. Well, I suppose that's a possibility."

"Thanks," I said, and started to turn away.

"An unpaid personal day," he added.

I just nodded and hurried off to where I'd parked my patrol vehicle.

****

I didn't have all that far to go. The Reznar place was back in the woods a ways, maybe eight miles into the Big Thicket and not near any main roads, but I knew the way well enough. I'd been out there once a year since I left high school, checking up on things. Each time I came, the place looked a little shabbier and the pine trees that ringed it had marched a little further into the yard. This time they were so close it looked like their needles might scratch on the windows at night. It had been a good spread once, a three story house built of good cedar wood and painted a happy yellow color with green trim. Now the paint was peeling and a bunch of the old sash windows had been replaced with cheap single panes that wouldn't open, not even to catch an evening breeze. There were no cars in the three slot garage even though one of the doors was hanging open—looking like it was stuck that way for good.

I suppose if I was a better man I would have been out that way every weekend cleaning up the lawn and doing all the little repairs a big house needs. I suppose if I was a better man, maybe it would be called the Clark place now and I'd be living there myself. But there are things that are hard to forget, even for a man who hopes to get into heaven, and for someone like me they can be downright unforgivable. My yearly visits had staved off most of my guilt and I hardly thought about the place for months at a time anymore. It was beginning to look like that had been a mistake.

Sighing to myself, I switched off the radio rig attached to my dashboard. Then I took off my badge and put it in the glove compartment. I took my hat off, too, since it was shady enough back in the pines. I kept my sidearm in its holster.

I knocked at the front door but didn't expect an answer. It was unlocked, which is not rare in these parts, so I let myself in. I knew where Sarah was going to be so I headed straight there—the family parlor in back, a dim room full of antique chairs that needed to be refinished, a big round table covered in a yellowing cloth, and a fancy two thousand dollar computer internet setup with an ergonomic back chair. Sarah Reznar was sitting in it wearing nothing but an old housedress, plugged tight into her keyboard and screen. She was playing one of those online games where you get to look just like yourself but ten years younger and twenty pounds lighter and she didn't even seem aware of my entrance.

I watched the screen for a little while as her virtual reality self flirted with a computerized fellow in a turtleneck and little square glasses. It looked like they were in some kind of big town coffee bar and little hearts kept floating up from the tops of their heads. I suppose I was waiting for her to get to a good stopping place but eventually I cleared my throat and looked down at the carpet as she jumped right out of her chair and spun around to face me.

It did bad things to my chest to see how she'd changed. The sun was drained right out of her cheeks and her red hair was streaked with gray so it looked like a used-up, rusted old Brillo pad. Her eyes were big as they always were, but instead of looking dewy and bright like they used to, now they just looked watery and like they couldn't quite focus on me.

"It's not October yet," she said. "You're not due, Tommy Clark."

"No, ma'am, I suppose I'm not," I said. This, I figured, was going to be the hardest part.

Now I knew for a fact that Sarah Reznar never did anything wrong in her life, not since the one time in her summer after high school, back when she and I were an item. We were both a little wilder back then. One time we went into a cave down by the quarry and she ate what she thought were peyote buttons (long story short, they were *not*). I should have known enough to stop her, but I guess I was thinking that if she got high she might let me take off her tight jeans for once. We never got around to it, though, not that day or ever since.

Before that day, she'd had a chance to go to college the next year, and not just to ETU in town. Instead she'd had to stay here in the house where she was born, the place where she would most likely live out her days, atoning for her one paltry sin. I'd had a chance to get out as well, with a football scholarship, but after that day in the cave neither of us were going anywhere.

"You gave your word," she said, because she knew why I'd come three months early. We'd both known it would come to this eventually.

"And you gave yours, so I guess we're even. One promise broken each," I said, which came out harder than I would have liked. "You told me you'd keep him out of trouble. Just tell me now where your boy is. You won't have to handle the details. I'll take care of everything."

"He never touched that girl!"

I didn't say anything. I suppose maybe I'd been holding out a thread of hope, that Frances Bucknell did get eaten by a gator after all. The look on her face told me otherwise. Sarah and I never could lie to each other.

"I'm guessing he's close by," I said, and her eyes darted to the door to the kitchen. The one that led to the back porch. I started to head that way when she grabbed me. I managed to fend her off without hurting her.

"You're as good as his daddy!"

"His daddy," I said, very slowly, "was a bug the size of a Doberman pinscher that died eighty million years ago." It was a hurtful thing to say but it was enough to make her let me go.

I suppose I ought to tell you, at this point, the truth about Sarah Reznar's one moment of weakness. Those things she thought were peyote buttons? They were wolf weevil eggs, left in a dry cave by a creature that should never have existed in the first place. A creature God did not create without some help from the Other Fellow.

Those wolf weevils weren't just big bugs that hung around irritating dinosaurs. Judging by what we found in that cave, they had some pretty advanced tools and a complex social structure. We got all that from paintings they left in the cave. Very detailed paintings.

We also got how they had eggs that could take over a mama dinosaur's body and make it start pumping out little baby weevils. Eggs that looked like something a dinosaur would eat, you see.

The one Sarah ate might have been a little past its use-by date, though.

The thing she gave birth to looked like one of them, sure, but he was also kind of human. He was covered in thick, bristly black hair most places, except where he was shiny and smooth and segmented. One of his arms ended in a pincer, and he had four tiny clasper legs sticking out of his belly. One of his eyes was compound, like a bee's, and the other just looked nasty, squinty and tiny and black. There were some patches of bright yellow fur on his face and shoulders that were always kind of moist, and we never did figure out why. He would have been about nine feet tall if he could stand up straight, which he could not. She named him Tommy Junior.

He was out on the back porch, just as I expected, sitting in a rocking chair and watching birds fly in and out of the big tractor shed at the edge of the back lawn. He didn't so much as look up as I approached, just rubbed his jointed shoulder like it was paining him.

"Boy," I said.

I gave him a second. When he didn't move, I said "Look at me, boy, when I talk to you."

He turned around a little in the chair. His neck didn't quite turn as far as a human's ought to. "Hey, sir," he said, because I never let him call me anything else. His voice was the most human thing about him. It sounded a lot like Sarah's, because it never broke no matter how old he got.

"I figure you know why I'm here."

"I sure don't," he tried, but I just stared hard at him and then he looked down at his lap. "Sir," he added.

"You're going to tell me you don't know what happened to Frances Bucknell? That you had nothing to do with it? Your mama seems to think different."

He looked up at the outhouse again and I thought for a second he was going to cry. I didn't know if he could do that or not. The yellow fur on his face got darker, though, and all laid down flat. "She didn't run away. Most times, they run off when they see me."

I leaned against the porch railing and waited. That's an old trick the Sheriff taught me. You want somebody to confess, you don't beat it out of them, or yell in their face until you're blue. You just shut your own yap and wait. A guilty conscience needs to talk, is how Butch put it, because it can't stand the silence. In the silence it can hear itself think. Give 'em enough time and they'll tell all.

"She said she was from the University, she was studying biology," he told me. "She came out to the Thicket looking for the Piney Devil."

"And instead she found you," I said.

"Yes, sir." He tried to sit up in his chair. "She had real pretty hair. I wanted to—I mean, before I—before she tripped and hit her head, I was thinking maybe she and I could—"

"That's enough," I told him. "You remember, now, what I told you, way back. About what we would have to do if there was ever any trouble again. After what happened with your mama's pet cat, we had a talk, you remember?"

"Yes, sir," he told me, and started getting up out of the chair. It wasn't so easy because his left leg bent in such a way it kept getting caught in the runners. Then he stepped down off the porch, onto the grass of the back yard. I suppose I thought he was going to do the decent thing, so I was a little slow on drawing my piece and stepping down after him.

He got about halfway to the outhouse before he turned around to look at me. I nodded in respect, figuring that was where he wanted it done.

Then the little freak pulled a fast one on me. A wing-case on his strong leg popped open and a thin, glassy fan spread out. Another case opened on his back and a second wing fluttered out and went stiff.

Didn't even know he had them.

They weren't so big or strong that he could fly, luckily for me, but they buzzed something nasty in the air and suddenly he was jumping over the outhouse, right over it so only his weak leg scratched along the roof, and by the time I ran around the other side he was gone, into the woods.

****

Most people would get lost in the Big Thicket within ten minutes. It's a dark place, even on a sunny day, with pine trees seventy, a hundred feet tall and branches so thick they block out all the sunlight. There aren't a lot of roads through that forest, and almost no development at all, just tree trunks so thick they're nearly touching and a carpet of dead stuff underfoot a good foot thick in places, so walking in those woods is like walking on a trampoline. There is so much underbrush that one place in the woods looks almost exactly the same as another and without a compass you'd be hard pressed to know if you were getting anywhere or just walking in circles.

The boy, though, he grew up in between those trees. His mama never let him out into the daylight, where somebody might see him and start asking questions. He'd spent his boyhood running around that patch of woods playing games with himself, eating whatever little furry animals he could catch, since the suppers Sarah made for him didn't fill him up. The trees might have been custom-built, as well, for his strange anatomy. Where the trees got thick he could jump up into the lower branches, and hop along from one to another. So my chances of catching him back there were not good.

Except, I grew up in the Thicket myself. And I knew that what looked like a random assortment of trees was anything but. The places where a man can walk in there aren't just thin patches, they're animal trails. Not exactly what you would call clear-cut paths, but wide enough that you can follow them. The trails don't run in straight lines. They double back on themselves and they follow what water there is back there. So the forest isn't just primeval chaos, it's a maze, and if you've threaded that maze enough times you know where a boy running away from authority is going to head, and you know there's a smaller, less obvious trail that cuts that way a lot faster.

I caught sight of him coming through a narrow little clearing, a notch in the woods where lightning took down a couple dozen trees fifteen years ago. He emerged from the dark trees with not a little noise, stumbling and breaking twigs in his haste, so I ducked back into the woods and watched him come, looking over his shoulder for me, scared out of his wits.

He didn't even see me as I came up on him, weapon drawn and held out at arm's length. "Do what you're told, boy," I said, "and stop right there."

He turned himself around to peer at me with his squinty eye and I saw the fur on his face turn orange with surprise.

"You gonna behave?" I asked.

He raised both his arms in the air and for a second I thought I had him. Then one of the clasper arms on his belly reached up and swatted the gun out of my hand. Then his good leg came up and kicked me straight across the clearing.

I landed in the needles, which probably saved me from a broken arm or worse, and rolled with the tumble. I looked around and saw my gun lying half-buried in the underbrush, maybe ten feet away. I got to my feet and ran over to scoop it up, but before I could reach it he grabbed me from behind, those claspers digging into my ribs and back. He lifted me off the ground like I would lift a sand bag and held me up kicking in the air. Then his pincer came up and clacked near my throat.

It's funny the things that come to you at moments like that. I was thinking about how if he killed me and left my body right there, nobody would ever find it, most likely. Animals would get to me and eat the soft parts, and then my bones would be buried by the pine needles within a single summer. How long would it be before some idiot camper stumbled on my skeleton and wondered who this fellow had been, so far away from civilization?

"Aw, heck," I said, as the pincer worked its way around my throat. Just like it had Frances Bucknell's. It wasn't sharp enough to cut my head clean off, but it was strong enough to pull it off. Just like hers. "You didn't just kill her, did you, boy? You had to go and play with what was left of her. How long did you keep her head around as a toy?"

"Just till it stopped being so pretty. Just a little while," he said, sounding surprised to hear me talk so calm.

"That's long enough." Then I bashed my head backward against his face and felt the hard part of my skull turn that soft, wet yellow fur to muck. He screamed in pain and dropped me to the ground. It was the work of a second to dash over, pick up my weapon, and spin around to face him again.

He was in a bad condition. The whole left side of his face had caved in and was leaking black goo like a rusty tap. He had his human hand up pressed against the wound and the fur on his shoulders and his other cheek had turned a bright screaming red.

"What'd you do that for?" he demanded. "I didn't mean to do nothing wrong. I didn't know she would break so easy! Daddy! Please don't do this."

"I'm not your daddy," I told him.

Then I did what I came for and put a bullet in his brains. I did it the way you shoot a dog that's got the rabies. Face to face.

****

When I went back on the radio and headed for town it was already getting dark. I checked in at the station and found Sheriff Anderson sitting behind his desk, reading a Mack Bolan paperback. He glanced up when I came in and frowned. "You're back," he said. "You had yourself a good personal day?"

"I got done what needed doing," I told him. I started to head back to the locker room, wanting to change, but I figured I should say something. "I have a feeling, sir, that we won't ever figure out who killed Frances Bucknell. But that it's alright because the perpetrator won't be repeating the crime."

"That's some kind of feeling you got," the Sheriff said. The look on his face didn't change. "I suppose feelings don't come under the heading of things that get written up in official paperwork, do they?"

"No, sir," I told him. "I don't suppose they should."

He shrugged. "Don't matter. Wasn't in our jurisdiction, anyway." Then he gave me a big, toothy smile and went back to his book.

****

*David Wellington is the author of seven novels. His zombie novels Monster Island, Monster Nation and Monster Planet (Thunder's Mouth Press) form a complete trilogy. He has also written a series of vampire novels including (so far) Thirteen Bullets, Ninety-Nine Coffins, Vampire Zero, and Twenty-Three Hours (Three Rivers Press).*

*As an undergraduate he attended Syracuse University; in 1996 he received an MFA in Creative Writing from Penn State; and in 2006 he received an MLS from the Pratt Institute. Mr. Wellington currently resides in New York City with his wife Elisabeth and their dog, Mary.*

*Mr. Wellington got his start in publishing in an interesting way. In 2004 he began serializing his horror fiction online, posting short chapters of a novel three times a week on a friend's blog. The book was written in "real-time"; that is, each chapter was conceived, outlined, researched, composed and edited within twenty-four hours of its initial posting. By word of mouth, readers learned of the project and returned to watch the story evolve. Response to the project was so great that in 2004 Thunder's Mouth Press approached Mr. Wellington about publishing Monster Island as a print book. The novel has been featured in Rue Morgue, Fangoria, and the New York Times. For more information please visit davidwellington.net.*

# ~Last Exit to Pinebox~

*by JD Wiker*

"Is it dead?"

Mark Whitman looked back toward his car, where his wife Emma stood supporting herself on the open passenger door. The concern on her face was evident by the glow from the dome light.

"Yeah, I think so," he told her. He looked down at what he assumed was an armadillo, crushed and bloody on the highway. It twitched, seemingly trying to claw at his leg. *But I don't think it knows it yet. Still, no reason to upset Emma—not while she's due any day now, and we're in the middle of nowhere.*

"You should move it off the road," Emma called back to him. She frowned. "I'd feel bad ..."

Mark debated whether he agreed or not. True, it wasn't entirely dead, and moving it might spare it further indignity. But he was pretty sure it didn't have long to live, anyway. Besides, if another car hit it again, it would be more of a mercy than the agony it would endure from him trying to carry it off the highway so it could bleed to death in peace.

He looked back the way they had come. In the dark, he could barely see the highway, and he certainly didn't see any headlights coming this way. Truth to tell, he wasn't sure if there was *any* other traffic on this road. His GPS had told him to take Highway 96 to the nearest gas station, but he had gone 20 miles with no sign of another soul sharing the road, let alone this supposed gas station. There was a kind of glow on the horizon ahead which might be a town, or at least an interchange, but, at this hour, that was no guarantee of a fill-up. Small-town gas stations, in his experience, closed up around dinner time and didn't open until the locals were on their way to work the next morning.

He breathed out a heartfelt curse. *Nothing is ever easy*, he reflected. Emma could go into labor any day now, and he would have preferred to have stayed home in Albuquerque, close to their doctor, close to a hospital he could drive to in less than fifteen minutes. But Emma's family in Louisiana were having "a traditional family Christmas," and had put pressure on her to be there—never mind that she was expecting, never mind that her doctor had ordered her not to fly, never mind that they had to *drive* across the biggest state in the contiguous forty-eight on Christmas Eve. No, her family had made up their minds and then made up hers.

Mark really hated his in-laws. He himself had grown up in a loving, supportive family, taught right from wrong, and given every opportunity to better himself that middle-class parents in the 70s could afford.

Emma, though, had family that were just a step above trailer trash—on a good day. They were poor and uneducated, feuded for decades over otherwise trivial issues, and spent most of their welfare checks on drugs, alcohol, mismatched garage-sale furniture, and hideously ugly knick-knacks. Their homes, their clothes, their very *skin* was stained with years of chain smoking, and it always set off his asthma just to spend a couple of hours with them. And now they had committed to spending the whole of Christmas day there.

But Mark Whitman loved his wife, and would do anything for her, even if it meant having to endure her relatives. She really didn't like them any more than he did—in fact, she'd once confessed of being molested as a child by her oldest cousin (who was now mercifully in prison)—but the Kilgores had, between them, almost three-hundred years of experience in manipulating people, and they knew exactly how to press her buttons. "Went off to college and got too good for *us*." "Got that computer job in New Mexico and don't never call *us*." "Don't even talk like normal people no more." Emma was proud of having made something of herself, of having gotten an education, of having found a good husband, of having found a well-paying job—of having gotten out of Lower Junction, Louisiana—but she was still emotionally fragile, particularly now, and it didn't take long for her family to make her remember that Pride was one of the Seven Deadly Sins.

So now they were driving through God-Knows-Where, Texas, low on gas—and he was standing shivering on the road, watching an armadillo die because he hadn't swerved just a little farther or just a little faster.

He looked down at it again. *Better to put it out of its misery*, he thought. But he knew that there was no way he could do that, noble as it might be, with Emma watching. She'd cry for hours, and, between the stress of the trip, not having had enough sleep, and worrying about his wife and unborn son, his nerves were wearing pretty thin right now.

"It's already dead," he lied to her, starting back to the car. "Besides, I don't have anything to pick it up with." He reached her side of the car and gently nudged her back inside. "You need to stay off your feet, baby," he reminded her. "Rest. Try to get some sleep. Anyway, I'm sure they have road crews who take care of this sort of thing all the time."

*Well, not that sure.* The deeper they penetrated into East Texas, the more frequently they encountered roadkill. They must have passed a splattered animal corpse at least once a mile, and it had gotten worse after they'd taken the 96 interchange, as if all the animals just threw themselves into the paths of oncoming cars on the highway rather than face another day in the thick, menacing forest lining the road. Hell, if he lived here, didn't have a job, couldn't pay his bills, had a cheating bitch for a wife, and a bottle and a gun as his only real friends, he could do it, himself. Just put one between Emma's eyes while she was asleep, then another in her stomach to make sure the baby was dead, then lay down on the bed next to them and jam the gun up under his chin and pull the trigger—

The roar of a passing semi and the blare of its horn snapped him out of it. *What the hell?* he thought. *Where did that come from*? Not just the ghoulish, suicidal thoughts, but that damned eighteen-wheeler? He was certain it hadn't been there when he looked back up the highway a few seconds ago. He sure hadn't noticed any lights. Had he been standing there, daydreaming, while a huge truck bore down on him, and he just hadn't noticed? Was he that tired? Had he dozed off walking around the car to his side? And it had been close, too. He must have been just about to step into traffic. *Jesus,* he thought, *I could have died just then.*

With an effort, he pulled himself together and continued around to the driver's side—this time, checking both ways for oncoming vehicles. He slipped into his seat and gave his wife what he hoped was a reassuring smile as he buckled his seat belt.

"What was that all about?" she asked.

"What was what about?"

"Did you not see that truck that went by?"

"Oh," he said, embarrassed. "No, I didn't. I guess I'm just tired. I'll get some coffee when we get gas."

She turned to stare after the truck, already receding toward the faint glow in the distance. "It was weird," she said. "Just a bunch of wrecked cars, stacked on top of each other."

"Probably a wrecker truck," Mark suggested.

"They all had numbers painted on them," Emma told him. "Ones, twos, and threes ... nothing higher. Mostly twos."

Mark stared after the truck himself, but it was little more than an indistinct configuration of red taillights now. "I didn't notice." He shrugged. "Too busy trying not to get hit by it."

His wife gave him a frightened look, but he wasn't sure it was about him nearly being killed just now. "It was red paint," she said. "It looked like blood."

Mark took her hand and gave it a reassuring squeeze. "In this light, I'm not surprised," he said. He started the car again. "It's probably a code for the junk yard. 'One' means it's drivable, 'two' means it's only good for parts, 'three' means scrap it."

Emma managed a weak smile. "I guess," she said. "How much gas do we have?"

"Not much," Mark said. "In fact, I'm really hoping that's a town ahead, or we may have to turn around and go back to the main highway and take our chances."

He checked his mirrors and carefully pulled back out onto the highway, still a bit rattled about the near miss with the semi. They drove in silence for a few moments, then Emma spoke up. "It's a town," she said, pointing at a green highway sign on the roadside ahead.

Mark could make it out now that they were approaching it. "Pinebox," he read.

"Ugh," Emma said. "Thank God *that's* not ominous-sounding."

****

Pinebox was bigger than Mark expected, but small enough that he'd driven almost all the way through town before he finally saw another person.

The Pinebox Diner was the only place Mark could find that was open, so he pulled in and parked. Emma waited in the car. Moving her at this stage in her pregnancy wasn't easy, and he saw no reason to drag her in with him if they weren't going to be there all that long. All he needed was some hot coffee and directions to the nearest open gas station.

"Coffee, hon?" called a pink-uniformed waitress from behind the counter.

"Black, two sugars," he replied. "To go, please."

The waitress smiled. "Sure," she said. "Just let me put it on." She turned her back to him and busied herself at the big coffee urn.

Mark looked around the diner. It was one of those old-fashioned, railway-car-turned-diner places he remembered seeing in his youth, though he couldn't recall ever being inside one. This one was dingy with bad lighting, though he couldn't really identify any one spot that was particularly dirty or dark; it was as though he was looking at the place with blinders on. In fact, it took him a moment to realize he wasn't the only customer.

"Good morning," said a large black man from one of the booths. He had a deep, full voice, with a fatherly tone that Mark found at once soothing and authoritative. As he focused in, he realized the man was a minister.

"Good morning," he replied automatically. "Sorry, I didn't see you there."

"No one ever does," the man replied. "A black man in a black suit—and Gloria isn't very good about replacing the burned-out lights in here. I blend in."

"Um," said Mark, not sure how to take that.

The minister chuckled, low and friendly. "My apologies," he said, "I sometimes forget that not everyone shares my sense of humor." He extended a hand. "Reverend Porter."

Mark shook the Reverend's hand. "Mark Whitman."

"Traveling on Christmas Eve, Mister Whitman?"

"Yes," Mark replied. "Visiting my wife's family, in Louisiana."

"Is that her in the car outside?"

"Yes," he said. "Emma. She's trying to sleep." He glanced over at Gloria, still fussing with the coffee urn. "I'm trying to stay awake."

"A sensible policy," Reverend Porter agreed.

"And direction," Mark said. "I mean, directions."

"To Louisiana?"

"No," Mark chuckled. "A gas station. We're almost on empty."

The Reverend *tsk*ed. "No gas stations open around here," he said. "Not for a few hours yet—especially not on Christmas Eve."

"What about back on the highway?" Mark asked. "I can probably make it another twenty miles or so …"

"We're pretty far off the beaten trail here in Pinebox," Reverend Porter said. "The flow of traffic usually avoids us, though the university brings folks in pretty regularly." He smiled. "Just not during the holidays."

"Well, crap," Mark said. "Oh. Sorry."

Reverend Porter chuckled again. "Oh, that's alright, Mister Whitman. This is a farming community. It's unusual when folks *don't* mention fertilizer."

Mark smiled thinly. There was something about talking to the reverend that made him uncomfortable, as though he were somehow being tested, and had best tread lightly. He glanced again at the waitress behind the counter. She stood watching the conversation, eyes bright and attentive, while the coffee pot percolated behind her. The clock on the wall over her other shoulder clicked loudly from 1:22 to 1:23.

*This is a weird town*, Mark thought.

"So," he said, turning to the Reverend again, "There's no hope of getting gas before six A.M.?"

"Oh, there's always hope," Reverend Porter said. "In fact, if you wait here a little while, old Nick might just come by a little early."

"Old Nick?" Mark asked.

"He runs the gas station, just up the road." Reverend Porter nodded his head in the general direction of the highway. Mark looked. In the darkness, he could just make out the dim shape of gas pumps, not half a mile from where he stood. As he peered out, he heard the roar of a semi, and a moment later the wrecker truck drove by, laden with its crushed cars, numbers from one to three painted blood-red on their buckled door panels. Now that Mark was seeing them with his own eyes, he could tell that these were all wrecks—cars that had been destroyed in various collisions, and turned over to the local junkyard for disposal. He wondered about the circumstances of those accidents—why they had happened, and how long ago, and whether anyone had survived.

The bell over the door rang, announcing another customer. Mark tore his eyes away from the grim spectacle of the passing truck and looked hopefully to the door for a sign that the next late-night diner patron might be the aforementioned Nick.

Instead, it was a family of three—husband, wife, and young son—who all looked every bit as tired as he was. At a glance, he could tell that, like he and Emma, they were en route to visit family for Christmas, and had found themselves stuck in the middle of nowhere, with no place to stop and rest but the morbidly-named Pinebox.

"Coffee, hons?" Gloria asked them. They nodded mutely. "Be ready in a minute. Make yourselves comfortable."

The family shuffled to a nearby booth and collapsed into their seats, the mother putting her arm around her son, and the father staring blankly out the window.

"Good morning," Reverend Porter said, and they looked bleakly up at him.

"You folks traveling, too?" Mark asked them.

They seemed not to have noticed him until he spoke. They stared at him for a moment, their expressions unreadable, until the man broke the ominous silence.

"Traveling," he said. "On Christmas Eve."

"Where are you headed?" Mark asked.

"Corpus Christi," the man replied. The woman hugged the boy tighter. He seemed on the verge of dozing off—or of passing out.

"Been driving long?" Mark asked. "Your son there looks like he's fading."

The woman started to cry. Her husband put his arm around her, all but ignoring Mark—for which he found himself grateful. He didn't know what he'd said, but it was obviously making these people every bit as uncomfortable as he felt, just being here.

"Getting cold out there," Reverend Porter observed. "Are you sure you don't want to bring your wife inside while you wait?"

"Plenty warm in here," Gloria agreed.

"That's probably not a bad idea," Mark said, then noticed the man in the next booth looking intently at him, and shaking his head, almost imperceptibly, *No.*

Mark looked out at the car. Emma was dozing in the passenger seat, her face angelic in the moonlight. In a moment their life together flashed before his eyes, from their first meeting to their first kiss to the moment he knew that he wanted to be with her for the rest of his life. He saw their wedding, their honeymoon in

Maui, the look in her eyes when she told him she was pregnant, and the thought hit him like a revelation: *I have to protect her. I have to protect my family.*

"Y'know," he said, "on second thought, maybe we'll just head on out. At the very least, we can go back the way we came. We may lose a little time, but I'm sure we'll find an open gas station on the main highway." He glanced back at the family. The man was subtly nodding his head, his eyes shining.

"You sure, hon?" Gloria asked. "Your wife sure looks cold. Can't be good for the baby."

"*Baby*?" the woman in the next booth suddenly gasped. "Your wife is pregnant?"

"Yes," Mark told her, confused by her concern. "She's due any day now. I—" He stopped abruptly, and turned to look at Gloria, behind the counter. "I didn't tell you my wife was pregnant," he said quietly.

"Are you sure?" Reverend Porter asked. "I could've sworn you said something."

"Oh, my God," the woman said, slightly louder. "*Oh, my God.*"

"Well, a woman just knows these things," Gloria smiled. For the first time, Mark noticed that her teeth were stained a dark brown, like she had been eating gravedirt and washing it down with motor oil. Her breath stank, even at this distance, and he found himself taking a step backward.

"No," said the man in the next booth, staring hard at Reverend Porter. "*No*. I don't care. We *won't* do that."

"It's not your decision, Mister Josephsen," Reverend Porter said. "It's up to Mister Whitman. He's the one in the driver's seat."

"What—" Mark began, but his throat had gone dry. He swallowed hard and tried again. "What's going on? What are you people talking about?"

"You need to go, Mister Whitman," Josephsen said, rising from his seat to stand between Mark and the reverend. "Just get out of here. It has nothing to do with you."

"By all means, Mister Whitman," Reverend Porter said. "You should go back the way you came. Head back to the main highway. I'm sure you'll find a gas station there."

"Don't listen to him!" Josephsen said. "Don't drink that!" He slapped something out of Mark's hand, and Mark suddenly realized he'd been holding a coffee cup, though he couldn't remember Gloria handing him one. It hit the floor and spilled, looking like brown blood spattering across the linoleum tiles. "Get out of here!" Josephsen roared at him.

Mark stumbled backward until he felt the diner door behind him. The bell jingled merrily as he pushed out in the parking lot. He looked over his shoulder at the car, saw Emma smile at him and start to open the door. Back in the diner,

Gloria flashed her dead-teeth grin again, and Reverend Porter favored him with another hearty chuckle that seemed to reverberate through his bones. He turned and rushed back to the car, urging Emma to stay inside.

"Did you get directions?" she asked him. "Is there a gas station open?"

"We have to go back to the highway," he told her. "Nothing's open here."

"Oh," she said, "I guess not."

He followed her gaze back to the diner. The lights were out now, and Mark could see not even a hint of movement from within. It was as though the place had just *shut off*, somehow, that even the barest signs of life had been utterly and completely snuffed out.

Mark rushed around to the driver's side of the car and threw himself inside, starting the car as fast as he could. He threw the car in reverse and didn't stop until he was back on the street. Still rolling backward, he slammed the car into drive and gunned it, aiming directly for the highway.

"Slow down," Emma said. "You should try to conserve gas."

He looked blankly at her. She had been dozing—hadn't seen any of what he'd seen inside the diner. She didn't *know*.

"Oh!" she said suddenly. "You forgot your coffee."

"Too late now," he said. *Far, far too late.*

"Are you sure?" Emma said, glancing in the sideview mirror. "It looks like they just closed. They're probably still there."

"I'm sure they are," Mark said. *I get the feeling that they can never leave.*

****

Mark drove like a man possessed. He sped up the highway on-ramp and onto the 96, almost tipping the car over on the cloverleaf. Emma gripped the armrests of her seat as hard as she could, staring at him in surprise and fear, but never once saying a word—terrified at her husband's inexplicable panic, yet trusting him all the same. It wasn't until he could no longer see the glow of Pinebox behind him that Mark finally let up on the accelerator—and realized that he had been driving at over a hundred miles per hour. He let the car gradually slow down to a safe speed, then pulled off to the shoulder and put the car in neutral.

It seemed like a long time before Emma's voice snapped him back to reality. "Mark?" she asked. "What's the matter? What happened back there?"

He looked at her mutely. *How do I explain this? I don't believe in ghosts, or demons, or the supernatural, in any way, shape, or form—but what I saw back there, what happened in that eerie diner, there's no way that was real. She's going to think I'm lying, trying to find a way out of visiting her family, or that I'm crazy—and, then again, maybe I am. Maybe I imagined all of that, just now ... that weird waitress with the rotten teeth and the creepy Reverend, that family that he could've sworn had just sort of appeared out of nowhere, and the way they looked! Like they had been driving all night, over and over again, for an eternity ...*

"Mark?" Emma asked again, taking his hand. "It's okay, baby. You can tell me. Just tell me."

Mark opened his mouth and there was a hellish roar and a blinding light and a crashing jolt from behind and Mark was slammed back in his seat, his eyes locked with Emma's as they both fought the force of the impact without knowing where it came from or why, both of them just suddenly swept down the highway like rag doll's in a child's toy car and then they were free of the light and the sound but still moving, effortlessly, through the air, first looking down at the ground then up at the sky and back again. In some detached part of his mind, Mark recognized that they had been hit by something big, something that had sent them careening down the highway and off an embankment, and now they were flying, end over end, somersaulting to oblivion. Emma's eyes were wide with terror, and he could see in her expression that she was prepared to die, if only her unborn son could survive, and she was silently pleading with her husband to somehow make it happen, to protect their son if she couldn't, even as he knew that they were moving too fast, too high off the ground, for the impact not to kill them all, and there was nothing she or he or even God could do to save any of them now.

Unless ...

****

"Coffee, hon?" Gloria asked.

Mark staggered in through the door of the Pinebox Diner, the bell jingling merrily. He helped Emma to a booth and got her settled in before dropping in beside her. He wrapped his arm around her to comfort her, but she was cold, so cold, from the long walk back from the highway, from the twisted wreckage of their car.

"It'll warm you up," Gloria supplied. "Keep you awake for the rest of your trip."

"Yeah," Mark said, his voice raspy through his dry throat. "Black, two sugars. Cream for her."

"Be just a minute," Gloria said.

Mark peered around the dimly-lit diner until he found the shadow he was expecting to see, that cold, dark area that he knew was always here, had always been here, and would always be.

"Good morning," said Reverend Porter's voice from the gloom. He seemed to appear out of nowhere as he leaned forward into the light. "Still traveling on Christmas Eve, I see."

"What are you?" Mark asked.

The Reverend smiled, and his eyes glittered like points of flickering fire. "No one special. Just a fellow having a cup of coffee in a diner, waiting on his meal to arrive. Nothing more than that."

"The Josephsens?" Mark said.

"Nice family," Reverend Porter said. "Drove a '75 Cutlass Supreme, but had a little trouble on the road. Had to walk all the way back to town. In the cold." The Reverend gave Mark a serious look. "In the dark."

"What happened to them?"

"They headed on to their final destination," the Reverend told him. "Finally found a ride to take them on the rest of the way." The Reverend stirred his coffee for a moment. "Could be you'll get lucky like that, too—find someone willing to help you on your way."

"Someone to—?" Mark said. Emma was starting to cry, watching them talk, instinctively understanding what his mind refused to accept. He stared at the Reverend, sitting in the shadows, blending in with the dark.

"You can't get there without help," Reverend Porter explained. "You just have to wait until someone comes along who's willing to do for you the same as was done for Mister and Misses Josephsen and their boy. Just some kindly folks, traveling on Christmas Eve, who find themselves in just the right position to help out a few poor souls."

Emma pressed her face into him, sobbing. He was starting to understand it now, to accept it. They had to get out of there, to keep driving, no matter how long it took. Sooner or later, someone like he and his wife and their unborn child would come along and help them to move on, and then it would be their turn. In the meantime, he would have to get back behind the wheel, and just keep driving, not stopping or sleeping or ever getting there, but always hoping that the next night would be the right night, and he could finally, finally pull over and rest.

"Best get going," the reverend said. "Be light soon. Not much of the night left."

Gloria appeared at the table, handing them their coffees. "On the house," she said, smiling that ghastly smile. "You'll be needing it."

Mark lurched up out of his seat and helped Emma up. He nodded grimly at Gloria and Reverend Porter, and guided Emma out, into the parking lot. Beside his car sat the wrecking truck, empty now, no driver evident, though someone had just painted a big, blood-red "3" on the passenger side of his car. Mark ran his fingers over it as he helped Emma get inside. The paint was cold, like ice water. He walked around to his side and got in, and started the car.

"You want the heater?" he asked Emma.

"Sure," she said, numbly, holding herself. She looked at him, her eyes hopeless and dark. "How much longer?" she asked.

Mark thought about it. *How long had they been driving?* He couldn't remember the last time they'd stopped. He couldn't remember much of anything, before tonight. He just had the impression that he had been driving for a long time, and that they should have arrived by now. The trip was taking longer than he'd expected.

"Can't be much longer," he told her.

"I wish I could just close my eyes," she said. "And sleep until we're there."

Mark took a sip of coffee. It didn't seem particularly warm, and it didn't seem to rouse him, but it filled him with determination to see their journey through to the end.

"We'll drive until morning," he said. "Then we'll pull off the road somewhere and get some sleep."

"I was hoping we'd be there by morning," Emma said.

Mark put the car in reverse and pulled out carefully. The streets were deserted, but he wasn't taking a chance on getting rear-ended now, not with a pregnant wife in the car. It had happened to him once before—*when was that, exactly?*—and he had no desire to go through that, ever again.

"Can't be much longer," he said again. "But we'll need to stop for gas soon." He reached for his coffee, but the cup was empty. "And I should get some more coffee." He put the car in gear, and yawned.

"Just to keep me going."

****

*JD Wiker has been writing since he got his first (toy) typewriter at age 8. After years of struggling along as a stockboy, gas station attendant, disc jockey, computer systems operator, game designer, and IP developer, he returned to his first calling, and is currently working on his first novel. JD lives in Virginia with his wife Keri. This story was inspired in part by their drive across northern Texas when they relocated from southern California.*

# Body Found

PINEBOX, TX - The body of an unidentified woman was found near the railroad tracks in southern Golan County Sunday. It was found by Byron Brown, who lives in the area.

"I saw something blue in the ditch, and stopped to see what it was. It was the girl's blue jacket," Byron said.

Sheriff Butch Anderson issued the following statement.

"We are doing everything we can to identify the body and the cause of death and will release that information to the public when we know."

When asked if the woman was murdered, Sheriff Anderson replied, "We don't know yet. It could have been some sort of animal attack. We just don't know yet."

The body has proven difficult to identify as the fingerprints are not on file and the head is currently missing from the scene. Anyone with information about this case is asked to immediately contact the Sheriff's department at 800-555-4357.

# Head Discovered

PINEBOX, TX - A woman's head was discovered in a drainage ditch off Cane Bottom Road in Pinebox by several boys who were playing in the area.

Pinebox Police Detective David West stated that the head belonged to "Francis Bucknell, who has been missing since last Saturday, and whose body was discovered last Sunday near the railroad line in southern Golan County."

It is unknown how or why the head was discovered more than two miles from where the body was found. The Sheriff's Department is working with the Pinebox Police Department in this investigation. Detective West is treating this as a murder case, though there is still a chance that it was some sort of wild animal attack.

Francis Bucknell was a Sophomore student at East Texas University and was a Forestry major. She often hiked in the Thicket and left the dorms last Saturday morning and did not return.

Her roommate, Jenny Knowls, claims that Bucknell was fascinated by the legend of the Piney Devil and various Bigfoot sightings, and spent many weekends hiking and camping in the Thicket hoping to spot or find evidence of one.

Bucknell body was discovered near the railroad tracks in southern Golan County on Sunday, but remained unidentified until her head was discovered on Tuesday.

The Pinebox Police Department and the Golan County Sheriffs Department is asking for anyone with information about this case to contact them immediately at 800-555-4357.

# Lake Greystone Boaters Missing

PINEBOX, TX - Two men are missing after a day of fishing and noodling on Lake Greystone, and a third is currently being investigated by the Sheriff's Department for possibly having played a role in the disappearances.

According to a Sheriff's Department spokesperson, last Saturday Clay Matthews and Peter Johnson met Dr. Robert Newhouse, a visting professor from Massachusetts, while fishing on Lake Greystone and took him noodling east of Dale Island.

Noodling is the practice of placing one's arm into underwater holes as a form of fishing. Large catfish, usually flathead, bite down on the arm and can be fought to the surface by the fisherman.

"Noodling is a dangerous practice," reminds Golan County Gamewarden Jim Bohay. "You could just as easily stick your arm into a nest of water mocassins or disturb an alligator. Some of those catfish weigh as much as seventy pounds and it is not unknown for noodlers to break their arms or even be drowned."

Local authorities are dredging the area for the bodies of Clay Matthews and Dr. Robert Newhouse, but the bodies have not yet been recovered. Divers have been brought in from Houston and it is hoped that the bodies will soon be recovered.

"The area where the accident happened is not very deep, but there is a channel that runs to a deeper part of the lake with enough flow that the bodies could have been carried further out into the lake," Bohay explained. "We will find them."

The Sheriff's Department is also investigating possible foul play in the case.

"There are questions about what really happened out there that day," said Sheriff Butch Anderson. The Sheriff's Department has named Peter Johnson as a "person of interest" in this case.

"First, though, it is absolutely essential that the bodies of these men be recovered for their families to have closure and to be certain as to what actually happened out there last weekend."

# Ninth Girl Missing

PINEBOX, TX - Police continue to work around the clock with no results as the "Pinebox Strangler" case continues to go unsolved. Three girls have been found strangled while five remain unaccounted for. Police Chief Dennis Taylor reiterated his refused to comment on an ongoing investigation. He also refused to speculate whether this latest missing girl is the ninth of the strangler's victims, noting that many ETU students have gone home until the current crisis is over.

The first victim, Anna Schulty, was found near the Shepherd's Cemetery. Her throat had been cut, but forensics evidence points to her having been strangled first. The body was assaulted after the murder occurred, though the Pinebox Police and the Federal Bureau of Investigations have not released any evidence from the crime scene.

Anna Schulty was murdered around the 3rd or 4th of last month and the killer has been continuing his murderous rampage by striking on average two times a week since, though all the victims have been found in different areas in and around the Pinebox area.

Local, state, and federal law enforcement agencies have descended on Golan County and have made many statements about "protecting the community" and "bringing the killer to justice." Armed citizen patrols have begun at night and some are concerned about vigilantism.

"We are going to protect our own. You can believe that," said Nathan Roper, a Pinebox native and Junior Animal Science major at ETU. "He's out there, and he will strike again. We have to be ready."

Many female students have returned home and ETU officials are considering cancelling all classes until the killer is brought to justice. "We will do whatever we have to, as student safety is our primary concern," said Sandra Day, a spokeswoman for the university.

Sheriff Butch Anderson reported that, "It's getting real hairy out here. We keep getting all kinds of crazy reports ranging from Jack the Ripper stuff, to werewolves and who knows what else. Do us all a favor, and let law enforcement do its job. These kids carrying guns and knives around at night is going to get somebody killed. Probably them."

# Pinebox Diner to Reopen

In the 1960s, the Pinebox Diner was a meeting place for Raven's students, locals, and was known as having the best fresh pies in all of East Texas. However, in 1974, the Pinebox Diner shut its doors after thirteen years of serving our fair city. The owner, Tim Simmons, disappeared and as there was no owner, the enterprise had to end.

But now, Jimmy Tyler, a class of 65 alum of ETU, has purchased the diner's remnants and is in the process of rebuilding the Pinebox icon. "It meant so much to me and I want to bring that same spirit back to our town."

Mr. Tyler is planning a grand reopening on August first of this year. "The diner is going to be retro, like it was in the early 1960s. Authentic booths, a soda bar, and we are going to serve the biggest burgers in Texas, with huge orders of homestyle French fries, malts, and follow it up with homemade cherry and apple pies."

The entire building has undergone basic reconstruction with a new roof, siding, and windows. "It's been a dream of mine for many years, and now I am in a place where I can make it a reality," Mr. Tyler said. "We have even purchased an authentic jukebox, though the music will be a mix of modern as well as the best of the sixties."

"The place has great ambiance, and it's like the spirits of the those who went ahead of us are there with us, hoping to make the diner come alive again."

# Dr. Louise Frazier Recognized for Service

Dr. Louise Frazier, a Professor of Biology at ETU, and the current Coroner for Golan County is to receive a community service award for her many contributions to the citizens of Pinebox.

Mayor Flowers stated, "She has proven time and again how valuable she is in helping us solve various murder cases. Being with her is like being in an episode of CSI."

Dr. Frazier has successfully identified over twenty bodies in the past two years and has been "invaluable to the Pinebox Police department. Her aid and expertise has led to the conviction of seven murderers."

She has also worked with the March of Quarters, the Pinebox Hospice Board, and with the Pinebox Dramatics Society. She is to be honored next Tuesday evening by the local Panther's Club who will bestow the Panther's Honor Plaque and Award to her. The Panther's Club banquet will begin at 7 pm and tickets are available for twenty dollars a seat.

"Come on out and help us honor a pillar of our community," invited Mayor Flowers, who also serves as the President of the Panther's Club.

# Local Boy Dies in Biking Accident

Jimmy Berry, a twelve year old boy died Saturday as he rode his bike down Linda Lane. While police are investigating the accident, Detective Parker of the Pinebox Police Department stated that "it is apparent that he hit something while traveling at a fast pace, and was thrown over his handlebars and unfortunately landed on his head on the concrete pavement, causing massive head trauma."

The boy and his friends had been riding their bikes down the hill of Linda Lane and were turning onto a cul de sac when the accident occurred.

Berry was a seventh grade student at Pinebox Middle School, and a member of Troop 1224 of the Boy Scouts. His parents have requested that anyone wishing to make a donation contact the Raven's State Bank and give to the Berry Memorial Fund which is to help Pinebox Middle School students purchase school supplies and to help teacher's in the classroom. "While Jimmy did not love school, he was a good student, and we want to do something to help others remember him," his father said.

Jimmy was pronounced dead at the scene,. The funeral is set for 2 p.m. Wednesday at the Shepherd's Cemetery.

# Fielding Building Sold

The downtown Fielding building, which has sat idle and empty for over a year, has been sold to an Italian businessman, Alistor Strega. Mr. Strega stated that he has "fallen in love with Pinebox. It's unique ambience calls to me. I think I have found a new home."

The Fielding building is a local landmark and was built in 1873. Originally it was a boarding house, then it served as a local tavern and bar from 1886 to 1902. It was converted into business apartments and was leased for various businesses until the 1970s, when it was closed for a time.

The building was remodeled and reopened in 1976 and served as a focal building for the Independence Day 200 year anniversary celebration in Pinebox where it was made an official historic site by the city and recognized as such by the state.

The building closed late last year after the disappearance of Ms. Suzanne Marie Whitcomb, the owner of Pinebox Realty, which offices were in the building.

Mr. Strega has stated he may be looking into opening a new business, "perhaps antiques." Mayor Flowers expressed his joy at having the building purchased and hopefully reopened to the public. "I just have one thing to say, Welcome to Pinebox, Mr. Strega."

# Big Thicket Legends: Skinwalkers

By Jackson Green

Welcome back readers of the weird and wired. Today I'm continuing my series of articles on Big Thicket Legends. Have you heard of Skinwalkers? Legends state that they are powerful witches from various Native American tribes, though most commonly associated with the Apache and Comanche of the Southwest.

These powerful shamans have given themselves over to dark spirits of the earth and are bloodthirsty murderers, who kill for power. The reward for their crimes...new bodies. Skins to be exact.

Legends state that these once-human creatures take the skin of those they kill and can wear it, magically welding the new skin over their bodies and taking on the likeness of their victims. They even take the eyes and teeth of their victims. Other stories state that Skinwalkers may even turn into animals and that their bodies, pulsing with strange powers, may change, by growing or shrinking, and taking on the form of whatever skin the shaman collects.

These shaman are the center of many terrifying stories and legends of the Native Americans, as well as the early settlers of the southwest.

In 1842, Big Pine, a Caddoan shaman, whose mother reportedly was a Comanche witch, resisted the Texas Rangers as they attempted to drive the Native Americans out of East Texas. Legends and stories from the time state that the towns of Nacogdoches and Sabinetown were besieged by the Skinwalker, Big Pine. He walked among them, unknown, and killed many people out of revenge for what was being done to his people.

One legend states that the famous blue woman of Sabinetown finally defeated Big Pine in a great release of arcane energies. Other legends state that Captain Edmund Dale of the Texas Rangers tracked the Skinwalker through the Big Thicket and killed him somewhere near the Six Mile Bridge.

One thing is for sure. Native Americans believe these stories to be true, and there is much cultural evidence to support that belief.

Sweet dreams, kiddies. Until next time, be safe.

# Explosion Unexplained

PINEBOX, TX - An old house exploded last Tuesday night. The home, which had been abandoned for several years, was completely destroyed by the blast, the cause of which is unknown.

"The gas lines have been turned off for years, so unless some strange mistake was made, we have no idea what caused the explosion," said Sheriff Butch Anderson at the scene.

"There was a two-tone brown, 1983, Buick Regal with expired plates, license number U81-OIC, was found abandoned nearby on the Pinebox Cutoff Road. We are asking that anyone with information about this explosion or this car contact us at 1-800-555-4357."

## Guitar Game Tournament Set for Saturday

The Guitar Hero phenomenon continues to grow as tournaments and competitions have taken the nation by storm. The second Annual Guitar Hero tournament is set to begin at 9 am this Saturday at the Ravens Student Center.

The tournament is open to everyone from the age of 12 to 99 and the entry fee is $20. The tournament is double elimination and is a head to head seeded competition and is expected to go late into the night before the Champion is crowned. The winner of the contest will receive a $2000 scholarship and $500 in gaming gift certificates from various stores. The winner will also be sent to Austin next October for the Texas State Championship and receive free transportation, motel room, and $200 spending money.

Second and third place prizes include new guitars, game disks, t-shirts, and gift certificates to local restaurants. Last year's winner, Calvin Griffis, is expected to make another run for the prize, though it is expected that this year there will be more than 200 contestants, compared to 96 last year.

"This is good, wholesome fun with great music and is a true event. Who knows, maybe so many people will want to play that we have to do it in Raven's Stadium next year," said ETU President Nelson. "I invite everyone to come on out, bring your family, and have fun."

# Pinebox Welcomes New Public Defender

Judges Howard Lindsey and Marie Derousseau teamed with the Pinebox City Council and current Public Defender Franklin Perkins, and have announced the hiring of a new public defender for Golan County. After a two-month search, they settled on Louis Rainer, who will be replacing Mr. Perkins, who is retiring after over a decade of service in the Public Defender's office.

"Mr. Rainer is a top Texas lawyer from the University of Texas with an extensive background from stints in Dallas and Houston. He's seen a lot and will serve our county well," said Judge Derousseau.

Mr. Perkins is retiring for medical reasons. "My ticker ain't tickin' right," he said. "I'm ready to retire anyway, and I am proud of how my office has worked tirelessly for the people of Golan County and the great city of Pinebox. I'm happy with the selection of Louis, and I'm certain he will serve our community for many years to come."

Louis Rainer was not available for comment, but did send the following via email communications: "My wife and I are very excited to be moving to East Texas. The Big Thicket is beautiful and with great access to lakes and rivers, we are excited to be moving to what we consider paradise. I hope to help the people of Golan County and to give everyone the proper representation they are due according to our wonderful Constitution."

Mr. Rainer is scheduled to begin his service early next week.

Printed in the United States
147493LV00001B/1/P

9 780981 963723